B L O W - U P
AND OTHER STORIES

JULIO CORTÁZAR

. . . .

BLOW-UP
AND OTHER STORIES

ORIGINALLY TITLED
END OF THE GAME
AND OTHER STORIES

TRANSLATED FROM THE SPANISH
BY PAUL BLACKBURN

PANTHEON BOOKS, NEW YORK

All rights reserved under International and Pan-American Copyright Conventions. Published in the United States by Pantheon Books, a division of Random House, Inc., New York, and simultaneously in Canada by Random House of Canada Limited, Toronto. Originally published in Spanish in the following volumes: *Bestiario; Las Armas Secretas;* and *Final del Juego.* Translation first published in the United States under the title *End of the Game and Other Stories* by Pantheon Books, a division of Random House, Inc., in 1967.

Library of Congress Cataloging in Publication Data

Cortázar, Julio.
Blow-up, and other stories.
(Pantheon modern writers)
Previously published under title: End of the game, and other stories.
1. Cortázar, Julio—Translations, English. I. Title.
PQ7797.C7145A23   1985   863   84—22792
ISBN 0-394-72881-5

Manufactured in the United States of America

CONTENTS

. . . .

O N E

AXOLOTL

· · · · · · · · · · · · · · · · ·

There was a time when I thought a great deal about the axolotls. I went to see them in the aquarium at the Jardin des Plantes and stayed for hours watching them, observing their immobility, their faint movements. Now I am an axolotl.

I got to them by chance one spring morning when Paris was spreading its peacock tail after a wintry Lent. I was heading down the boulevard Port-Royal, then I took Saint-Marcel and L'Hôpital and saw green among all that grey and remembered the lions. I was friend of the lions and panthers, but had never gone into the dark, humid building that was the aquarium. I left my bike against the gratings and went to look at the tulips. The lions were sad and ugly and my panther was asleep. I decided on the aquarium, looked obliquely at banal fish until, unexpectedly, I hit it off with the axolotls. I stayed watching them for an hour and left, unable to think of anything else.

In the library at Sainte-Geneviève, I consulted a dictionary and learned that axolotls are the larval stage (provided with gills) of a species of salamander of the genus Ambystoma. That they were Mexican I knew already by looking at them and their little pink Aztec faces and the placard at the top of the tank. I read that specimens of them had been found in Africa capable of living on dry land during the periods of drought, and continuing their life under water when the rainy season came. I found their Spanish name, *ajolote*, and the mention that they were edible, and that their oil was used (no longer used, it said) like cod-liver oil.

I didn't care to look up any of the specialized works, but the next day I went back to the Jardin des Plantes. I began to go every morning, morning and afternoon some days. The aquarium guard smiled perplexedly taking my ticket. I would lean up against the iron bar in front of the tanks and set to watching them. There's nothing strange in this, because after the first minute I knew that we were linked, that something infinitely lost and distant kept pulling us together. It had been enough to detain me that first morning in front of the sheet of glass where some bubbles rose through the water. The axolotls huddled on the wretched narrow (only I can know how narrow and wretched) floor of moss and stone in the tank. There were nine specimens, and the majority pressed their heads against the glass, looking with their eyes of gold at whoever came near them. Disconcerted, almost ashamed, I felt it a lewdness to be peering at these silent and immobile figures heaped at the bottom of the tank. Mentally I isolated one, situated on the right and somewhat apart from the others, to study it better. I saw a rosy little body, translucent (I thought of those Chinese figurines of milky glass), looking like a small lizard about six inches long, ending in a fish's tail of extraordinary delicacy, the most sensitive part of our body. Along the back ran a transparent fin which joined with the tail, but what obsessed me was the feet, of the slenderest nicety, ending in tiny fingers with minutely human nails. And then I discovered its eyes, its face. Inexpressive features, with no other trait save the eyes, two orifices, like brooches, wholly of transparent gold, lacking any life but looking, letting themselves be penetrated by my look, which seemed to travel past the golden level and lose itself in a diaphanous interior mystery. A very slender black halo ringed the eye and etched it onto the pink flesh, onto the rosy stone of the head, vaguely triangular, but with curved and irregular sides which gave it a total likeness to a statuette corroded by time. The mouth was masked by the triangular plane of the face, its considerable size would be guessed only in profile; in front a delicate crevice barely slit the lifeless stone. On both sides of the head where the ears should have been, there grew three tiny sprigs red as coral, a vegetal outgrowth, the gills, I suppose. And they were the only thing quick about it; every ten or fifteen seconds the sprigs pricked up stiffly and again subsided. Once in a while a foot would barely move, I saw the diminutive toes poise mildly on the moss. It's that we don't enjoy moving a lot, and the tank is so cramped—we barely move in any direction and we're hitting one of the others with our tail or our head—difficulties arise, fights, tiredness. The time feels like it's less if we stay quietly.

It was their quietness that made me lean toward them fascinated the first time I saw the axolotls. Obscurely I seemed to understand their secret will, to abolish space and time with an indifferent immobility. I knew better later; the gill contraction, the tentative reckoning of the delicate feet on the stones, the abrupt swimming (some of them swim with a simple undulation of the body) proved to me that they were capable of escaping that mineral lethargy in which they spent whole hours. Above all else, their eyes obsessed me. In the standing tanks on either side of them, different fishes showed me the simple stupidity of their handsome eyes so similar to our own. The eyes of the axolotls spoke to me of the presence of a different life, of another way of seeing. Glueing my face to the glass (the guard would cough fussily once in a while), I tried to see better those diminutive golden points, that entrance to the infinitely slow and remote world of these rosy creatures. It was useless to tap with one finger on the glass directly in front of their faces; they never gave the least reaction. The golden eyes continued burning with their soft, terrible light; they continued looking at me from an unfathomable depth which made me dizzy.

And nevertheless they were close. I knew it before this, before being an axolotl. I learned it the day I came near them for the first time. The anthropomorphic features of a monkey reveal the reverse of what most people believe, the distance that is traveled from them to us. The absolute lack of similarity between axolotls and human beings proved to me that my recognition was valid, that I was not propping myself up with easy analogies. Only the little hands . . . But an eft, the common newt, has such hands also, and we are not at all alike. I think it was the axolotls' heads, that triangular pink shape with the tiny eyes of gold. That looked and knew. That laid the claim. They were not *animals*.

It would seem easy, almost obvious, to fall into mythology. I began seeing in the axolotls a metamorphosis which did not succeed in revoking a mysterious humanity. I imagined them aware, slaves of their bodies, condemned infinitely to the silence of the abyss, to a hopeless meditation. Their blind gaze, the diminutive gold disc without expression and nonetheless terribly shining, went through me like a message: "Save us, save us." I caught myself mumbling words of advice, conveying childish hopes. They continued to look at me, immobile; from time to time the rosy branches of the gills stiffened. In that instant I felt a muted pain; perhaps they were seeing me, attracting my strength to penetrate into the impenetrable thing of their lives. They were not human beings, but I had found in no animal such a profound relation with myself. The axolotls were like witnesses of something, and at times like horrible judges. I felt ignoble in front of them; there was such a terrifying purity in those transparent eyes. They were larvas, but larva means disguise and also phantom. Behind those Aztec faces, without expression but of an implacable cruelty, what semblance was awaiting its hour?

I was afraid of them. I think that had it not been for feeling the proximity of other visitors and the guard, I would not have been bold enough to remain alone with them. "You eat them alive with your eyes, hey," the guard said, laughing; he likely thought I was a little cracked. What he didn't notice was that it was they devouring me slowly with their eyes, in a cannibalism of gold. At any distance from the aquarium, I had only to think of them, it was as though I were being affected from a distance. It got to the point that I was going every day, and at night I thought of them immobile in the darkness, slowly putting a hand out which immediately encountered another. Perhaps their eyes could see in the dead of night, and for them the day continued indefinitely. The eyes of axolotls have no lids.

I know now that there was nothing strange, that that

had to occur. Leaning over in front of the tank each morning, the recognition was greater. They were suffering, every fiber of my body reached toward that stifled pain, that stiff torment at the bottom of the tank. They were lying in wait for something, a remote dominion destroyed, an age of liberty when the world had been that of the axolotls. Not possible that such a terrible expression which was attaining the overthrow of that forced blankness on their stone faces should carry any message other than one of pain, proof of that eternal sentence, of that liquid hell they were undergoing. Hopelessly, I wanted to prove to myself that my own sensibility was projecting a nonexistent consciousness upon the axolotls. They and I knew. So there was nothing strange in what happened. My face was pressed against the glass of the aquarium, my eyes were attempting once more to penetrate the mystery of those eyes of gold without iris, without pupil. I saw from very close up the face of an axolotl immobile next to the glass. No transition and no surprise, I saw my face against the glass, I saw it on the outside of the tank, I saw it on the other side of the glass. Then my face drew back and I understood.

Only one thing was strange: to go on thinking as usual, to know. To realize that was, for the first moment, like the horror of a man buried alive awaking to his fate. Outside, my face came close to the glass again, I saw my mouth, the lips compressed with the effort of understanding the axolotls. I was an axolotl and now I knew instantly that no understanding was possible. He was outside the aquarium, his thinking was a thinking outside the tank. Recognizing him, being him himself, I was an axolotl and in my world. The horror began—I learned in the same moment —of believing myself prisoner in the body of an axolotl, metamorphosed into him with my human mind intact, buried alive in an axolotl, condemned to move lucidly among unconscious creatures. But that stopped when a foot just grazed my face, when I moved just a little to one side and saw an axolotl next to me who was looking at me, and understood that he knew also, no communication possible, but very clearly. Or I was also in him, or all of us were thinking humanlike, incapable of expression, limited to the golden splendor of our eyes looking at the face of the man pressed against the aquarium.

He returned many times, but he comes less often now. Weeks pass without his showing up. I saw him yesterday, he looked at me for a long time and left briskly. It seemed to me that he was not so much interested in us any more, that he was coming out of habit. Since the only thing I do is think, I could think about him a lot. It occurs to me that at the beginning we continued to communicate, that he felt more than ever one with the mystery which was claiming him. But the bridges were broken between him and me, because what was his obsession is now an axolotl, alien to his human life. I think that at the beginning I was capable of returning to him in a certain way—ah, only in a certain way—and of keeping awake his desire to know us better. I am an axolotl for good now, and if I think like a man it's only because every axolotl thinks like a man inside his rosy stone semblance. I believe that all this succeeded in communicating something to him in those first days, when I was still he. And in this final solitude to which he no longer comes, I console myself by thinking that perhaps he is going to write a story about us, that, believing he's making up a story, he's going to write all this about axolotls.

HOUSE TAKEN OVER

· · · · · · · · · · · · ·

We liked the house because, apart from its being old and spacious (in a day when old houses go down for a profitable auction of their construction materials), it kept the memories of great-grandparents, our paternal grandfather, our parents and the whole of childhood.

Irene and I got used to staying in the house by ourselves, which was crazy, eight people could have lived in that place and not have gotten in each other's way. We rose at seven in the morning and got the cleaning done, and about eleven I left Irene to finish off whatever rooms and went to the kitchen. We lunched at noon precisely; then there was nothing left to do but a few dirty plates. It was pleasant to take lunch and commune with the great hollow, silent house, and it was enough for us just to keep it clean. We ended up thinking, at times, that that was what had kept us from marrying. Irene turned down two suitors for no particular reason, and María Esther went and died on me before we could manage to get engaged. We were easing into our forties with the unvoiced concept that the quiet, simple marriage of sister and brother was the indispensable end to a line established in this house by our grandparents. We would die here someday, obscure and distant cousins would inherit the place, have it torn down, sell the bricks and get rich on the building plot; or more justly and better yet, we would topple it ourselves before it was too late.

Irene never bothered anyone. Once the morning housework was finished, she spent the rest of the day on the sofa in her bedroom, knitting. I couldn't tell you why she knitted so much; I think women knit when they discover that it's a fat excuse to do nothing at all. But Irene was not like that, she always knitted necessities, sweaters for winter, socks for me, handy morning robes and bedjackets for herself. Sometimes she would do a jacket, then unravel it the next moment because there was something that didn't please her; it was pleasant to see a pile of tangled wool in her knitting basket fighting a losing battle for a few hours to retain its shape. Saturdays I went downtown to buy wool; Irene had faith in my good taste, was pleased with the colors and never a skein had to be returned. I took advantage of these trips to make the rounds of the bookstores, uselessly asking if they had anything new in French literature. Nothing worthwhile had arrived in Argentina since 1939.

But it's the house I want to talk about, the house and Irene, I'm not very important. I wonder what Irene would have done without her knitting. One can reread a book, but once a pullover is finished you can't do it over again, it's some kind of disgrace. One day I found that the drawer at the bottom of the chiffonier, replete with moth-balls, was filled with shawls, white, green, lilac. Stacked amid a great smell of camphor—it was like a shop; I didn't have the nerve to ask her what she planned to do with them. We didn't have to earn our living, there was plenty coming in from the farms each month, even piling up. But Irene was only interested in the knitting and showed a wonderful dexterity, and for me the hours slipped away watching her, her hands like silver sea-urchins, needles flashing, and one or two knitting baskets on the floor, the balls of yarn jumping about. It was lovely.

How not to remember the layout of that house. The din-ing room, a living room with tapestries, the library and three large bedrooms in the section most recessed, the one that faced toward Rodríguez Peña. Only a corridor with its massive oak door separated that part from the front wing, where there was a bath, the kitchen, our bedrooms and the hall. One entered the house through a vestibule with enameled tiles, and a wrought-iron grated door opened onto the living room. You had to come in through the vestibule and open the gate to go into the living room; the doors to our bedrooms were on either side of this, and opposite it was the corridor leading to the back section; going down the passage, one swung open the oak door be-yond which was the other part of the house; or just before the door, one could turn to the left and go down a nar-rower passageway which led to the kitchen and the bath. When the door was open, you became aware of the size of the house; when it was closed, you had the impression of an apartment, like the ones they build today, with barely enough room to move around in. Irene and I always lived in this part of the house and hardly ever went beyond the oak door except to do the cleaning. Incredible how much dust collected on the furniture. It may be Buenos Aires is a clean city, but she owes it to her population and nothing else. There's too much dust in the air, the slightest breeze and it's back on the marble console tops and in the diamond patterns of the tooled-leather desk set. It's a lot of work to get it off with a feather duster; the motes rise and hang in the air, and settle again a minute later on the pianos and the furniture.

I'll always have a clear memory of it because it happened so simply and without fuss. Irene was knitting in her bedroom, it was eight at night, and I suddenly decided to put the water up for *mate*. I went down the corridor as far as the oak door, which was ajar, then turned into the hall toward the kitchen, when I heard something in the library or the dining room. The sound came through muted and indistinct, a chair being knocked over onto the carpet or the muffled buzzing of a conversation. At the same time or a second later, I heard it at the end of the passage which led from those two rooms toward the door. I hurled myself against the door before it was too late and shut it, leaned on it with the weight of my body; luckily, the key was on our side; moreover, I ran the great bolt into place, just to be safe.

I went down to the kitchen, heated the kettle, and when I got back with the tray of *mate*, I told Irene:

"I had to shut the door to the passage. They've taken over the back part."

She let her knitting fall and looked at me with her tired, serious eyes.

"You're sure?"

I nodded.

"In that case," she said, picking up her needles again, "we'll have to live on this side."

I sipped at the *mate* very carefully, but she took her time starting her work again. I remember it was a grey vest she was knitting. I liked that vest.

The first few days were painful, since we'd both left so many things in the part that had been taken over. My collection of French literature, for example, was still in the library. Irene had left several folios of stationery and a pair of slippers that she used a lot in the winter. I missed my briar pipe, and Irene, I think, regretted the loss of an ancient bottle of Hesperidin. It happened repeatedly (but only in the first few days) that we would close some drawer or cabinet and look at one another sadly.

"It's not here."

One thing more among the many lost on the other side of the house.

But there were advantages, too. The cleaning was so much simplified that, even when we got up late, nine thirty for instance, by eleven we were sitting around with our arms folded. Irene got into the habit of coming to the kitchen with me to help get lunch. We thought about it and decided on this: while I prepared the lunch, Irene would cook up dishes that could be eaten cold in the evening. We were happy with the arrangement because it was always such a bother to have to leave our bedrooms in the evening and start to cook. Now we made do with the table in Irene's room and platters of cold supper.

Since it left her more time for knitting, Irene was content. I was a little lost without my books, but so as not to inflict myself on my sister, I set about reordering papa's stamp collection; that killed some time. We amused ourselves sufficiently, each with his own thing, almost always getting together in Irene's bedroom, which was the more comfortable. Every once in a while, Irene might say:

"Look at this pattern I just figured out, doesn't it look like clover?"

After a bit it was I, pushing a small square of paper in front of her so that she could see the excellence of some stamp or another from Eupen-et-Malmédy. We were fine, and little by little we stopped thinking. You can live without thinking.

(Whenever Irene talked in her sleep, I woke up immediately and stayed awake. I never could get used to this voice from a statue or a parrot, a voice that came out of the dreams, not from a throat. Irene said that in my sleep I flailed about enormously and shook the blankets off. We had the living room between us, but at night you could hear everything in the house. We heard each other breathing, coughing, could even feel each other reaching for the light switch when, as happened frequently, neither of us could fall asleep.

Aside from our nocturnal rumblings, everything was quiet in the house. During the day there were the household sounds, the metallic click of knitting needles, the rustle of stamp-album pages turning. The oak door was massive, I think I said that. In the kitchen or the bath, which adjoined the part that was taken over, we managed to talk loudly, or Irene sang lullabies. In a kitchen there's always too much noise, the plates and glasses, for there to be interruptions from other sounds. We seldom allowed ourselves silence there, but when we went back to our rooms or to the living room, then the house grew quiet, half-lit, we ended by stepping around more slowly so as not to disturb one another. I think it was because of this that I woke up irremediably and at once when Irene began to talk in her sleep.)

Except for the consequences, it's nearly a matter of repeating the same scene over again. I was thirsty that night, and before we went to sleep, I told Irene that I was going to the kitchen for a glass of water. From the door of the bedroom (she was knitting) I heard the noise in the kitchen; if not the kitchen, then the bath, the passage off at that angle dulled the sound. Irene noticed how brusquely I had paused, and came up beside me without a word. We stood listening to the noises, growing more and more sure that they were on our side of the oak door, if not the kitchen then the bath, or in the hall itself at the turn, almost next to us.

We didn't wait to look at one another. I took Irene's arm and forced her to run with me to the wrought-iron door, not waiting to look back. You could hear the noises, still muffled but louder, just behind us. I slammed the grating and we stopped in the vestibule. Now there was nothing to be heard.

"They've taken over our section," Irene said. The knitting had reeled off from her hands and the yarn ran back toward the door and disappeared under it. When she saw that the balls of yarn were on the other side, she dropped the knitting without looking at it.

"Did you have time to bring anything?" I asked hopelessly.

"No, nothing."

We had what we had on. I remembered fifteen thousand pesos in the wardrobe in my bedroom. Too late now.

I still had my wrist watch on and saw that it was 11 P.M. I took Irene around the waist (I think she was crying) and that was how we went into the street. Before we left, I felt terrible; I locked the front door up tight and tossed the key down the sewer. It wouldn't do to have some poor devil decide to go in and rob the house, at that hour and with the house taken over.

THE DISTANCES

The Diary of Alina Reyes

JANUARY 12

Last night it happened again, I so tired of bracelets and cajoleries, of pink champagne and Renato Viñes' face, oh that face like a spluttering seal, that picture of Dorian Gray in the last stages. It was a pleasure to go to bed to the *Red Bank Boogie*, with a chocolate mint, mama ashen-faced and yawning (as she always comes back from parties, ashen and half-asleep, an enormous fish and not even that).

Nora who says to fall asleep when it's light, the hubbub already starting in the street in the middle of the urgent chronicles her sister tells half-undressed. How happy they are, I turn off the lights and the hands, take all my clothes off to the cries of daytime and stirring, I want to sleep and I'm a terrible sounding bell, a wave, the chain the dog trails all night against the privet hedges. Now I lay me down to sleep . . . I have to recite verses, or the system of looking for words with *a*, then with *a* and *e*, with five vowels, with four. With two and one consonant (obo, emu), with four consonants and a vowel (crass, dross), then the poems again, The moon came down to the forge/ in its crinoline of tuberoses./ The boy looks and looks./ The boy is looking at it. With three and three in alternate order, cabala, bolero, animal; pavane, Canada, repose, regale.

So hours pass: with four, with three and two, then later palindromes: easy ones like hah, bob, mom, did, dad, gag, radar; then more complicated or nice silly ones like oho Eve oho, or the Napoleon joke, "able was I ere I saw Elba." Or the beautiful anagrams: Salvador Dalí, *avida dollars;* Alina Reyes, *es la reina y* . . . That one's so nice because it opens a path, because it does not close. Because the queen and . . . *la reina y* . . .

No, horrible. Horrible because it opens a path to this one who is not the queen and whom I hate again at night. To her who is Alina Reyes but not the queen of the anagram; let her be anything, a Budapest beggar, a beginner at a house of prostitution in Jujuy, a servant in Quetzaltenango, any place that's far away and not the queen. But yes Alina Reyes and because of that last night it happened again, to feel her and the hate.

JANUARY 20

At times I know that she's cold, that she suffers, that they beat her. I can only hate her so much, detest the hands that throw her to the ground and her as well, her even more because they beat her, because I am I and they beat

●   18

her. Oh, I'm not so despondent when I'm sleeping or when I cut a suit or it's the hours mama receives and I'm serving tea to señora Regules or to the boy from the Rivas'. Then it's less important to me, it's a little more like something personal, I with myself; I feel she is more mistress of her adversity, far away and alone, but the mistress. Let her suffer, let her freeze; I endure it from here, and I believe that then I help her a little. Like making bandages for a soldier who hasn't been wounded yet, and to feel that's acceptable, that one is soothing him beforehand, providentially.

Let her suffer. I give a kiss to señora Regules, tea to the boy from the Rivas', and I keep myself for that inner resistance. I say to myself, "Now I'm crossing a bridge, it's all frozen, now the snow's coming in through my shoes. They're broken." It's not that she's feeling nothing. I only know it's like that, that on one side I'm crossing a bridge at the same instant (but I don't know if it is at the same instant) as the boy from the Rivas' accepts the cup of tea from me and puts on his best spoiled face. And I stand it all right because I'm alone among all these people without sensitivity and I'm not so despondent. Nora was petrified last night, and asked, "But what's happening to you?" It was happening to that one, to me far off. Something horrible must have happened to her, they were beating her or she was feeling sick and just when Nora was going to sing Fauré and I at the piano gazing happily at Luis María leaning with his elbows on the back of it which made him look like a model, he gazing at me with his puppy-look, the two of us so close and loving one another so much. It's worse when that happens, when I know something about her just at the moment I'm dancing with Luis María, kissing him, or just near him. Because in the distances they do not love me—her. That's the part they don't like and as it doesn't suit me to be rent to pieces inside and to feel they are beating me or that the snow is coming in through my shoes when Luis María is dancing with me and his hand on my waist makes the strong odor of oranges, or of cut hay, rise in me like heat at midday, and they are beating her and it's impossible to fight back, and I have to tell Luis María that I don't feel well, it's the humidity, humidity in all that snow which I do not feel, which I do not feel and it's coming in through my shoes.

JANUARY 25

Sure enough, Nora came to see me and made a scene. "Look, doll, that's the last time I ask you to play piano for me. We were quite an act." What did I know about acts, I accompanied her as best I could, I remember hearing her as though she were muted. *Votre âme est un paysage choisi* . . . but I watched my hands on the keys and it seemed to me they were playing all right, that they accompanied Nora decently. Luis María also was watching my hands. Poor thing, I think that was because it didn't cheer him up particularly to look at my face. I must look pretty strange.

Poor little Nora. Let someone else accompany her. (Each time this seems more of a punishment, now I know myself there only when I'm about to be happy, when I am happy, when Nora is singing Fauré I know myself there and only the hate is left.)

NIGHT

At times it's tenderness, a sudden and necessary tenderness toward her who is not queen and walks there. I would like to send her a telegram, my respects, to know that her sons are well or that she does not have sons—because I don't think there I have sons—and could use consolation, compassion, candy. Last night I fell asleep thinking up messages, places to meet. WILL ARRIVE THURSDAY STOP MEET ME AT BRIDGE. What bridge? An idea that recurs just as Budapest always recurs, to believe in the beggar in Budapest where they'll have lots of bridges and percolating snow. Then I sat straight up in bed and almost bawling, I almost run and wake mama, bite her to make her wake up. I keep on thinking about it. It is still not easy to say it. I keep on thinking that if I really wanted to, if it struck my fancy, I would be able to go to Budapest right away. Or to Jujuy or Quetzaltenango. (I went back to look up those names, pages back.) Useless, it would be the same as saying Tres Arroyos, Kobe, Florida Street in the 400-block. Budapest just stays because *there* it's cold, there they beat me and abuse me. There (I dreamed it, it's only a dream, but as it sticks and works itself into my wakefulness) there's someone called Rod—or Erod, or Rodo—and he beats me and I love him, I don't know if I love him but I let him beat me, that comes back day after day, so I guess I do love him.

LATER

A lie. I dreamed of Rod or made him from some dream figure already worn out or to hand. There's no Rod, they're punishing me there, but who knows whether it's a man, an angry mother, a solitude.

Come find me. To say to Luis María, "We're getting married and you're taking me to Budapest, to a bridge where there's snow and someone." I say: and if I am? (Because I think all that from the secret vantage point of not seriously believing it. And if I am?) All right, if I am . . . But plain crazy, plain. . . ? What a honeymoon!

JANUARY 28

I thought of something odd. It's been three days now that nothing has come to me from the distances. Maybe they don't beat her now, or she could have come by a coat. To send her a telegram, some stockings . . . I thought of something odd. I arrived in the terrible city and it was afternoon, a green watery afternoon as afternoons never are if one does not help out by thinking of them. Beside the Dobrina Stana, on the Skorda Prospect equestrian statues bristling with stalagmites of hoarfrost and stiff policemen, great smoking loaves of coarse bread and flounces of wind puffing in the windows. At a tourist's pace, walking by the Dobrina, the map in the pocket of my blue suit (in this freezing weather and to leave my coat in the Burglos), until I come to a plaza next to the river, nearly in the river thundering with broken ice floes and barges and some kingfisher which is called there *sbunáia tjèno* or something worse.

I supposed that the bridge came after the plaza. I thought that and did not want to go on. It was the afternoon of Elsa Piaggio de Tarelli's concert at the Odeón, I fussed over getting dressed, unwilling, suspecting that afterwards only insomnia would be waiting for me. This thought of the night, so much of night . . . Who knows if I would not get lost. One invents names while traveling, thinking, remembers them at the moment: Dobrina Stana, *sbunáia tjéno*, the Burglos. But I don't know the name of the square, it is a little as though one had really walked into a plaza in Budapest and was lost because one did not know its name; if there's no name, how can there be a plaza?

I'm coming, mama. We'll get to your Bach all right, and your Brahms. The way there is easy. No plaza, no Hotel

Burglos. We are here, Elsa Piaggio there. Sad to have to interrupt this, to know that I'm in a plaza (but that's not sure yet, I only think so and that's nothing, less than nothing). And that at the end of the plaza the bridge begins.

NIGHT

Begins, goes on. Between the end of the concert and the first piece I found the name and the route. Vladas Square and the Market Bridge. I crossed Vladas Square to where the bridge started, going along slowly and wanting to stop at times, to stay in the houses or store windows, in small boys all bundled up and the fountains with tall heroes with their long cloaks all white, Tadeo Alanko and Vladislas Néroy, tokay drinkers and cymbalon players. I saw Elsa Piaggio acclaimed between one Chopin and another, poor thing, and my orchestra seat gave directly onto the plaza, with the beginning of the bridge between the most immense columns. But I was thinking this, notice, it's the same as making the anagram *es la reina y* . . . in place of Alina Reyes, or imagining mama at the Suarez's house instead of beside me. Better not to fall for that nonsense; that's something very strictly my own, to give in to the desire, the real desire. Real because Alina, well, let's go— Not the other thing, not feeling her being cold or that they mistreat her. I long for this and follow it by choice, by knowing where it's going, to find out if Luis María is going to take me to Budapest. Easier to go out and look for that bridge, to go out on my own search and find myself, as now, because now I've walked to the middle of the bridge amid shouts and applause, between "Albéniz!" and more applause and "The Polonaise!" as if that had any meaning amid the whipping snow which pushes against my back with the wind-force, hands like a thick towel around my waist drawing me to the center of the bridge.

(It's more convenient to speak in the present tense. This was at eight o'clock when Elsa Piaggio was playing the third piece, I think it was Julián Aguirre or Carlos Guastavino, something with pastures and little birds.) I have grown coarse with time, I have no respect for her now. I remember I thought one day: "There they beat me, there the snow comes in through my shoes and I know it at that moment, when it is happening to me there I know it at the same time. But why at the same time? Probably I'm coming late, probably it hasn't happened yet. Probably they will beat her within fourteen years or she's already a cross and an epitaph in the Sainte-Ursule cemetery." And that seemed to me pleasant, possible, quite idiotic. Because behind that, one falls always into the matching time. If now she were really starting over the bridge, I know I would feel it myself, from here. I remember that I stopped to look at the river which was like spoiled mayonnaise thrashing against the abutments, furiously as possible, noisy and lashing. (This last I was thinking.) It was worth it to lean over the parapet of the bridge and to hear in my ears the grinding of the ice there below. It was worth it to stop a little bit for the view, a little bit from fear too which came from inside—or it was being without a coat, the light snowfall melting and my topcoat at the hotel—And after all, for I am an unassuming girl, a girl without petty prides, but let them come tell me that the same thing could have happened to anyone else, that she could have journeyed to Hungary in the middle of the Odeón. Say, that would give anyone the shivers!

But mama was pulling at my sleeve, there was hardly anyone left in the orchestra section. I'm writing to that point, not wishing to go on remembering what I thought. I'm going to get sick if I go on remembering. But it's certain, certain; I thought of an odd thing.

JANUARY 30

Poor Luis María, what an idiot to get married to me. He doesn't know what he'll get on top of that. Or underneath that, Nora says, posing as an emancipated intellectual.

JANUARY 31

We'll be going there. He was so agreeable about it I almost screamed. I was afraid, it seemed to me that he entered into this game too easily. And he doesn't know anything, he's like a queen's pawn that sews up the game without even suspecting it. The little pawn Luis María beside his queen. Beside the queen and—

FEBRUARY 7

What's important now is to get better. I won't write the end of what I had thought at the concert. Last night again I sensed her suffering. I know that they're beating me there again. I can't avoid knowing it, but enough chronicle. If I had limited myself to setting this down regularly just as a whim, as alleviation . . . It was worse, a desire to understand in reading it over; to find keys in each word set to paper after those nights. Like when I thought of the plaza, the torn river and the noises and afterwards . . . But I'm not writing that, I'll never, ever, write that.

To go there to convince myself that celibacy has been no good for me, that it's nothing more than that, to be twenty-seven years old and never to have had a man. Now he will be my puppy, my penguin, enough to think and to be, to be finally and for good.

Nevertheless, now that I shall close this diary, for one gets married or one keeps a diary, the two things don't go well together—even now I don't want to finish it up without saying this with the happiness of hope, with hope for happiness. We will go there but it doesn't have to be what I thought the night of the concert. (I'll write it, and enough of the diary as far as I'm concerned.) I will find her on the bridge and we will look at one another. The night of the concert I felt echo in my ears the grinding of the ice there below. And it will be the queen's victory over that malignant relationship, that soundless and unlawful encroachment. If I am really I, she will yield, she will join my radiant *zone*, my lovelier and surer life; I have only to go to her side and lay a hand on her shoulder.

Alina Reyes de Aráoz and her husband arrived in Budapest April sixth, and took accommodations at the Ritz. That was two months before their divorce. On the afternoon of the second day, Alina went out to get to know the city and enjoy the thaw. As it pleased her to walk alone— she was brisk and curious—she went in twenty different directions looking vaguely for something, but without thinking about it too much, content to let her desire choose, that it express itself in abrupt changes of direction which led her from one store window to another, crossing streets, moving from one showcase to another.

She came to the bridge and crossed it as far as the middle, walking now with some difficulty because the snow hindered her and from the Danube a wind comes up from below, a difficult wind which hooks and lashes. She felt as though her skirt were glued to her thighs (she was not dressed properly for the weather) and suddenly a desire to turn around, to go back to the familiar city. At the center of the desolate bridge the ragged woman with black straight hair waited with something fixed and anxious in the lined face, in the folding of the hands, a little closed but already outstretched. Alina was close to her, repeating, now she knew, facial expressions and distances as if after a dress rehearsal. Without foreboding, liberating herself at last—she believed it in one terrible, jubilant, cold leap—she was beside her and also stretched out her hands, refusing to think, and the woman on the bridge hugged her against her chest and the two, stiff and silent, embraced one another on the bridge with the crumbling river hammering against the abutments.

Alina ached: it was the clasp of the pocketbook, the strength of the embrace had run it in between her breasts with a sweet, bearable laceration. She surrounded the slender woman feeling her complete and absolute within her arms, with a springing up of happiness equal to a hymn, to loosing a cloud of pigeons, to the river singing. She shut her eyes in the total fusion, declining the sensations from outside, the evening light; suddenly very tired but sure of her victory, without celebrating it as so much her own and at last.

It seemed to her that one of the two of them was weeping softly. It should have been her because she felt her cheeks wet, and even the cheekbone aching as though she had been struck there. Also the throat, and then suddenly the shoulders, weighed down by innumerable hardships. Opening her eyes (perhaps now she screamed) she saw that they had separated. Now she did scream. From the cold, because the snow was coming in through her broken shoes, because making her way along the roadway to the plaza went Alina Reyes, very lovely in her grey suit, her hair a little loose against the wind, not turning her face. Going off.

THE IDOL OF
THE CYCLADES
· · · · · · · · · · · · · · ·

"It strikes me the same whether you listen to me or not," Somoza said. "That's how it is, and it seems only fair to me that you know that."

Morand was startled, as though he'd come back from very far off. He remembered that before he'd been drowsing in a half-dream, it had occurred to him that Somoza was going crazy.

"Forgive me, I was distracted for a moment," he said. "Will you concede that all this . . . Anyway, to get here and find you in the middle of . . ."

But that Somoza was going crazy, to take that for granted was too easy.

"That's right, there are no words for it," Somoza said. "At least in our words."

They looked at one another for a second, and Morand was the first to avert his eyes while Somoza's voice rose again in that impersonal tone typical of these explanations which, the next moment, went beyond all intelligibility. Morand chose not to look at him, but then fell again into a helpless contemplation of the small statue set upon the column, and it was like a return to that golden afternoon of cigar smoke and the smell of herbs when, incredibly, Somoza and he had dug her up out of the island. He remembered how Teresa, a few yards off stretched out on a boulder from which she was trying to make out the coastline of Paros, had whirled around hearing Somoza's cry, and after a second's hesitation had run toward them, forgetting that she had the upper half of her red bikini in her hand. She had leaned over the excavation out of which Somoza's hand sprang with the statuette almost unrecognizable under its moldiness and chalk deposits, until Morand, angry and laughing at the same moment, yelled at her to cover herself, and Teresa stood up staring at him as if she had not understood, suddenly turned her back on them and hid her breasts between her hands while Somoza handed the statuette up to Morand and jumped out of the pit. Nearly without transition Morand remembered the hours that followed, the night in the big camping tents on the banks of the rushing stream, Teresa's shadow walking in the moonlight under the olives, and it was as though Somoza's voice now, echoing monotonously in the almost-empty studio with its sculptures, would come to him again out of that night, making part of his memory, when Somoza had confusedly intimated his ridiculous hopes to him, and he, between two swallows of retsina, had laughed happily and had accused him of being a phony archaeologist and an incurable poet.

"There are no words for it," Somoza had just said. "At least in our words."

In the great tent at the bottom of the Skyros valley, his hands had held the statuette up and caressed it so as to end by stripping it of its false clothes, time and oblivion (Teresa among the olives was still infuriated by Morand's reproach, by his stupid prejudices), and the night turned slowly while Somoza confided to him his senseless hope that someday he would be able to approach the statue by ways other than the hands and the eyes of science, meanwhile the wine and tobacco mixed into the conversation with the crickets and the waters of the stream until there was nothing left but a confused sense of not being able to understand one another. Later, when Somoza had gone back to his tent carrying the statuette with him, and Teresa got tired of being by herself and came back to lie down, Morand talked with her about Somoza's daydreams, and they asked one another with that amiable Parisian irony if everyone from the Río de la Plata had such a simple-minded imagination. Before going to sleep, they discussed what had taken place that afternoon, until, finally, Teresa accepted Morand's excuses, finally kissed him, and everything was as usual on the island, everywhere, it was he and she and the night overhead and the long oblivion.

"Anyone else know about it?" Morand asked.

"No. You and I. Seems to me that was right," Somoza said. "These last months, I've hardly stepped out of here. At first there was an old woman came to clean up the studio and wash my clothes for me, but she got on my nerves."

"It seems incredible that one could live like this in the suburbs of Paris. The silence . . . Listen, at least you have to go down to the town to do the shopping."

"Before, yes, I told you already. Now nothing's missing. Everything that's necessary's here."

Morand looked in the direction that Somoza's finger pointed, past the statuette and the reproductions abandoned on the shelves. He saw wood, whitewash, stone, hammers, dust, the shadow of trees against the windows. The finger seemed to indicate a corner of the studio where nothing was, hardly a dirty rag on the floor.

But these last two years very little had changed between them, there'd also been a far corner emptied of time, with a dirty rag which was like all they had not said to one another and which perhaps they should have said. The island expedition, a romantic and crazy idea conceived on a café terrace on the boulevard Saint-Michel, had ended as soon as they discovered the idol in the valley ruins. Perhaps the fear that they would be found out finished off the cheerfulness of the first few weeks, and the day came finally when Morand intercepted a glance of Somoza's while the three of them were going down to the beach, and that night he discussed it with Teresa and they decided to come back as early as possible, because they guessed that Somoza, and it seemed to them almost unfair, that he was beginning—so unexpectedly—to be falling for her. In Paris, they continued to see one another at great intervals, almost always for professional reasons, but Morand went to the appointments alone. Somoza asked after Teresa the first time, but afterward she seemed to be of no importance to him. Everything that they should have been saying weighed heavily between the two, perhaps the three of them. Morand agreed that Somoza should keep the statuette for a while. It would be impossible to sell it before a couple of years anyway; Marcos, the man who knew a colonel who was acquainted with an Athens customs official, had imposed the time-lapse as a condition of allow-

31

ing himself to be bribed. Somoza took the statue to his apartment, and Morand saw it each time that they met. It was never suggested that sometimes Somoza visit Morand and his wife, like so many other things they did not mention any more and which at bottom were always Teresa. Somoza seemed to be completely occupied with his *idée fixe*, and if once in a while he invited Morand to come back to his apartment for a cognac, there was nothing more to it than that. Nothing very extraordinary, after all Morand knew very well Somoza's tastes for certain marginal literatures, just as he was put off by Somoza's longing. The thing that surprised him most was the fanaticism of that hope which emerged during those hours of almost automatic confidences, and when he felt his own presence as highly unnecessary, the repeated caressing of the beautiful and expressionless statue's little body, repeating the spells in a monotone until it became tiresome, the same formulas of passage. As seen by Morand, Somoza's obsession was susceptible to analysis: in some sense, every archaeologist identifies himself with the past he explores and brings to light. From that point to believing that intimacy with one of those vestiges could alienate, alter time and space, open a fissure whereby one could comply with . . . Somoza never used that kind of vocabulary; what he said was always more or less than that, a haphazard language full of allusions and exorcisms moving from obstinate and irreducible levels. For that reason, then, he had begun to work clumsily on replicas of the statuette; Morand had managed to see the first of them even before Somoza had left Paris, and he listened with a friendly courtesy to those stiffheaded commonplaces re: the repetition of gesture and situation as a way of abrogation, Somoza's cocksureness that his obstinate approach would come to identify itself with the initial structure, with a superimposition which would be more than that because,

32

as yet, there was no duality, just fusion, primordial contact (not his words, but Morand had to translate them in some way, later, when he reconstructed them for Teresa). Contact which, Somoza finally said, had been established forty-eight hours before, on the night of the summer solstice.

"All right," Morand admitted, lighting another cigarette, "but I'd be happy if you could explain to me why you're so sure that . . . okay, that you've gotten to the bottom of it."

"Explain? . . . don't you see it?"

He stretched out his hand once more toward a castle in the air, to a corner of the loft; it described an arc which included the roof and the statuette set on its thin column of marble, enveloped in the brilliant cone of light from the reflector. Incongruously enough, Morand remembered that Teresa had crossed the frontier, carrying the statuette hidden in the toy chest Marcos had made in a basement in Plaka.

"It couldn't be that it wasn't going to happen," Somoza said almost childishly. "I was getting a little bit closer every replica I made. The form was becoming familiar to me. I want to say that . . . Ah, it would take days to explain it to you . . . and the absurd thing is that there everything comes in one . . . But when it's this . . . "

His hand waved about, came and went, marking out the *that* and the *this*.

"The truth of the matter is that you've managed to become a sculptor," Morand said, hearing himself speak and it sounding stupid. "The last two replicas are perfect. Whenever you get around to letting me keep the statue, I'll never know if you've given me the original or not."

"I'll never give her to you," Somoza said simply. "And don't think that I've forgotten that she belongs to both of us. But I'll never give her to you. The only thing I would

33

have wished is that Teresa and you had stayed with me, had matched me. Yes, I would have liked it had you been with me the evening it came."

It was the first time in almost two years that Morand had heard him mention Teresa, as if until that moment she had been somehow dead for him, but his manner of naming Teresa was hopelessly antique, it was Greece that morning when they'd gone down to the beach. Poor Somoza. Still. Poor madman. But even more strange was to ask oneself why, at the last minute, before getting into the car after Somoza's telephone call, he had felt it necessary to call Teresa at her office to ask her to meet them later at the studio. He would have to ask her about it later, to know what Teresa had been thinking while she listened to his instructions on how to get to the solitary summerhouse on the hill. He'd have Teresa repeat exactly, word for word, what she'd heard him say. Silently Morand damned this mania for systems which made him reconstitute life as though he were restoring a Greek vase for the museum, glueing the tiniest particles with minute care, and Somoza's voice there, mixed with the coming and going gestures of his hands which also seemed to want to glue pieces of air, putting together a transparent vase, his hands which pointed out the statuette, obliging Morand to look once more against his will at that white lunar body, a kind of insect antedating all history, worked under inconceivable circumstances by someone inconceivably remote, thousands of years ago, even further back, the dizzying distances of the animal, of the leap, vegetal rites alternating with tides and syzygies and seasons of rut and humdrum ceremonies of propitiation, the expressionless face where only the line of the nose broke its blind mirror of insupportable tension, the breasts hardly visible, the triangle of the sex and the arms crossed over the belly, embracing it, the idol of beginnings, the primeval terror under the rites from time immemorial, the hachet of stone from the immolations on the altars high on the hills. It was enough to make him believe that he also was turning into an imbecile, as if being an archaeologist were not sufficient.

"Please," said Morand, "couldn't you make some effort to explain to me even though you believe that none of it can be explained? The only thing I'm definitely sure of is that you've spent these months carving replicas, and that two nights ago . . ."

"It's so simple, Somoza said, "I've always felt that the flesh was still in contact with the other. But I had to retrace five thousand years of wrong roads. Curious that they themselves, the descendants of the Aegeans, were guilty of that mistake. But nothing's important now. *Look, it goes like this.*"

Close to the idol, he raised one hand and laid it gently over the breasts and the belly. The other caressed the neck, went up to the statue's absent mouth, and Morand heard Somoza speaking in a stifled and opaque voice, a little as if it were his hands or perhaps that nonexistent mouth, they that were speaking of the hunt in the caverns of smoke, of the number of deer in the pen, of the name which had to be spoken only afterwards, of the circle of blue grease, of the swing of the double rivers, of Pohk's childhood, of the procession to the eastern steps and the high ones in the accursed shadows. He wondered if, in one of Somoza's lapses of attention, he could manage to telephone and reach Teresa and warn her to bring Dr. Vernet with her. But Teresa would already have started and be on the way, and at the edge of the rocks where The Many was roaring, the master of the greens struck off the left horn of the handsomest buck and was handing it to the master of those who guarded the salt, to renew the pact with Haghesa.

"Listen, let me breathe," Morand said, rising and taking a step forward. "It's fabulous, and furthermore I have a terrible thirst. Let's drink something, I can go out and get a . . ."

"The whiskey is there," said Somoza, slowly removing his hands from the statue. "I shall not drink, I must fast before the sacrifice."

"Pity," Morand said, looking for the bottle. "I hate to drink alone. What sacrifice?"

He poured a whiskey up to the brim of the glass.

"That of the union, to use your words. Don't you hear them? The double flute, like the one on the statuette we saw in the Athens Museum. The sound of life on the left, and that of discord on the right. Discord is also life for Haghesa, but when the sacrifice is completed, the flutists cease to blow into the pipe on the right and one will hear only the piping of the new life that drinks the spilt blood. And the flutists will fill their mouths with blood and blow on the left pipe, and I shall anoint her face with blood, you see, like this, and the eyes shall appear and the mouth beneath the blood."

"Stop talking nonsense," Morand said, taking a good slug of the whiskey. "Blood would not go very well with our marble doll. Yeah, it's hot."

Somoza had taken off his smock with a leisurely and deliberate movement. When he saw that he was unbuttoning his trousers, Morand told himself that he had been wrong to let him get excited, in consenting to this explosion of his mania. Austere and brown, Somoza drew himself up erect and naked under the light of the reflector and seemed to lose himself in contemplation of a point in space. From a corner of his half-open mouth there fell a thread of spittle and Morand, setting the glass down quickly on the floor, figured that to get to the door he had to trick him in some way. He never found out where the

stone hatchet had come from which was swinging in Somoza's hand. He understood.

"That was thoughtful," he said backing away slowly.
"The pact with Haghesa, eh? And poor Morand's going to
donate the blood, you're sure of that?"

Without looking at him, Somoza began to move toward
him delineating an arc of a circle, as if he were following
a precharted course.

"If you really want to kill me," Morand shouted at him,
backing into the darkened area, "why this big scene? Both
of us know perfectly well it's over Teresa. But what good's
it going to do you, she's never loved you and she'll never
love you!"

The naked body was already moving out of the circle
illuminated by the reflector. Hidden in the shadows of the
corner, Morand stepped on the wet rags on the floor and
figured he couldn't go further back. He saw the hatchet
lifted and he jumped as Nagashi had taught him at the
gym in the place des Ternes. Somoza caught the toe-kick
in the center of his thigh and the nishi hack on the left
side of his neck. The hatchet came down on a diagonal,
too far out, and Morand resiliently heaved back the torso
which toppled against him, and caught the defenseless
wrist. Somoza was still a muffled, dull yell when the cutting edge of the hatchet caught him in the center of his
forehead.

Before turning to look at him, Morand vomited in the
corner of the loft, all over the dirty rags. He felt emptied,
and vomiting made him feel better. He picked the glass up
off the floor and drank what was left of the whiskey,
thinking Teresa was going to arrive any minute and that
he had to do something, call the police, make some explanation. While he was dragging Somoza's body back into
the full light of the reflector, he was thinking that it
should not be difficult to show that he had acted in self-

defense. Somoza's eccentricities, his seclusion from the world, his evident madness. Crouching down, he soaked his hands in the blood running from the face and scalp of the dead man, checking his wrist watch at the same time, twenty of eight. Teresa would not be long now, better to go out and wait for her in the garden or in the street, to spare her the sight of the idol with its face dripping with blood, the tiny red threads that glided past the neck, slipped around the breasts, joined in the delicate triangle of the sex, ran down the thighs. The hatchet was sunk deep into the skull of the sacrifice, and Morand pulled it out, holding it up between his sticky hands. He shoved the corpse a bit more with his foot, leaving it finally up next to the column, sniffed the air and went over to the door. Better open it so that Teresa could come in. Leaning the hatchet up against the door, he began to strip off his clothes, because it was getting hot and smelled stuffy, the caged herd. He was naked already when he heard the noise of the taxi pulling up and Teresa's voice dominating the sound of the flutes; he put the light out and waited, hatchet in hand, behind the door, licking the cutting edge of the hatchet lightly and thinking that Teresa was punctuality itself.

LETTER TO A
YOUNG LADY IN PARIS
· · · · · · · · · · · · · · · ·

Andrea, I didn't want to come live in your apartment in the calle Suipacha. Not so much because of the bunnies, but rather that it offends me to intrude on a compact order, built even to the finest nets of air, networks that in your environment conserve the music in the lavender, the heavy fluff of the powder puff in the talcum, the play between the violin and the viola in Ravel's quartet. It hurts me to come into an ambience where someone who lives beautifully has arranged everything like a visible affirmation of her soul, here the books (Spanish on one side, French and English on the other), the large green cushions there, the crystal ashtray that looks like a soap-bubble that's been cut open on this exact spot on the little table, and always a perfume, a sound, a sprouting of plants, a photograph of the dead friend, the ritual of tea trays and sugar tongs . . . Ah, dear Andrea, how difficult it is to stand counter to, yet to accept with perfect submission of one's whole being, the elaborate order that a woman establishes in her own gracious flat. How much at fault one feels taking a small metal tray and putting it at the far end of the table, setting it there simply because one has brought one's English dictionaries and it's at this end, within easy reach of the hand, that they ought to be. To move that tray is the equivalent of an unexpected horrible crimson in the middle of one of Ozenfant's painterly cadences, as if suddenly the strings of all the double basses snapped at the same time with the same dreadful whiplash at the most hushed instant in a Mozart symphony. Moving that tray alters the play of relationships in the whole house, of each object with another, of each moment of their soul with the soul of the house and its absent inhabitant. And I cannot bring my fingers close to a book, hardly change a lamp's cone of light, open the piano bench, without a feeling of rivalry and offense swinging before my eyes like a flock of sparrows.

You know why I came to your house, to your peaceful living room scooped out of the noonday light. Everything looks so natural, as always when one does not know the truth. You've gone off to Paris, I am left with the apartment in the calle Suipacha, we draw up a simple and satisfactory plan convenient to us both until September brings you back again to Buenos Aires and I amble off to some other house where perhaps . . . But I'm not writing you for that reason, I was sending this letter to you because of the rabbits, it seems only fair to let you know; and because I like to write letters, and maybe too because it's raining.

I moved last Thursday in a haze overlaid by weariness, at five in the afternoon. I've closed so many suitcases in my life, I've passed so many hours preparing luggage that never manages to get moved anyplace, that Thursday was a day full of shadows and straps, because when I look at valise straps it's as though I were seeing shadows, as though they were parts of a whip that flogs me in some indirect way, very subtly and horribly. But I packed the bags, let your maid know I was coming to move in. I was going up in the elevator and just between the first and second floors I felt that I was going to vomit up a little rabbit. I have never described this to you before, not so much, I don't think, from lack of truthfulness as that, just naturally, one is not going to explain to people at large that from time to time one vomits up a small rabbit. Always I have managed to be alone when it happens, guarding the fact much as we guard so many of our privy acts, evidences of our physical selves which happen to us in total privacy. Don't reproach me for it, Andrea, don't blame me. Once in a while it happens that I vomit up a bunny. It's no reason not to live in whatever house, it's no reason for one to blush and isolate oneself and to walk around keeping one's mouth shut.

When I feel that I'm going to bring up a rabbit, I put two fingers in my mouth like an open pincer, and I wait to feel the lukewarm fluff rise in my throat like the effervescence in a sal hepatica. It's all swift and clean, passes in the briefest instant. I remove the fingers from my mouth and in them, held fast by the ears, a small white rabbit. The bunny appears to be content, a perfectly normal bunny only very tiny, small as a chocolate rabbit, only it's white and very thoroughly a rabbit. I set it in the palm of my hand, I smooth the fluff, caressing it with two fingers; the bunny seems satisfied with having been born and waggles and pushes its muzzle against my skin, moving it with that quiet and tickling nibble of a rabbit's mouth against the skin of the hand. He's looking for something to eat, and then (I'm talking about when this happened at my house on the outskirts) I take him with me out to the balcony and set him down in the big flowerpot among the clover that I've grown there with this in mind. The bunny raises his ears as high as they can go, surrounds a tender clover leaf with a quick little wheeling motion of his snout, and I know that I can leave him there now and go on my way for a time, lead a life not very different from people who buy their rabbits at farmhouses.

Between the first and the second floors, then, Andrea, like an omen of what my life in your house was going to be, I realized that I was going to vomit a rabbit. At that point I was afraid (or was it surprise? No, perhaps fear of the same surprise) because, before leaving my house, only two days before, I'd vomited a bunny and so was safe for a month, five weeks, maybe six with a little luck. Now, look, I'd resolved the problem perfectly. I grew clover on the balcony of my other house, vomited a bunny, put it in with the clover and at the end of a month, when I suspected that any moment . . . then I made a present of the rabbit, already grown enough, to señora de Molina, who believed I had a hobby and was quiet about it. In another flowerpot tender and propitious clover was already growing, I awaited without concern the morning when the tickling sensation of fluff rising obstructed my throat, and the new little rabbit reiterated from that hour the life and habits of its predecessor. Habits, Andrea, are concrete forms of rhythm, are that portion of rhythm which helps to keep us alive. Vomiting bunnies wasn't so terrible once one had gotten into the unvarying cycle, into the method. You will want to know why all this work, why all that clover and señora de Molina. It would have been easier to kill the little thing right away and . . . Ah, you should vomit one up all by yourself, take it in two fingers and set it in your opened hand, still attached to yourself by the act itself, by the indefinable aura of its proximity, barely now broken away. A month puts a lot of things at a distance; a month is size, long fur, long leaps, ferocious eyes, an absolute difference. Andrea, a month is a rabbit, it really makes a real rabbit; but in the maiden moment, the warm bustling fleece covering an inalienable presence . . . like a poem in its first minutes, "fruit of an Idumean night" as much one as oneself . . . and afterwards not so much one, so distant and isolated in its flat white world the size of a letter.

With all that, I decided to kill the rabbit almost as soon as it was born. I was going to live at your place for four months: four, perhaps with luck three—tablespoonsful of alcohol down its throat. (Do you know pity permits you to kill a small rabbit instantly by giving it a tablespoon of alcohol to drink? Its flesh tastes better afterward, they say, however, I . . . Three or four tablespoonsful of alcohol, then the bathroom or a package to put in the rubbish.)

Rising up past the third floor, the rabbit was moving in the palm of my hand. Sara was waiting upstairs to help me get the valises in . . . Could I explain that it was a whim? Something about passing a pet store? I wrapped the tiny creature in my handkerchief, put him into my overcoat pocket, leaving the overcoat unbuttoned so as not to squeeze him. He barely budged. His minuscule consciousness would be revealing important facts: that life is a movement upward with a final click, and is also a low ceiling, white and smelling of lavender, enveloping you in the bottom of a warm pit.

Sara saw nothing, she was too fascinated with the arduous problem of adjusting her sense of order to my valise-and-footlocker, my papers and my peevishness at her elaborate explanations in which the words "for example" occurred with distressing frequency. I could hardly get the bathroom door closed; to kill it now. A delicate area of heat surrounded the handkerchief, the little rabbit was extremely white and, I think, prettier than the others. He wasn't looking at me, he just hopped about and was being content, which was even worse than looking at me. I shut him in the empty medicine chest and went on unpacking, disoriented but not unhappy, not feeling guilty, not soaping up my hands to get off the feel of a final convulsion.

I realized that I could not kill him. But that same night I vomited a little black bunny. And two days later another white one. And on the fourth night a tiny grey one.

You must love the handsome wardrobe in your bedroom, with its great door that opens so generously, its empty shelves awaiting my clothes. Now I have them in there. Inside there. True, it seems impossible; not even Sara would believe it. That Sara did not suspect anything, was the result of my continuous preoccupation with a task that takes over my days and nights with the singleminded crash of the portcullis falling, and I go about hardened inside, calcined like that starfish you've put above the bathtub, and at every bath I take it seems all at once to swell with salt and whiplashes of sun and great rumbles of profundity.

They sleep during the day. There are ten of them. During the day they sleep. With the door closed, the wardrobe is a diurnal night for them alone, there they sleep out their night in a sedate obedience. When I leave for work I take the bedroom keys with me. Sara must think that I mistrust her honesty and looks at me doubtfully, every morning she looks as though she's about to say something to me, but in the end she remains silent and I am that much happier. (When she straightens up the bedroom between nine and ten, I make noise in the living room, put on a Benny Carter record which fills the whole apartment, and as Sara is a *saetas* and *pasodobles* fan, the wardrobe seems to be silent, and for the most part it is, because for the rabbits it's night still and repose is the order of the day.)

Their day begins an hour after supper when Sara brings in the tray with the delicate tinkling of the sugar tongs, wishes me good night—yes, she wishes me, Andrea, the most ironic thing is that she wishes me good night—shuts herself in her room, and promptly I'm by myself, alone with the closed-up wardrobe, alone with my obligation and my melancholy.

I let them out, they hop agilely to the party in the living room, sniffing briskly at the clover hidden in my pockets which makes ephemeral lacy patterns on the carpet which they alter, remove, finish up in a minute. They eat well, quietly and correctly; until that moment I have nothing to say, I just watch them from the sofa, a useless book in my hand—I who wanted to read all of Giraudoux, Andrea, and López's Argentine history that you keep on the lower shelf—and they eat up the clover.

There are ten. Almost all of them white. They lift their warm heads toward the lamps in the living room, the three motionless suns of their day; they love the light because their night has neither moon nor sun nor stars nor streetlamps. They gaze at their triple sun and are content. That's when they hop about on the carpet, into the chairs, ten tiny blotches shift like a moving constellation from one part to another, while I'd like to see them quiet, see them at my feet and being quiet—somewhat the dream of any god, Andrea, a dream the gods never see fulfilled—something quite different from wriggling in behind the portrait of Miguel de Unamuno, then off to the pale green urn, over into the dark hollow of the writing desk, always fewer than ten, always six or eight and I asking myself where the two are that are missing, and what if Sara should get up for some reason, and the presidency of Rivadavia which is what I want to read in López's history.

Andrea, I don't know how I stand up under it. You remember that I came to your place for some rest. It's not my fault if I vomit a bunny from time to time, if this moving changed me inside as well—not nominalism, it's not magic either, it's just that things cannot alter like that all at once, sometimes things reverse themselves brutally and when you expect the slap on the right cheek—. Like that, Andrea, or some other way, but always like that.

It's night while I'm writing you. It's three in the afternoon, but I'm writing you during their night. They sleep during the day. What a relief this office is! Filled with shouts, commands, Royal typewriters, vice presidents and mimeograph machines! What relief, what peace, what horror, Andrea! They're calling me to the telephone now. It was some friends upset about my monasterial nights, Luis inviting me out for a stroll or Jorge insisting—he's bought a ticket for me for this concert. I hardly dare to say no to them, I invent long and ineffectual stories about my poor health, I'm behind in the translations, any evasion possible. And when I get back home and am in the elevator—that stretch between the first and second floors—night after night, hopelessly, I formulate the vain hope that really it isn't true.

I'm doing the best I can to see that they don't break your things. They've nibbled away a little at the books on the lowest shelf, you'll find the backs repasted, which I did so that Sara wouldn't notice it. That lamp with the porcelain belly full of butterflies and old cowboys, do you like that very much? The crack where the piece was broken out barely shows, I spent a whole night doing it with a

46

special cement that they sold me in an English shop—you know the English stores have the best cements—and now I sit beside it so that one of them can't reach it again with its paws (it's almost lovely to see how they like to stand on their hind legs, nostalgia for that so-distant humanity, perhaps an imitation of their god walking about and looking at them darkly; besides which, you will have observed —when you were a baby, perhaps—that you can put a bunny in the corner against the wall like a punishment, and he'll stand there, paws against the wall and very quiet, for hours and hours).

At 5 A.M. (I slept a little stretched out on the green sofa, waking up at every velvety-soft dash, every slightest clink) I put them in the wardrobe and do the cleaning up. That way Sara always finds everything in order, although at times I've noticed a restrained astonishment, a stopping to look at some object, a slight discoloration in the carpet, and again the desire to ask me something, but then I'm whistling Franck's *Symphonic Variations* in a way that always prevents her. How can I tell you about it, Andrea, the minute mishaps of this soundless and vegetal dawn, half-asleep on what staggered path picking up butt-ends of clover, individual leaves, white hunks of fur, falling against the furniture, crazy from lack of sleep, and I'm behind in my Gide, Troyat I haven't gotten to translating, and my reply to a distant young lady who will be asking herself already if . . . why go on with all this, why go on with this letter I keep trying to write between telephone calls and interviews.

Andrea, dear Andrea, my consolation is that there are ten of them and no more. It's been fifteen days since I held the last bunny in the palm of my hand, since then nothing, only the ten of them with me, their diurnal night and growing, ugly already and getting long hair, adolescents now and full of urgent needs and crazy whims, leaping on top of the bust of Antinoös (it is Antinoös, isn't it, that boy who looks blindly?) or losing themselves in the living room where their movements make resounding thumps, so much so that I ought to chase them out of there for fear that Sara will hear them and appear before me in a fright and probably in her nightgown—it would have to be like that with Sara, she'd be in her nightgown—and then . . . Only ten, think of that little happiness I have in the middle of it all, the growing calm with which, on my return home, I cut past the rigid ceilings of the first and second floors.

I was interrupted because I had to attend a committee meeting. I'm continuing the letter here at your house, Andrea, under the soundless grey light of another dawn. Is it really the next day, Andrea? A bit of white on the page will be all you'll have to represent the bridge, hardly a period on a page between yesterday's letter and today's. How tell you that in that interval everything has gone smash? Where you see that simple period I hear the circling belt of water break the dam in its fury, this side of the paper for me, this side of my letter to you I can't write with the same calm which I was sitting in when I had to put it aside to go to the committee meeting. Wrapped in their cube of night, sleeping without a worry in the world, eleven bunnies; perhaps even now, but no, not now— In the elevator then, or coming into the building; it's not important now where, if the when is now, if it can happen in any now of those that are left to me.

Enough now, I've written this because it's important to me to let you know that I was not all that responsible for the unavoidable and helpless destruction of your home. I'll leave this letter here for you, it would be indecent if the mailman should deliver it some fine clear morning in Paris. Last night I turned the books on the second shelf in the other direction; they were already reaching that high, standing up on their hind legs or jumping, they gnawed off the backs to sharpen their teeth—not that they were hungry, they had all the clover I had bought for them, I store it in the drawers of the writing desk. They tore the curtains, the coverings on the easy chairs, the edge of Augusto Torres' self-portrait, they got fluff all over the rug and besides they yipped, there's no word for it, they stood in a circle under the light of the lamp, in a circle as though they were adoring me, and suddenly they were yipping, they were crying like I never believed rabbits could cry.

I tried in vain to pick up all the hair that was ruining the rug, to smooth out the edges of the fabric they'd chewed on, to shut them up again in the wardrobe. Day is coming, maybe Sara's getting up early. It's almost queer, I'm not disturbed so much about Sara. It's almost queer, I'm not disturbed to see them gamboling about looking for something to play with. I'm not so much to blame, you'll see when you get here that I've repaired a lot of the things that were broken with the cement I bought in the English shop, I did what I could to keep from being a nuisance . . . As far as I'm concerned, going from ten to eleven is like an unbridgeable chasm. You understand: ten was fine, with a wardrobe, clover and hope, so many things could happen for the better. But not with eleven, because to say eleven is already to say twelve for sure, and Andrea, twelve would be thirteen. So now it's dawn and a cold solitude in which happiness ends, reminiscences, you and perhaps a good deal more. This balcony over the street is filled with dawn, the first sounds of the city waking. I don't think it will be difficult to pick up eleven small rabbits splattered over the pavement, perhaps they won't even be noticed, people will be too occupied with the other body, it would be more proper to remove it quickly before the early students pass through on their way to school.

A YELLOW FLOWER

. . . .

We are immortal, I know it sounds like a joke. I know because I met the exception to the rule, I know the only mortal there is. He told me his story in a bar in the rue Cambronne, drunk enough so it didn't bother him to tell the truth, even though the bartender (who owned the place) and the regulars at the counter were laughing so hard that the wine was coming out of their eyes. He must have seen some flicker of interest in my face—he drifted steadily toward me and we ended up treating ourselves to a table in the corner where we could drink and talk in peace. He told me that he was a retired city employee and that his wife had gone back to her parents for the summer, as good a way as any of letting it be known that she'd left him. He was a guy, not particularly old and certainly not stupid, with a sort of dried-up face and consumptive eyes. In honesty, he was drinking to forget, a fact which he proclaimed by the time we were starting the fifth glass of red. But he did not smell of Paris, that signature of Paris which apparently only we foreigners can detect. And his nails were decently pared, no specks under them.

He told how he'd seen this kid on the number 95 bus, oh, about thirteen years old, and after looking at him for a spell it struck him that the boy looked very much like him, at least very much as he remembered himself at that age. He continued little by little admitting that the boy seemed completely like him, the face, the hands, the mop of hair flopping over the forehead, eyes very widely spaced, even more strongly in his shyness, the way he took refuge in a short-story magazine, the motion of his head in tossing his hair back, the hopeless awkwardness of his movements. The resemblance was so exact that he almost laughed out loud, but when the boy got down at the rue de Rennes, he got off too, leaving a friend waiting for him in Montparnasse. Looking for some pretext to speak with the kid, he asked directions to a particular street, and without surprise heard himself answered by a voice that had once been his own. The kid was going as far as the street, and they walked along together shyly for several blocks. At that tense moment, a kind of revelation came over him. Not an explanation, but something that could dispense with explanation, that turned blurred or stupid somehow when—as now—one attempted to explain it.

To make a long story short, he figured a way to find out where the kid lived, and with the prestige of having spent some time as a scoutmaster, he managed to gain entrance to that fortress of fortresses, a French home. He found an air of decent misery, a mother looking older than she should have, a retired uncle, two cats. Afterward, it was not too difficult; a brother of his entrusted him with his son who was going on fourteen, and the two boys became friends. He began to go to Luc's house every week; the mother treated him to heated-up coffee, they talked of the war, of the occupation, of Luc also. What had started as a blunt revelation was developing now like a theorem in geometry, taking on the shape of what people used to call fate. Besides, it could be said in everyday words: Luc was him again, there was no mortality, we were all immortals.

"All immortals, old man. Nobody'd been able to prove it, and it had to happen to me, and on a 95 bus. Some slight imperfection in the mechanism, a crimp and doubling back of time, I mean an overlap, a re-embodiment incarnate, simultaneously instead of consecutively. Luc should never have been born until after I'd died, and on the other hand, I . . . never mind the fantastic accident of meeting him on a city bus. I think I told you this already, it was a sort of absolute surety, no words needed. That was that, and that was the end of it. But the doubts began afterwards, because in a case like that, you either think that you're an imbecile, or you start taking tranquilizers. As for the doubts, you kill them off, one by one, the proofs that you're not crazy keep coming. And what made those dopes laugh the hardest when, once in a while, I said something to them about it, well, I'll tell you now. Luc wasn't just me another time, he was going to become like me, like this miserable sonofabitch talking to you. You only had to watch him playing, just watch, he always fell down and hurt himself, twisting a foot or throwing his clavicle out, flushes of feeling that'd make him break out in hives, he could hardly even ask for anything without blushing horribly. On the other hand his mother would talk to you about anything and everything with the kid standing there squirming with embarrassment, the most

53

incredible, intimate, private . . . anecdotes about his
first teeth, drawings he made when he was eight, illnesses
. . . she liked to talk. The good lady suspected nothing,
that's for sure, and the uncle played chess with me, I was
like family, even lending them money to get to the end of
the month. No, it was easy to get to know Luc's history,
just edging questions into discussions his elders were interested in: the uncle's rheumatism, politics, the venality
of the concierge, you know. So between bishop calling
check to my king and serious discussions of the price of
meat, I learned about Luc's childhood, and the bits of evidence stockpiled into an incontrovertible proof. But I want
you to understand me, meanwhile let's order another
glass: Luc was me, what I'd been as a kid, but don't think
of him as the perfect copy. More like an analogous figure,
understand? I mean, when I was seven I dislocated my
wrist, with Luc it was the clavicle, and at nine I had German measles and he had scarlet fever, the measles had
me out some two weeks, Luc was better in five days, well,
you know, the strides of science, etc. The whole thing was
a repeat and so, give you another example somewhat to
the point, the baker on the corner is a reincarnation of
Napoleon, and he doesn't know because the pattern hasn't
changed, I mean, he'll never be able to meet the real arti-
cle on a city bus; but if in some way or another he becomes aware of the truth, he might be able to understand
that he's a repeat of, is still repeating Napoleon, that the
move from being a dishwasher to being the owner of a
decent bakery in Montparnasse is the same pattern as the
jump from Corsica to the throne of France, and that if he
dug carefully enough through the story of his life, he'd
find moments that would correspond to the Egyptian
Campaign, to the Consulate, to Austerlitz, he might even
figure that something is going to happen to his bakery in a
few years and that he'll end on St. Helena, say, some fur-

nished room in a sixth-floor walkup, a big defeat, no? and surrounded by the waters of loneliness, also still proud of that bakery of his which was like a flight of eagles. You get it?"

Well, I got it all right, but I figured that we all get childhood diseases about the same time, and that almost all of us break something playing football.

"I know, I haven't mentioned anything other than the usual coincidences, very visible. For example, even that Luc looked like me is of no serious importance, even if you're sold on the revelation on the bus. What really counted was the sequence of events, and that's harder to explain because it involves the character, inexact recollections, the mythologies of childhood. At that time, I mean when I was Luc's age, I went through a very bad time that started with an interminable sickness, then right in the middle of the convalescence broke my arm playing with some friends, and as soon as that was healed I fell in love with the sister of a buddy of mine at school, and God, it was painful, like you can't look at a girl's eyes and she's making fun of you. Luc fell sick also, and just as he was getting better they took him to the circus, and going down the bleacher seats he slipped and dislocated his ankle. Shortly after that his mother came on him accidentally one afternoon with a little blue kerchief twisted up in his hands, standing at a window crying: it was a handkerchief she'd never seen before."

As someone has to be the devil's advocate, I remarked that puppy love is the inevitable concomitant of bruises, broken bones and pleurisy. But I had to admit that the business of the airplane was a different matter. A plane with a propeller driven by rubber bands that he'd gotten for his birthday.

"When he got it, I remembered the erector set my mother gave me as a present when I was fourteen, and what happened with that. It happened I was out in the garden in spite of the fact that a summer storm was ready to break, you could already hear the thunder cracking, and I'd just started to put a derrick together on the table under the arbor near the gate to the street. Someone called me from the house and I had to go in for a minute. When I got back, the box and the erector set were gone and the gate was wide open. Screaming desperately, I ran out into the street and there was no one in sight, and at that same moment a bolt of lightning hit the house across the road. All of this happened as a single stroke, and I was remembering it as Luc was getting his airplane and he stood there gazing at it with the same happiness with which I had eyed my erector set. The mother brought me a cup of coffee and we were trading the usual sentences when we heard a shout. Luc had run to the window as though he were going to throw himself out of it. His face white and his eyes streaming, he managed to blubber out that the plane had swerved in its trajectory and had gone exactly through the small space of the partly opened window. We'll never find it again, we'll never find it again, he kept saying. He was still sobbing when we heard a shout from downstairs, his uncle came running in with the news that there was a fire in the house across the street. Understand now? Yes, we'd better have another glass."

Afterward, as I was saying nothing, the man continued. He had begun thinking exclusively of Luc, of Luc's fate. His mother had decided to send him to a vocational school, so that what she referred to as "his life's road" would be open to him in some decent way, but that road was already open, and only he, who would not have been able to open his mouth, they would have thought him insane and kept him away from Luc altogether, would have been able to tell the mother and the uncle that there was no use whatsoever, that whatever they might do the result would be the same, humiliation, a deadly routine, the monotonous years, calamitous disasters that would continue to nibble away at the clothes and the soul, taking refuge in a resentful solitude, in some local bistro. But Luc's destiny was not the worst of it; the worst was that Luc would die in his turn, and another man would relive Luc's pattern and his own pattern until he died and another man in his turn enter the wheel. Almost as though Luc were already unimportant to him; at night his insomnia mapped it out even beyond that other Luc, to others whose names would be Robert or Claude or Michael, a theory of infinite extension, an infinity of poor devils repeating the pattern without knowing it, convinced of their freedom of will and choice. The man was crying in his beer, only it was wine in this case, what could you do about it, nothing.

"They laugh at me now when I tell them that Luc died a few months later, they're too stupid to realize . . . Yeah, now don't you start looking at me like that. He died a few months later, it started as a kind of bronchitis, like at the same age I'd come down with a hepatitis infection. Me, they put in the hospital, but Luc's mother persisted in keeping him at home to take care of him, and I went almost every day, sometimes I brought my nephew along to play with Luc. There was so much misery in that house that my visits were a consolation in every sense, company for Luc, a package of dried herrings or Damascus tarts. After I mentioned a drugstore where they gave me a special discount, it was taken for granted when I took charge of buying the medicines. It wound up by their letting me be Luc's nurse, and you can imagine how, in a case like that, where the doctor comes in and leaves without any special concern, no one pays much attention if the final symptoms have anything at all to do with the first diagnosis . . . Why are you looking at me like that? Did I say anything wrong?"

No, no, he hadn't said anything wrong, especially as he was crocked on the wine. On the contrary, unless you imagine something particularly horrible, poor Luc's death seemed to prove that anyone given enough imagination can begin a fantasy on the number 95 bus and finish it beside a bed where a kid is dying quietly. I told him no to calm him down. He stayed staring into space for a spell before resuming the story.

"All right, however you like. The truth is that in those weeks following the funeral, for the first time I felt something that might pass for happiness. I still went every once in a while to visit Luc's mother, I'd bring a package of cookies, but neither she nor the house meant anything to me now, it was as though I were waterlogged by the marvelous certainty of being the first mortal, of feeling that my life was continuing to wear away, day after day, wine after wine, and that finally it would end some place or another, some time or another, reiterating until the very end the destiny of some unknown dead man, nobody knows who or when, but me, I was going to be really dead, no Luc to step into the wheel to stupidly reiterate a stupid life. Understand the fullness of that, old man, envy me for all that happiness while it lasted."

Because apparently it had not lasted. The bistro and the cheap wine proved it, and those eyes shining with a fever that was not of the body. Nonetheless he had lived some months savoring each moment of the daily mediocrity of his life, the breakup of his marriage, the ruin of his fifty years, sure of his inalienable mortality. One afternoon, crossing the Luxembourg gardens, he saw a flower.

"It was on the side of a bed, just a plain yellow flower. I'd stopped to light a cigarette and I was distracted, looking at it. It was a little as though the flower were looking at me too, you know, those communications, once in a while . . . You know what I'm talking about, everyone feels that, what they call beauty. It was just that, the flower was beautiful, it was a very lovely flower. And I was damned, one day I was going to die and forever. The flower was handsome, there would always be flowers for men in the future. All at once I understood nothing, I mean nothingness, nothing, I'd thought it was peace, it was the end of the chain. I was going to die, Luc was already dead, there would never again be a flower for anyone like us, there would never be anything, there'd be absolutely nothing, and that's what nothing was, that there would never again be a flower. The lit match burned my fingers, it smarted. At the next square I jumped on a bus going, it wasn't important where, anywhere, I didn't know, and foolishly enough I started looking around, looking at everything, everyone you could see in the street, everyone on the bus. When we came to the end of the line I got off and got onto another bus going out to the suburbs. All afternoon, until night fell, I got off and on buses, thinking of the flower and of Luc, looking among the passengers for someone who resembled Luc, someone who looked like me or Luc, someone who could be me again, someone I could look at knowing it was myself, that it was me, and then let him go on, to get off without saying anything, protecting him almost so that he would go on and live out his poor stupid life, his imbecilic, abortive life until another imbecilic abortive life, until another imbecilic abortive life, until another . . ."

I paid the bill.

T W O

CONTINUITY

OF PARKS

· · · · · · · · · · · · · · · · · · ·

He had begun to read the novel a few days before. He had put it down because of some urgent business conferences, opened it again on his way back to the estate by train; he permitted himself a slowly growing interest in the plot, in the characterizations. That afternoon, after writing a letter giving his power of attorney and discussing a matter of joint ownership with the manager of his estate, he returned to the book in the tranquillity of his study which looked out upon the park with its oaks. Sprawled in his favorite armchair, its back toward the door—even the possibility of an intrusion would have irritated him, had he thought of it—he let his left hand caress repeatedly the green velvet upholstery and set to reading the final chapters. He remembered effortlessly the names and his mental image of the characters; the novel spread its glamour over him almost at once. He tasted the almost perverse pleasure of disengaging himself line by line from the things around him, and at the same time feeling his head rest comfortably on the green velvet of the chair with its high back, sensing that the cigarettes rested within reach of his hand, that beyond the great windows the air of afternoon danced under the oak trees in the park. Word by word, licked up by the sordid dilemma of the hero and heroine, letting himself be absorbed to the point where the images settled down and took on color and movement, he was witness to the final encounter in the mountain cabin. The woman arrived first, apprehensive; now the lover came in, his face cut by the backlash of a branch. Admirably, she stanched the blood with her kisses, but he rebuffed her caresses, he had not come to perform again the ceremonies of a secret passion, protected by a world of dry leaves and furtive paths through the forest. The dagger warmed itself against his chest, and underneath liberty pounded, hidden close. A lustful, panting dialogue raced down the pages like a rivulet of snakes, and one felt it had all been decided from eternity. Even to those caresses which writhed about the lover's body, as though wishing to keep him there, to dissuade him from it; they sketched abominably the frame of that other body it was necessary to destroy. Nothing had been forgotten: alibis, unforeseen hazards, possible mistakes. From this hour on, each instant had its use minutely assigned. The cold-blooded, twice-gone-over reexamination of the details was barely broken off so that a hand could caress a cheek. It was beginning to get dark.

Not looking at one another now, rigidly fixed upon the task which awaited them, they separated at the cabin door. She was to follow the trail that led north. On the path leading in the opposite direction, he turned for a moment to watch her running, her hair loosened and flying. He ran in turn, crouching among the trees and hedges until, in the yellowish fog of dusk, he could distinguish the avenue of trees which led up to the house. The dogs were not supposed to bark, they did not bark. The estate manager would not be there at this hour, and he was not there. He went up the three porch steps and entered. The woman's words reached him over the thudding of blood in his ears: first a blue chamber, then a hall, then a carpeted stairway. At the top, two doors. No one in the first room, no one in the second. The door of the salon, and then, the knife in hand, the light from the great windows, the high back of an armchair covered in green velvet, the head of the man in the chair reading a novel.

THE NIGHT FACE UP · · · · · · · · · · · · · · · ·

Halfway down the long hotel vestibule, he thought that probably he was going to be late, and hurried on into the street to get out his motorcycle from the corner where the next-door superintendent let him keep it. On the jewelry store at the corner he read that it was ten to nine; he had time to spare. The sun filtered through the tall downtown buildings, and he—because for himself, for just going along thinking, he did not have a name—he swung onto the machine, savoring the idea of the ride.

N.B. The war of the blossom was the name the Aztecs gave to a ritual war in which they took prisoners for sacrifice. It is metaphysics to say that the gods see men as flowers, to be so uprooted, trampled, cut down. —ED.

The motor whirred between his legs, and a cool wind whipped his pantslegs.

He let the ministries zip past (the pink, the white), and a series of stores on the main street, their windows flashing. Now he was beginning the most pleasant part of the run, the real ride: a long street bordered with trees, very little traffic, with spacious villas whose gardens rambled all the way down to the sidewalks, which were barely indicated by low hedges. A bit inattentive perhaps, but tooling along on the right side of the street, he allowed himself to be carried away by the freshness, by the weightless contraction of this hardly begun day. This involuntary relaxation, possibly, kept him from preventing the accident. When he saw that the woman standing on the corner had rushed into the crosswalk while he still had the green light, it was already somewhat too late for a simple solution. He braked hard with foot and hand, wrenching himself to the left; he heard the woman scream, and at the collision his vision went. It was like falling asleep all at once.

He came to abruptly. Four or five young men were getting him out from under the cycle. He felt the taste of salt and blood, one knee hurt, and when they hoisted him up he yelped, he couldn't bear the presssure on his right arm. Voices which did not seem to belong to the faces hanging above him encouraged him cheerfully with jokes and assurances. His single solace was to hear someone else confirm that the lights indeed had been in his favor. He asked about the woman, trying to keep down the nausea which was edging up into his throat. While they carried him face up to a nearby pharmacy, he learned that the cause of the accident had gotten only a few scrapes on the legs. "Nah, you barely got her at all, but when ya hit, the impact made the machine jump and flop on its side . . ." Opinions, recollections of other smashups, take it easy, work him in

shoulders first, there, that's fine, and someone in a dust-
coat giving him a swallow of something soothing in the
shadowy interior of the small local pharmacy.

Within five minutes the police ambulance arrived, and
they lifted him onto a cushioned stretcher. It was a relief
for him to be able to lie out flat. Completely lucid, but realizing that he was suffering the effects of a terrible shock,
he gave his information to the officer riding in the ambulance with him. The arm almost didn't hurt; blood
dripped down from a cut over the eyebrow all over his
face. He licked his lips once or twice to drink it. He felt
pretty good, it had been an accident, tough luck; stay quiet
a few weeks, nothing worse. The guard said that the
motorcycle didn't seem badly racked up. "Why should it,"
he replied. "It all landed on top of me." They both laughed,
and when they got to the hospital, the guard shook his
hand and wished him luck. Now the nausea was coming
back little by little; meanwhile they were pushing him on
a wheeled stretcher toward a pavilion further back, rolling
along under trees full of birds, he shut his eyes and
wished he were asleep or chloroformed. But they kept him
for a good while in a room with that hospital smell, filling
out a form, getting his clothes off, and dressing him in a
stiff, greyish smock. They moved his arm carefully, it
didn't hurt him. The nurses were constantly making wise-
cracks, and if it hadn't been for the stomach contractions
he would have felt fine, almost happy.

They got him over to X-ray, and twenty minutes later,
with the still-damp negative lying on his chest like a black
tombstone, they pushed him into surgery. Someone tall
and thin in white came over and began to look at the X-
rays. A woman's hands were arranging his head, he felt
that they were moving him from one stretcher to another.
The man in white came over to him again, smiling, some-

thing gleamed in his right hand. He patted his cheek and made a sign to someone stationed behind.

It was unusual as a dream because it was full of smells, and he never dreamt smells. First a marshy smell, there to the left of the trail the swamps began already, the quaking bogs from which no one ever returned. But the reek lifted, and instead there came a dark, fresh composite fragrance, like the night under which he moved, in flight from the Aztecs. And it was all so natural, he had to run from the Aztecs who had set out on their manhunt, and his sole chance was to find a place to hide in the deepest part of the forest, taking care not to lose the narrow trail which only they, the Motecas, knew.

What tormented him the most was the odor, as though, notwithstanding the absolute acceptance of the dream, there was something which resisted that which was not habitual, which until that point had not participated in the game. "It smells of war," he thought, his hand going instinctively to the stone knife which was tucked at an angle into his girdle of woven wool. An unexpected sound made him crouch suddenly stock-still and shaking. To be afraid was nothing strange, there was plenty of fear in his dreams. He waited, covered by the branches of a shrub and the starless night. Far off, probably on the other side of the big lake, they'd be lighting the bivouac fires; that part of the sky had a reddish glare. The sound was not repeated. It had been like a broken limb. Maybe an animal that, like himself, was escaping from the smell of war. He stood erect slowly, sniffing the air. Not a sound could be heard, but the fear was still following, as was the smell, that cloying incense of the war of the blossom. He had to press forward, to stay out of the bogs and get to the heart of the forest. Groping uncertainly through the dark, stooping every other moment to touch the packed earth of the trail, he took a few steps. He would have liked to have broken into a run, but the gurgling fens lapped on either side of him. On the path and in darkness, he took his bearings. Then he caught a horrible blast of that foul smell he was most afraid of, and leaped forward desperately.

"You're going to fall off the bed," said the patient next to him. "Stop bouncing around, old buddy."

He opened his eyes and it was afternoon, the sun already low in the oversized windows of the long ward. While trying to smile at his neighbor, he detached himself almost physically from the final scene of the nightmare. His arm, in a plaster cast, hung suspended from an apparatus with weights and pulleys. He felt thirsty, as though he'd been running for miles, but they didn't want to give him much water, barely enough to moisten his lips and make a mouthful. The fever was winning slowly and he would have been able to sleep again, but he was enjoying the pleasure of keeping awake, eyes half-closed, listening to the other patients' conversation, answering a question from time to time. He saw a little white pushcart come up beside the bed, a blond nurse rubbed the front of his thigh with alcohol and stuck him with a fat needle connected to a tube which ran up to a bottle filled with a milky, opalescent liquid. A young intern arrived with some metal and leather apparatus which he adjusted to fit onto the good arm to check something or other. Night fell, and the fever went along dragging him down softly to a state in which things seemed embossed as through opera glasses, they were real and soft and, at the same time, vaguely distasteful; like sitting in a boring movie and thinking that, well, still, it'd be worse out in the street, and staying.

A cup of a marvelous golden broth came, smelling of leeks, celery and parsley. A small hunk of bread, more precious than a whole banquet, found itself crumbling little by little. His arm hardly hurt him at all, and only in the eyebrow where they'd taken stitches a quick, hot pain sizzled occasionally. When the big windows across the way turned to smudges of dark blue, he thought it would not be difficult for him to sleep. Still on his back so a little uncomfortable, running his tongue out over his hot, too-dry lips, he tasted the broth still, and with a sigh of bliss, he let himself drift off.

First there was a confusion, as of one drawing all his sensations, for that moment blunted or muddled, into himself. He realized that he was running in pitch darkness, although, above, the sky criss-crossed with treetops was less black than the rest. "The trail," he thought, "I've gotten off the trail." His feet sank into a bed of leaves and mud, and then he couldn't take a step that the branches of shrubs did not whiplash against his ribs and legs. Out of breath, knowing despite the darkness and silence that he was surrounded, he crouched down to listen. Maybe the trail was very near, with the first daylight he would be able to see it again. Nothing now could help him to find it. The hand that had unconsciously gripped the haft of the dagger climbed like a fen scorpion up to his neck where the protecting amulet hung. Barely moving his lips, he mumbled the supplication of the corn which brings about the beneficent moons, and the prayer to Her Very Highness, to the distributor of all Motecan possessions. At the same time he felt his ankles sinking deeper into the mud, and the waiting in the darkness of the obscure grove of live oak grew intolerable to him. The war of the blossom had started at the beginning of the moon and had been going on for three days and three nights now. If he managed to hide in the depths of the forest, getting off the trail further up past the marsh country, perhaps the warriors wouldn't follow his track. He thought of the many prisoners they'd already taken. But the number didn't count, only the consecrated period. The hunt would continue until the priests gave the sign to return. Everything had its number and its limit, and it was within the sacred period, and he on the other side from the hunters.

He heard the cries and leaped up, knife in hand. As if the sky were aflame on the horizon, he saw torches moving among the branches, very near him. The smell of war was unbearable, and when the first enemy jumped him, leaped at his throat, he felt an almost-pleasure in sinking the stone blade flat to the haft into his chest. The lights were already around him, the happy cries. He managed to cut the air once or twice, then a rope snared him from behind.

"It's the fever," the man in the next bed said. "The same thing happened to me when they operated on my duodenum. Take some water, you'll see, you'll sleep all right."

Laid next to the night from which he came back, the tepid shadow of the ward seemed delicious to him. A violet lamp kept watch high on the far wall like a guardian eye. You could hear coughing, deep breathing, once in a while a conversation in whispers. Everything was pleasant and secure, without the chase, no . . . But he didn't want to go on thinking about the nightmare. There were lots of things to amuse himself with. He began to look at the cast on his arm, and the pulleys that held it so comfortably in the air. They'd left a bottle of mineral water on the night table beside him. He put the neck of the bottle to his mouth and drank it like a precious liqueur. He could now make out the different shapes in the ward, the thirty beds, the closets with glass doors. He guessed that his fever was down, his face felt cool. The cut over the eyebrow barely hurt at all, like a recollection. He saw himself leaving the hotel again, wheeling out the cycle. Who'd have thought that it would end like this? He tried to fix the moment of the accident exactly, and it got him very angry to notice that there was a void there, an emptiness he could not manage to fill. Between the impact and the moment that they picked him up off the pavement, the passing out or what went on, there was nothing he could see. And at the same time he had the feeling that this void, this nothingness, had lasted an eternity. No, not even time, more as if, in this void, he had passed across something, or had run back immense distances. The shock, the brutal dashing against the pavement. Anyway, he had felt an immense relief in coming out of the black pit while the people were lifting him off the ground. With pain in the broken arm, blood from the split eyebrow, contusion on the knee; with all that, a relief in returning to daylight, to the day, and to feel sustained and attended. That was weird. Someday he'd ask the doctor at the office about that. Now sleep began to take over again, to pull him slowly down. The pillow was so soft, and the coolness of the mineral water in his fevered throat. The violet light of the lamp up there was beginning to get dimmer and dimmer.

As he was sleeping on his back, the position in which he came to did not surprise him, but on the other hand the damp smell, the smell of oozing rock, blocked his throat and forced him to understand. Open the eyes and look in all directions, hopeless. He was surrounded by an absolute darkness. Tried to get up and felt ropes pinning his wrists and ankles. He was staked to the ground on a floor of dank, icy stone slabs. The cold bit into his naked back, his legs. Dully, he tried to touch the amulet with his chin and found they had stripped him of it. Now he was lost, no prayer could save him from the final . . . From afar off, as though filtering through the rock of the dungeon, he heard the great kettledrums of the feast. They had carried him to the temple, he was in the underground cells of Teocalli itself, awaiting his turn.

He heard a yell, a hoarse yell that rocked off the walls. Another yell, ending in a moan. It was he who was screaming in the darkness, he was screaming because he was alive, his whole body with that cry fended off what was coming, the inevitable end. He thought of his friends filling up the other dungeons, and of those already walking up the stairs of the sacrifice. He uttered another choked cry, he could barely open his mouth, his jaws were twisted back as if with a rope and a stick, and once in a while they would open slowly with an endless exertion, as if they were made of rubber. The creaking of the wooden latches jolted him like a whip. Rent, writhing, he fought to rid himself of the cords sinking into his flesh. His right arm, the strongest, strained until the pain became unbearable and he had to give up. He watched the double door open, and the smell of the torches reached him before the light did. Barely girdled by the ceremonial loincloths, the priests' acolytes moved in his direction, looking at him with contempt. Lights reflected off the sweaty torsos and off the black hair dressed with feathers. The cords went slack, and in their place the grappling of hot hands, hard as bronze; he felt himself lifted, still face up, and jerked along by the four acolytes who carried him down the passageway. The torchbearers went ahead, indistinctly lighting up the corridor with its dripping walls and a ceiling so low that the acolytes had to duck their heads. Now they were taking him out, taking him out, it was the end. Face up, under a mile of living rock which, for a succession of moments, was lit up by a glimmer of torchlight. When the stars came out up there instead of the roof and the great terraced steps rose before him, on fire with cries and dances, it would be the end. The passage was never going to end, but now it was beginning to end, he would see suddenly the open sky full of stars, but not yet, they trundled him along endlessly in the reddish shadow, hauling him roughly along and he did not want that, but how to stop it if they had torn off the amulet, his real heart, the life-center.

In a single jump he came out into the hospital night, to the high, gentle, bare ceiling, to the soft shadow wrapping him round. He thought he must have cried out, but his neighbors were peacefully snoring. The water in the bottle on the night table was somewhat bubbly, a translucent shape against the dark azure shadow of the windows. He panted, looking for some relief for his lungs, oblivion for those images still glued to his eyelids. Each time he shut his eyes he saw them take shape instantly, and he sat up, completely wrung out, but savoring at the same time the surety that now he was awake, that the night nurse would answer if he rang, that soon it would be daybreak, with the good, deep sleep he usually had at that hour, no images, no nothing . . . It was difficult to keep his eyes open, the drowsiness was more powerful than he. He made one last effort, he sketched a gesture toward the bottle of water with his good hand and did not manage to reach it, his fingers closed again on a black emptiness, and the passageway went on endlessly, rock after rock, with momentary ruddy flares, and face up he choked out a dull moan because the roof was about to end, it rose, was opening like a mouth of shadow, and the acolytes straightened up, and from on high a waning moon fell on a face whose eyes wanted not to see it, were closing and opening desperately, trying to pass to the other side, to find again the bare, protecting ceiling of the ward. And every time they opened, it was night and the moon, while they climbed the great terraced steps, his head hanging down backward now, and up at the top were the bonfires, red columns of perfumed smoke, and suddenly he saw the red stone, shiny with the blood dripping off it, and the spinning arcs cut by the feet of the victim whom they pulled off to throw him rolling down the north steps. With a last hope he shut his lids tightly, moaning to wake up. For a second he thought he had gotten there, because once more he was immobile in the bed, except that his head was hanging down off it, swinging. But he smelled death, and when he opened his eyes he saw the blood-soaked figure of the executioner-priest coming toward him with the stone knife in his hand. He managed to close his eyelids again, although he knew now he was not going to wake up, that he was awake, that the marvelous dream had been the other, absurd as all dreams are—a dream in which he was going through the strange avenues of an astonishing city, with green and red lights that burned without fire or smoke, on an enormous metal insect that whirred away between his legs. In the infinite lie of the dream, they had also picked him up off the ground, someone had approached him also with a knife in his hand, approached him who was lying face up, face up with his eyes closed between the bonfires on the steps.

BESTIARY

* * * * * * * * * * * * * * * *

Between the last spoonful of rice pudding with milk (very little cinnamon, a shame) and the goodnight kisses before going up to bed, there was a tinkling in the telephone room and Isabel hung around until Inés came from answering it and said something into their mother's ear. They looked at one another, then both of them looked at Isabel who was thinking about the broken birdcage and the long division problems and briefly of old lady Lucera being angry because she'd pushed her doorbell on the way back from school. She wasn't all that worried, Inés and her mother were looking as if they were gazing past her somewhere, almost taking her as an excuse; but they were looking at her.

"I don't like the idea of her going, believe you me," Inés said. "Not so much because of the tiger, after all they're very careful in that respect. But it's such a depressing house and only that boy to play with her . . ."

"I don't like the idea either," her mother said, and Isabel knew, as if she were on a toboggan, that they were going to send her to the Funes' for the summer. She flung herself into the news, into the great green wave, the Funes', the Funes', sure they were going to send her. They didn't like it, but it was convenient. Delicate lungs, Mar del Plata so very expensive, difficult to manage such a spoiled child, stupid, the way she always acted up with that wonderful Miss Tania, a restless sleeper, toys underfoot everyplace, questions, buttons to be sewn back on, filthy knees. She felt afraid, delighted, smell of the willow trees and the *u* in Funes was getting mixed in with the rice pudding, so late to be still up, and get up to bed, right now.

Lying there, the light out, covered with kisses and rueful glances from Inés and their mother, not fully decided but already decided in spite of everything to send her. She was enjoying beforehand the drive up in the phaeton, the first breakfast, the happiness of Nino, hunter of cockroaches, Nino the toad, Nino the fish (a memory of three years before, Nino showing her some small cutouts he'd glued in an album and telling her gravely, "This-is-a-toad, and THIS is-a-fish"). Now Nino in the park waiting for her with the butterfly net, and also Rema's soft hands—she saw them coming out of the darkness, she had her eyes open and instead of Nino's face—zap!—Rema's hands, the Funes' younger daughter. "Aunt Rema loves me a lot," and Nino's eyes got large and wet, she saw Nino again disjointedly floating in the dim light of the bedroom, looking at her contentedly. Nino the fish. Falling asleep wanting the week to be over that same night, and the goodbyes, the train, the last half-mile in the phaeton, the gate, the eucalyptus trees along the road leading up to the house. Just before falling asleep, she had a moment of terror when she imagined that she was maybe dreaming. Stretching out all at once, her feet hit the brass bars at the foot of the bed, they hurt through the covers, and she heard her mother and Inés talking in the big dining room, baggage, see the doctor about those pimples, cod-liver oil and concentrate of witch hazel. It wasn't a dream, it wasn't a dream.

It wasn't a dream. They took her down to Constitution Station one windy morning, small flags blowing from the pushcarts in the plaza, a piece of pie in the railroad station restaurant, and the enormous entrance to platform 14. Between Inés and her mother they kissed her so much that her face felt like it'd been walked on, soft and smelly, rouge and Coty powder, wet around the mouth, a squeamish feeling of filth that the wind eradicated with one large smack. She wasn't afraid to travel alone because she was a big girl, with nothing less than twenty pesos in her pocketbook, Sansinena Co., Frozen Meats a sweetish stink seeping in the window, the railroad trestle over the yellow brook and Isabel already back to normal from having had to have that crying spell at the station, happy, dead with fear, active, using fully the seat by the window, almost the only traveler in that portion of the coach from which one could examine all the different places and see oneself in the small mirrors. She thought once or twice of her mother, of Inés—they'd already be on the 97 car, leaving Constitution—she read no smoking, spitting is forbidden by law, seating capacity 42 passengers, they were passing through Banfield at top speed, vavooom! country more country more country intermingled with the taste of Milky Way and the menthol drops. Inés had reminded her that she would be working on the green wool in such a way that Isabel packed the knitting into the most inaccessible part of the suitcase, poor Inés, and what a stupid idea.

At the station she was a little bit worried because if the phaeton . . . But there it was, with don Nicanor very red and respectful, yes miss, this miss, that miss, was the trip fine, was her mother as well as ever, of course it had rained— Oh the swinging motion of the phaeton to get her back into the whole aquarium of her previous visit to Los Horneros. Everything smaller, more crystalline and pink, without the tiger then, don Nicanor with fewer white hairs, barely three years ago, Nino a toad, Nino a fish, and Rema's hands which made you want to cry and feel them on your head forever, a caress like death almost and pastries with vanilla cream, the two best things on earth.

They gave her a room upstairs all to herself, the loveliest room. A grownup's room (Nino's idea, all black curls and eyes, handsome in his blue overalls; in the afternoon, of course, Luis made him dress up, his slate-grey suit and a red tie) and inside, another tiny room with an enormous wild cardinal. The bathroom was two doors away (but inside doors through the rooms so that you could go without checking beforehand where the tiger was), full of spigots and metal things, though they did not fool Isabel easily, you could tell it was a country bathroom, things were not as perfect as in a city bath. And it smelled old, the second morning she found a waterbug taking a walk in the washbasin. She barely touched it, it rolled itself into a timid ball and disappeared down the gurgling drain.

Dear mama, I'm writing to— They were eating in the dining room with the chandelier because it was cooler. The Kid was complaining every minute about the heat,

Luis said nothing, but every once in a while you could see the sweat break out on his forehead or his chin. Only Rema was restful, she passed the plates slowly and always as if the meal were a birthday party, a little solemnly and impressively. (Isabel was secretly studying her way of carving and of ordering the servants.) For the most part, Luis was always reading, fist to brow, and the book leaning against a siphon. Rema touched his arm before passing him a plate, and the Kid would interrupt him once in a while to call him philosopher. It hurt Isabel that Luis might be a philosopher, not because of that, but because of the Kid, that he had an excuse then to joke and call him that.

They ate like this: Luis at the head of the table, Rema and Nino on one side, the Kid and Isabel on the other, so that there was an adult at the end and a child and a grownup at either side. When Nino wanted to tell her something serious, he'd give her a kick on the shin with his shoe. Once Isabel yelled and the Kid got angry and said she was badly brought up. Rema looked at her continuously until Isabel was comforted by the gaze and the potato soup.

Mama, before you go in to eat it's like all the rest of the time, you have to look and see if— Almost always it was Rema who went to see if they could go into the dining room with the crystal chandelier. The second day she came to the big living room and said they would have to wait. It was a long time before a farmhand came to tell them that the tiger was in the clover garden, then Rema took the children's hands and everyone went in to eat. The fried potatoes were pretty dry that morning, though only Nino and the Kid complained.

You told me I was not supposed to go around making— Because Rema seemed to hold off all questions with her terse sweetness. The setup worked so well that it was un-

81

necessary to worry about the business of the rooms. It was an absolutely enormous house, and at worst, there was only one room they couldn't go into; never more than one, so it didn't matter. Isabel was as used to it as Nino, after a couple of days. From morning until evening they played in the grove of willows, and if they couldn't play in the willow grove, there was always the clover garden, the park with its hammocks, and the edge of the brook. It was the same in the house, they had their bedrooms, the hall down the center, the library downstairs (except one Thursday when they couldn't go into the library) and the dining room with the chandelier. They couldn't go into Luis' study because Luis was reading all the time, once in a while he would call to his son and give him picture books; but Nino always took them out, they went to the living room or to the front garden to look at them. They never went into the Kid's study because they were afraid he would throw a tantrum. Rema told them that it was better that way, she said it as though she were warning them; they'd already learned how to read her silences.

After all's said, it was a sad life. Isabel wondered one night why the Funes' had invited her for the summer. She wasn't old enough to understand that it was for Nino not for her, a summer plaything to keep Nino happy. She only managed to see the sadness of the house, that Rema seemed always tired, that it hardly ever rained and that, nonetheless, things had that air of being damp and abandoned. After a few days she got used to the rules of the house and the not-difficult discipline of that summer at Los Horneros. Nino was beginning to learn to use the microscope Luis had given him; they spent a magnificent week growing insects in a trough with stagnant water and lily pads, putting drops on the glass slide to look at the microbes. "They're mosquito larvae, you're not going to see microbes with that microscope," Luis told them, his smile somewhat pained and distant. They could never believe that that wriggling horror was not a microbe. Rema brought them a kaleidoscope which she kept in her wardrobe, but they still preferred detecting microbes and counting their legs. Isabel carried a notebook and kept notations of their experiments, she combined biology with chemistry and putting together a medicine chest. They made the medicine chest in Nino's room after ransacking the whole house to get things for it. Isabel told Luis, "We want some of everything: things." Luis gave them Andreu lozenges, pink cotton, a test tube. The Kid came across with a rubber bag and a bottle of green pills with the label worn off. Rema came to see the medicine chest, read the inventory in the notebook, and told them that they were learning a lot of useful things. It occurred to her or to Nino (who always got excited and wanted to show off in front of Rema) to assemble an herbarium. As it was possible that morning to go down to the clover garden, they went about collecting samples and by nightfall they had both their bedroom floors filled with leaves and flowers on bits of paper, there was hardly room to step. Before going to bed, Isabel noted: "Leaf #74: green, heart-shaped, with brown spots." It annoyed her a little that almost all the leaves were green, nearly all smooth, and nearly all lanceolate.

The day they went out ant-hunting she saw the farmhands. She knew the foreman and the head groom because they brought reports to the house. But these other younger hands stood there against the side of the sheds with an air of siesta, yawning once in a while and watching the kids play. One of them asked Nino, "Why'ya collectin' all them bugs?" and tapped him on top of his head with all the curls, using two fingers. Isabel would have liked Nino to lose his temper, to show that he was the

boss's son. They already had the bottle crawling with ants
and on the bank of the brook they ran across a bug with
an enormous hard shell and stuck him in the bottle too, to
see what would happen. The idea of an ant-farm they'd
gotten out of *The Treasure of Youth*, and Luis loaned
them a big, deep glass tank. As they left, both of them
carrying it off, Isabel heard him say to Rema, "Better this
way, they'll be quiet in the house." Also it seemed to her
that Rema sighed. Before dropping off to sleep, when
faces appear in the darkness, she remembered again the
Kid going out onto the porch for a smoke, thin, humming
to himself, saw Rema who was bringing him out coffee
and he made a mistake taking the cup so clumsily that he
caught Rema's fingers while trying to get the cup, Isabel
had seen from the dining room Rema pulling her hand
back and the Kid was barely able to keep the cup from
falling and laughed at the tangle. Black ants better than
the red ones: bigger, more ferocious. Afterward let loose a
pile of red ones, watch the war from outside the glass, all
very safe. Except they didn't fight. Made two anthills, one
in each corner of the glass tank. They consoled one another by studying the distinctive habits, a special notebook
for each kind of ant. But almost sure they would fight,
look through the glass at war without quarter, and just
one notebook.

Rema didn't like to spy on them, she passed by the bedrooms sometimes and would see them with the ant-farm
beside the window, impassioned and important. Nino was
particularly good at pointing out immediately any new
galleries, and Isabel enlarged the diagram traced in ink on
double pages. On Luis' advice they collected black ants
only, and the ant-farm was already enormous, the ants
appeared to be furious and worked until nightfall, exca-
vating and moving earth with a thousand methods and

maneuvers, the careful rubbing of feelers and feet, abrupt fits of fury or vehemence, concentrations and dispersals for no apparent reason. Isabel no longer knew what to take notes on, little by little she put the notebook aside and hours would pass in studying and forgetting what had been discovered. Nino began to want to go back to the garden, he mentioned the hammocks and the colts. Isabel was somewhat contemptuous of him for that. The ant-farm was worth the whole of Los Horneros, and it gave her immense pleasure to think that the ants came and went without fear of any tiger, sometimes she tried to imagine a tiny little tiger like an eraser, roaming the galleries of the ant-farm; maybe that was why the dispersals and concentrations. And now she liked to rehearse the real world in the one of glass, now that she felt a little like a prisoner, now that she was forbidden to go down to the dining room until Rema said so.

She pushed her nose against one of the glass sides, promptly all attention because she liked for them to look at her; she heard Rema stop in the doorway, just silent, looking at her. She heard those things with such a sharp brightness when it was Rema.

"You're alone here? Why?"

"Nino went off to the hammocks. This big one must be a queen, she's huge."

Rema's apron was reflected in the glass. Isabel saw one of her hands slightly raised, with the reflection it looked as if it were inside the ant-farm; suddenly she thought about the same hand offering a cup of coffee to the Kid, but now there were ants running along her fingers, ants instead of the cup and the Kid's hand pressing the fingertips.

"Take your hand out, Rema," she asked.

"My hand?"

"Now it's all right. The reflection was scaring the ants."

85

"Ah. It's all right in the dining room now, you can go down."

"Later. Is the Kid mad at you, Rema?"

The hand moved across the glass like a bird through a window. It looked to Isabel as though the ants were really scared this time, that they ran from the reflection. You couldn't see anything now, Rema had left, she went down the hall as if she were escaping something. Isabel felt afraid of the question herself, a dull fear, made no sense, maybe it wasn't the question but seeing Rema run off that way, or the once-more-clear empty glass where the galleries emptied out and twisted like twitching fingers inside the soil.

It was siesta one afternoon, watermelon, handball against the wall which overlooked the brook, and Nino was terrific, catching shots that looked impossible and climbing up to the roof on a vine to get the ball loose where it was caught between two tiles. A son of one of the farmhands came out from beside the willows and played with them, but he was slow and clumsy and shots got away from him. Isabel could smell the terebinth leaves and at one moment, returning with a backhand an insidious low shot of Nino's, she felt the summer's happiness very deep inside her. For the first time she understood her being at Los Horneros, the vacation, Nino. She thought of the ant-farm up there and it was an oozy dead thing, a horror of legs trying to get out, false air, poisonous. She hit the ball angrily, happily, she bit off a piece of a terebinth leaf with her teeth, bitter, she spit it out in disgust, happy for the first time really, and at last, under the sun in the country.

The window glass fell like hail. It was in the Kid's study. They saw him rise in his shirtsleeves and the broad black eyeglasses.

"Filthy pains-in-the-ass!"

The little peon fled. Nino set himself alongside Isabel, she felt him shaking with the same wind as the willows.

"We didn't mean to do it, uncle."

"Honest, Kid, we didn't mean to do it."

He wasn't there any longer.

She had asked Rema to take away the ant-farm and Rema promised her. After, chatting while she helped her hang up her clothes and get into her pajamas, they forgot. When Rema put out the light, Isabel felt the presence of the ants, Rema went down the hall to say goodnight to Nino who was still crying and repentant, but she didn't have the nerve to call her back again. Rema would have thought that she was just a baby. She decided to go to sleep immediately, and was wider awake than ever. When the moment came when there were faces in the darkness, she saw her mother and Inés looking at one another and smiling like accomplices and pulling on gloves of phosphorescent yellow. She saw Nino weeping, her mother and Inés with the gloves on that now were violet hairdos that twirled and twirled round their heads, Nino with enormous vacant eyes—maybe from having cried too much—and thought that now she would see Rema and Luis, she wanted to see them, she didn't want to see the Kid, but she saw the Kid without his glasses with the same tight face that he'd had when he began hitting Nino and Nino fell backwards until he was against the wall and looked at him as though expecting that would finish it, and the Kid continued to whack back and forth across his face with a loose soft slap that sounded moist, until Rema intruded herself in front of Nino and the Kid laughed, his face almost touching Rema's, and then they heard Luis returning and saying from a distance that now they could go into the dining room. Everything had happened so fast because Nino had been there and Rema had come to tell them not to leave the living room until Luis found out what room the tiger was in and she stayed there with them watching the game of checkers. Nino won and Rema praised him, then Nino was so happy that he put his arms around her waist and wanted to kiss her. Rema had bent down, laughing, and Nino kissed her on the nose and eyes, the two of them laughing and Isabel also, they were so happy playing. They didn't see the Kid coming, when he got up to them he grabbed Nino, jerked at him, said something about the ball breaking the window in his room and started to hit him, he looked at Rema while he hit him, he seemed furious with Rema and she defied him with her eyes for a moment. Terrified, Isabel saw her face up to him, then she stepped in between to protect Nino. The whole evening meal was a deceit, a lie, Luis thought that Nino was crying from having taken a tumble, the Kid looked at Rema as if to order her to shut up, Isabel saw him now with his hard, handsome mouth, very red lips; in the dimness they were even more scarlet, she could see his teeth, barely revealed, glittering. A puffed cloud emerged from his teeth, a green triangle, Isabel blinked her eyes to wipe out the images and Inés and her mother appeared again with their yellow gloves; she gazed at them for a moment, then thought of the ant-farm: that was there and you couldn't see it; the yellow gloves were not there and she saw them instead as if in bright sunlight. It seemed almost curious to her, she couldn't make the ant-farm come out, instead she felt it as a kind of weight there, a chunk of thick, live space. She felt it so strongly that she reached about for the matches, the night-lamp. The ant-farm leaped from the nothingness, wrapped in shifting shadow. Isabel lifted the lamp and came closer. Poor ants, they were going to think that the sun was up. When she could see one of the sides, she was frightened;

the ants had been working in all that blackness. She
watched them swarm up and down, in silence, so visible,
palpable. They were working away inside there as though
they had not yet lost their hope of getting out.

It was almost always the foreman who kept them advised of the tiger's movements; Luis had the greatest confidence in him, and since he passed almost the whole day
working in his study, he neither emerged nor let those
who came down from the next floor move about until don
Roberto sent in his report. But they had to rely on one another also. Busy with the household chores inside, Rema
knew exactly what was happening upstairs and down. At
other times, it was the children who brought the news to
the Kid or to Luis. Not that they'd seen anything, just that
don Roberto had run into them outside, indicated the tiger's whereabouts to them, and they came back in to pass
it on. They believed Nino without question, Isabel less, she
was new and might make a mistake. Later, though, since
she always went about with Nino stuck to her skirt, they
finally believed both of them equally. That was in the
morning and afternoon; at night it was the Kid who went
out to check and see that the dogs were tied up or that no
live coals had been left close to the houses. Isabel noticed
that he carried the revolver and sometimes a stick with a
silver handle.

She hadn't wanted to ask Rema about it because Rema
clearly found it something so obvious and necessary; to
pester her would have meant looking stupid, and she
treasured her pride before another woman. Nino was
easy, he talked straight. Everything clear and obvious
when he explained it. Only at night, if she wanted to re-
construct that clarity and obviousness, Isabel noticed that
the important reasons were still missing. She learned
quickly what was really important: if you wanted to leave

the house, or go down to the dining room, to Luis' study, or to the library, find out first. "You have to trust don Roberto," Rema had said. Her and Nino as well. She hardly ever asked Luis because he hardly ever knew. The Kid, who always knew, she never asked. And so it was always easy, the life organized itself for Isabel with a few more obligations as far as her movements went, and a few less when it came to clothes, meals, the time to go to bed. A real summer, the way it should be all year round.

. . . see you soon. They're all fine. I have an ant-farm with Nino and we play and are making a very large herbarium. Rema sends her kisses, she is fine. I think she's sad, the same as Luis who is very nice. I think that Luis has some trouble although he studies all the time. Rema gave me some lovely colored handkerchiefs, Inés is going to like them. Mama, it's nice here and I'm enjoying myself with Nino and don Roberto, he's the foreman and tells us when we can go out and where, one afternoon he was almost wrong and sent us to the edge of the brook, when a farmhand came to tell us no, you should have seen how awful don Roberto felt and then Rema, she picked Nino up and was kissing him, and she squeezed me so hard. Luis was going about saying that the house was not for children, and Nino asked him who the children were, and everybody laughed, even the Kid laughed. Don Roberto is the foreman.

If you come to get me you could stay a few days and be with Rema and cheer her up. I think that she . . .

But to tell her mother that Rema cried at night, that she'd heard her crying going down the hall, staggering a little, stop at Nino's door, continue, go downstairs (she must have been drying her eyes) and Luis' voice in the distance: "What's the matter, Rema? Aren't you well?", a silence, the whole house like an enormous ear, then a murmur and Luis' voice again: "He's a bastard, a miserable bastard . . ." almost as though he were coldly confirming a fact, making a connection, a fate.

. . . is a little ill, it would do her good if you came and kept her company. I have to show you the herbarium and some stones from the brook the farmhands brought me. Tell Inés . . .

It was the kind of night she liked, insects, damp, reheated bread, and custard with Greek raisins. The dogs barked constantly from the edge of the brook, and an enormous praying mantis flew in and landed on the mantelpiece and Nino went to fetch the magnifying glass; they trapped it with a wide–mouthed glass and poked at it to make it show the color of its wings.

"Throw that bug away," Rema pleaded. "They make me so squeamish."

"It's a good specimen," Luis admitted. "Look how he follows my hand with his eyes. The only insect that can turn its head."

"What a goddamned night," the Kid said from behind his newspaper.

Isabel would have liked to cut the mantis' head off, a good snip with the scissors, and see what would happen.

"Leave it in the glass," she asked Nino. "Tomorrow we can put it in the ant-farm and study it."

It got hotter, by ten-thirty you couldn't breathe. The children stayed with Rema in the inside dining room, the men were in their studies. Nino was the first to say that he was getting sleepy.

"Go on up by yourself, I'll come see you later. Everything is all right upstairs." And Rema took him about the waist with that expression he liked so well.

"Tell us a story, Aunt Rema?"

"Another night."

They were down there alone, with the mantis which looked at them. Luis came to say his goodnights to them, muttering something about the hour that children ought to go to bed, Rema smiled at him when she kissed him.

"Growly bear," she said, and Isabel, bent over the mantis' glass, thought that she'd never seen Rema kissing the Kid or a praying mantis that was so so green. She moved the glass a little and the mantis grew frantic. Rema came over to tell her to go to bed.

"Throw that bug away, it's horrible."

"Rema, tomorrow."

She asked her to come up and say goodnight to her. The Kid had the door of his study left partly open and was pacing up and down in his shirtsleeves, the collar open. He whistled to her as she passed.

"I'm going to bed, Kid."

"Listen to me: tell Rema to make me a nice cold lemonade and bring it to me here. Then you go right up to your room."

Of course she was going to go up to her room, she didn't see why he had to tell her to. She went back to the dining room to tell Rema, she saw her hesitate.

"Don't go upstairs yet. I'm going to make the lemonade and you take it down yourself."

"He said for you . . ."

"Please."

Isabel sat down at the side of the table. Please. There were clouds of insects whirling under the carbide lamp, she would have stayed there for hours looking at nothing, repeating: Please, please. Rema, Rema. How she loved her, and that unhappy voice, bottomless, without any possible reason, the voice of sadness itself. Please. Rema, Rema . . . A feverish heat reached her face, a wish to throw herself at Rema's feet, to let Rema pick her up in her arms, a wish to die looking at her and Rema be sorry

for her, pass her cool, delicate fingers th
over the eyelids . . .

Now she was holding out a green tum
and sliced lemons.

"Take it to him."

"Rema . . ."

Rema seemed to tremble, she turned her back on the table so that she shouldn't see her eyes.

"I'll throw the mantis out right now, Rema."

One sleeps poorly in the viscous heat and all that buzzing of mosquitoes. Twice she was on the point of getting up, to go out into the hall or to go to the bathroom to put cold water on her face and wrists. But she could hear someone walking, downstairs, someone was going from one side of the dining room to the other, came to the bottom of the stairway, turned around . . . They weren't the confused, long steps of Luis' walk, nor was it Rema's. How warm the Kid had felt that night, how he'd drunk the lemonade in great gulps. Isabel saw him drinking the tumblerful, his hands holding the green tumbler, the yellow discs wheeling in the water under the lamp; but at the same time she was sure the Kid had never drunk the lemonade, that he was still staring at the glass she had brought him, over to the table, like someone looking at some kind of infinite naughtiness. She didn't want to think about the Kid's smile, his going to the door as though he were about to go into the dining room for a look, his slow turning back.

"She was supposed to bring it to me. You, I told you to go up to your room."

And the only thing that came to her mind was a very idiot answer:

"It's good and cold, Kid."

And the tumbler, green as the praying mantis.

Nino was the first one up, it was his idea that they go down to the brook to look for snails. Isabel had hardly slept at all, she remembered rooms full of flowers, tinkling bells, hospital corridors, sisters of charity, thermometers in jars of bichlorate, scenes from her first communion, Inés, the broken bicycle, the restaurant in the railroad station, the gypsy costume when she had been eight. Among all this, like a delicate breeze between the pages of an album, she found herself wide awake, thinking of things that were not flowers, bells, hospital corridors. She got out of bed grudgingly, washed her face hard, especially the ears. Nino said that it was ten o'clock and that the tiger was in the music room, so that they could go down to the brook right away. They went downstairs together, hardly saying good morning to Luis and the Kid who were both reading with their doors open. You could find the snails mostly on the bank nearest the wheatfields. Nino moved along blaming Isabel for her distraction, said she was no kind of friend at all and wasn't helping form the collection. She saw him suddenly as so childish, such a little boy with his snails and his leaves.

She came back first, when they raised the flag at the house for lunch. Don Roberto came from his inspection and Isabel asked him the same question as always. Then Nino was coming up slowly, carrying the box of snails and the rakes; Isabel helped him put the rakes away on the porch and they went in together. Rema was standing there, white and silent. Nino put a blue snail into her hand.

"The nicest one, for you."

The Kid was eating already, the newspaper beside him, there was hardly enough room for Isabel to rest her arm. Luis was the last to come from his room, contented as he always was at noon. They ate, Nino was talking about the snails, the snail eggs in the reeds, the collection itself, the sizes and the colors. He was going to kill them by himself, it hurt Isabel to do it, they'd put them to dry on a zinc sheet. After the coffee came and Luis looked at them with the usual question, Isabel got up first to look for don Roberto, even though don Roberto had already told her before. She made the round of the porch and when she came in again, Rema and Nino had their heads together over the snail box, it was like a family photograph, only Luis looked up at her and she said, "It's in the Kid's study," and stayed watching how the Kid shrugged his shoulders, annoyed, and Rema who touched a snail with a fingertip, so delicately that her finger even seemed part snail. Afterwards, Rema got up to go look for more sugar, and Isabel tailed along behind her babbling until they came back in laughing from a joke they'd shared in the pantry. When Luis said he had no tobacco and ordered Nino to look in his study, Isabel challenged him that she'd find the cigarettes first and they went out together. Nino won, they came back in running and pushing, they almost bumped into the Kid going to the library to read his newspaper, complaining because he couldn't use his study. Isabel came over to look at the snails, and Luis waiting for her to light his cigarette as always saw that she was lost, studying the snails which were beginning to ooze out slowly and move about, looking at Rema suddenly, but dropping her like a flash, captivated by the snails, so much so that she didn't move at the Kid's first scream, they were all running and she was still standing over the snails as if she did not hear the Kid's new choked cry, Luis beating against the library door, don Roberto coming in with the dogs, the Kid's moans amid the furious barking of the dogs, and Luis saying over and over again, "But if it was in his study! She said it was in his own study!", bent over the snails willowy as fingers, like Rema's fingers maybe, or it was Rema's hand on her shoulder, made her raise her head to look at her, to stand looking at her for an eternity, broken by her ferocious sob into Rema's skirt, her unsettled happiness, and Rema running her hand over her hair, quieting her with a soft squeeze of her fingers and a murmuring against her ear, a stuttering as of gratitude, as of an unnameable acquiescence.

THE GATES
OF HEAVEN
. . . .

José María came at eight with the information,
hardly beating around the bush at all he told me that Celina had just died. I remember that I noted the phrasing
with a flash, Celina just dying, almost with the sense that
she herself had decided the moment. It was almost night,
and José María's mouth was trembling when he told me.

"Mauro's taken it very hard, when I left he was like a
man out of his head. We'd better go."

I had to finish off some files, aside from which I'd promised a girl to take her to dinner. I knocked out a couple of
phone calls, then went out with José María to look for a

taxi. Mauro and Celina lived at Cánning and Santa Fe, so it took us only ten minutes from my place. Coming up we could see people standing about the hall door looking speechless and guilty; on the way I'd learned that Celina'd begun to vomit blood at six, that Mauro had fetched the doctor and that his mother was with them. It seems that the doctor had just begun to write out a long prescription when Celina opened her eyes and finally died with a sort of cough, more like a whistle.

"I held Mauro down, the doctor had to get out because Mauro wanted to beat him up. You know how he is when he gets sore."

I was thinking of Celina, of Celina's final face waiting for us inside the house. I hardly heard the old women crying and the commotion in the courtyard, but on the other hand I remember that the taxi cost two pesos sixty, and that the driver had a shiny cap. I saw two or three of Mauro's buddies from the neighborhood reading *La Razón* in the doorway. A little girl in a blue dress was holding a white cat with brown markings in her arms and smoothing its whiskers fastidiously. Further inside the laments began and the smell of a funeral.

"Go sit with Mauro," I told José María. "Make sure he gets high as a kite and stays that way."

The *mate* was already going strong. The wake was organizing itself, by itself: the faces, the drinks, the heat. Now that Celina had finished dying, it was incredible how the neighborhood could drop everything (even the quiz programs), and congregate at the scene of the disaster. A *mate* straw muttered very audibly when I passed the kitchen and looked into the death-room. Old lady Martita and another woman peered at me from the shadowy depths, where the bed seemed to be floating in a sea of dark jelly.

"The poor little thing passed away," old lady Martita said. "Come in, doctor, come in and see her. She looks as though she were sleeping."

I almost told her to go take a flying— I didn't even swear, and stuck my head into the hot soup. What a room. I looked at Celina for a long time without seeing her, and now I went over to her, black straight hair down the low forehead, which was bright as the mother-of-pearl on a guitar, to the beach-white platter of face, nothing to do. I realized there was nothing to do there, the room already belonged to the women, the mourners coming in the night. Not even Mauro could enter in peace and sit beside Celina, not even Celina was there waiting, that black and white thing had fallen over onto the side of the mourners, giving them the advantage of its immovable theme, repeating it. Better Mauro, better go look for Mauro, who was still on our side.

From the death-room to the dining room, deaf sentinels were smoking in the unlighted passageway. Peña, Crazy Bazán, Mauro's two younger brothers, and an unidentified old man. They greeted me respectfully.

"Thanks for coming, doctor," one brother said. "Yer always such a good friend of Mauro's, poor guy."

"Critical moments always show you who your friends are," the old man piped, with a handshake that felt like a live sardine.

All this was happening, but I was with Celina and Mauro again, the carnival, Luna Park, 1942, dancing, Celina in sky-blue which went badly with her dark color, Mauro with his Palm Beach suit, and I with six whiskeys in me and drunk as a monkey. I liked to go out with Mauro and Celina, a witness to their hard, hot happiness. The more I was reproached for this friendship, the more I leaned on them (my days and hours) to be witness to

99

what they themselves were never conscious of.

I dragged myself away from the dance, a wail rose from the room, lancing through the doors.

"That must be her mother," said Crazy Bazán, almost complacent.

"Perfect syllogism of the meek," I thought. "Celina dead, mother arrives, mother shrieks." It made me sick to my gut to think like that—for other people it's enough to feel that way—I have to think it. Mauro and Celina had not been my guinea pigs, no. I loved them, I still love them, very. Only that I could never enter their simplicity, only that I saw myself forced to feed myself on the reflection of their blood. I am Doctor Hardoy, a lawyer who doesn't fit in with Buenos Aires, not its law courts or its music or its racetracks; and I move as hard as I can in other directions, other bags. I know that my curiosity lies behind all this, notes that fill my files a bit at a time. But Celina and Mauro, no. Celina and Mauro no.

"Who would have thought . . ." I heard Peña, "so fast . . ."

"Right, but you know her lungs were very bad."

"Sure, but all the same . . ."

They were defending themselves against an open grave. Bad lungs, but even so and all that . . . Celina must not have anticipated dying either, for her and Mauro the tuberculosis was "a weakness." Again I saw her whirling enthusiastically in Mauro's arms, Canaro's Orchestra on the platform and the smell of cheap powder. She danced a *machicha* with me afterward, the floor was a hell of thick smoke and bodies. "How well you dance, Marcelo," as if surprised that a lawyer could follow a *machicha*. Neither she nor Mauro ever addressed me in the familiar; I used the intimate form with Mauro, but returned Celina's formalism. It was just hard for Celina to drop the "Doctor," maybe it gave her pride to use the title with her friends, "my friend, the Doctor." I asked Mauro to tell her, then she started using "Marcelo." So they came a little closer to me, but I was as far from them as ever. Not even going to the local dances together, or to the boxing matches or the football games (years ago Mauro had played with the Giants), or drinking *mate* in the kitchen until all hours. When the case was over and I'd won five thousand pesos for Mauro, Celina was the first to ask me not to drift off, but to come see them. She was already not very well; her voice, which was always a little hoarse, was getting weaker all the time. She coughed every night, Mauro bought her Escay Neurophosphate, which was stupid, and Bisleri iron quinine tablets—things people see in the magazines, and trust.

We went to the dances together and I watched them live.

"You ought to talk to Mauro," José María said, he'd just popped up next to me. "It'll do him good."

So I went, but I was thinking of Celina the whole time. It was an ugly thing to realize, but what I was doing was, really, collecting and reordering my data on Celina; they'd never been written out but I had it all in my head. Mauro was crying openly like any sane animal in this world, with no shame at all. He took my hands and wet them all up with his fevered sweat. When José María made him drink down a gin, he took it down between two sobs with a queer noise in his throat. And the phrases, that sputtering of stupidities with his whole life inside them, the obscure awareness of the irreparable thing that had happened to Celina but which he only resented and railed against. The great narcissism at last excused and free to make a spectacle of itself. I was disgusted with Mauro, but even more with myself, and started drinking cheap brandy which burned in the throat and tasted awful. By this time, the wake was moving like an express train; they were all perfect, from Mauro down, even the night was helpful, warm and even, so pleasant to stand around in the courtyard and speak of the poor deceased, let the dawn come while we stood around in the night dew and washed Celina's dirty linen.

That was on Monday, I had to go to Rosario later in the week for a lawyers' convention, where we did nothing but applaud one another and get blasted. On the train back that weekend, there were two dancers from the Moulin Rouge, I recognized the younger of the two, but she played dumb. All that morning I'd been thinking of Celina, not that Celina's dying was that important to me, but what mattered was the adjournment, the interruption of the system, the suspension of a necessary habit. When I saw the girls on the train, I thought of Celina's career and the expression on Mauro's face when he took her away from the Greek's, he took her from Kasidis' place to live with him. It needed a good deal of courage to expect anything from that woman at that time, and it was exactly at that period I got to know him, when he came to consult me in the matter of his old lady's lawsuit, some properties in Sanagasta. The second time Celina came with him, still in near-professional makeup, still swinging her hips in anything but housewifely fashion, but hanging very tight to his arm. It wasn't difficult to make a rational guess about them, to enjoy Mauro's aggressive simplicity and his unspoken assumption that he was taking Celina wholly for himself. When I began the business with them, it seemed to me he'd succeeded, at least outwardly and as far as daily demeanor went. I second-guessed the situation later, and better. Celina got out from under it a little by a certain capriciousness, her insistent taste for the local dances, her long daydreams beside the radio with some mending or

●   102

knitting in her hands. When I heard her sing (one night after the Giants had taken the Brooms, 4-1), I realized that she was still at Kasadis', far from a stable household and from Mauro, just a guy running a stall in the Abasto. I encouraged her cheap tastes, to get to know her better. The three of us went to an endless string of pizza joints, the jukeboxes turned up until you thought your eyes were going to fall out, the pizza bubbling away, the greasy floor strewn with little papers. But Mauro preferred the courtyard in his own house, long hours of bull session with the neighbors, and *mate*. He accepted the rest of it grudgingly, but he acquiesced without coming to terms. Then Celina pretended to accommodate herself, maybe it was true, she was getting used to being a housewife and not going out so often. I was the one who urged Mauro to go to the dances, and I knew she was grateful to me from the beginning. They loved one another, and Celina's happiness made up for the two, sometimes for the three of us.

It seemed like a good idea to get in and out of a tub, telephone Nilda that I'd pick her up Sunday on the way to the track, and then go see Mauro. He was sitting in the courtyard smoking between prolonged cups of *mate*. Two or three little holes in his shirt made me feel tender, and I put my hand on his shoulder by way of greeting. His face had the same expression as the last time, beside the grave, when he threw the fistful of earth and darted back as if bewildered. But I found a clear light in his eyes, his hand firm in our handshake.

"Thanks for coming over to see me. The time drags, Marcelo."

"Do you have to go to Abasto, or did you get someone to replace you?"

"I sent my brother, the gimpy one. I just haven't the

heart to go, even the day seems to last forever."

"Of course. You need some distraction. Get dressed and we'll take a drive around Palermo."

"Fine, let's go, it's all the same to me."

He put on a blue suit, stuck an embroidered handkerchief in the upper pocket, and I saw him put on some perfume from a bottle that had been Celina's. I liked the tilt of his hat with the brim snapped up, and his silent walk, loose and bouncy. I resigned myself to hearing "you can tell who your friends are at times like this," and with his second bottle of Quilmes Cristal he let me have everything he'd been sitting on full blast. We were at a back table in the café, almost by ourselves; I let him run on and from time to time I'd pour him some more beer. I hardly remember anything that he said, I think, really, it was always the same thing over again. I've remembered one phrase: "I have her here," and the gesture of driving his forefinger into the center of his chest as though he were indicating where a pain was, or a medal.

"I want to forget," he said also. "Anything, get loaded, go to a dancehall, pick up some chick, any chick. You understand me, Marcelo, you . . ." His forefinger rose, enigmatically, folded suddenly like a pocket knife. High as he was, he was ready to accept anything, and when I casually mentioned the Santa Fe Palace, he took it for granted that we were going to the dance and was the first to stand up and check his watch. We walked along not speaking, wiped out from the heat, and the whole time I suspected he was having a double-take, a recurrent feeling of surprise at not feeling on his arm Celina's warm happiness on the way to the dance.

"I never took her to this Palace," he said suddenly. "I used to come here before I met her. It's a place for very rough broads, do you come here?"

I have a good long description of the Santa Fe Palace in

my files. It's not called the Santa Fe nor is it on that street, though on one nearby. A shame that none of that can be accurately described, not its modest façade with posters that arouse man's hope and the filthy box office, even less the hangers-on killing time at the entrance and who check you out, hat to shoes. What follows is worse, not that it's disagreeable, just that there's nothing there that's precise; just plain chaos, confusion dissolving itself into a false order; hell and its circles. A hell like an amusement park with a 2 peso 50 admission and ladies at 0.50 centavos once around. Poorly isolated booths and a succession of sort of covered patios; in the first was a regular tango orchestra, in the second a group doing country music, and in the third a small combo from the north, guitars and drums, singers and *malambos*. Standing in a connecting passage (I was Virgil) we could see the three dance floors and hear all three musics; one could then choose whichever he wanted, or go from dance to dance looking for tables and women.

"It's not so bad," Mauro said in his gloomy mood. "Too bad it's so hot. They should install air conditioning."

(For the files: note, following Ortega, the contact between the common man and technology. Exactly where one would imagine a cultural shock, there is, on the contrary, a violent assimilation and enjoyment of the progress. Mauro talks about refrigeration units and audio-frequency amplification with the self-sufficiency of the Buenos Aires inhabitant who firmly believes he has everything coming to him.) I grabbed him by the arm and steered him into the aisle toward a table because he still seemed so distracted and was watching the bandstand of the tango orchestra and the singer who gripped the mike in both hands and moved it slowly back and forth in front of him. We rested our elbows comfortably in front of two brandies. Mauro took his down in a single shot.

"This puts a lid on the beer. Jesus, what a crowd in this joint!"

He called for another one and gave me a break in which to turn him off for a moment and look around me. Our table was next to the dance floor, on the other side there were chairs stretched along a long wall and a pile of women who replaced one another with that absent air taxi-dancers have when they're working or amusing themselves. There wasn't much talk and we heard the tango orchestra only too well, backed by squeeze-boxes and blasting away with a will. The singer was very heavy on the nostalgia and had a remarkable talent for making something dramatic out of a beat that was rather fast and basically without cutting-edge. *I cut my baby's head off and I carry it in a bag* . . . he held the microphone as if he were about to puke into it, with a kind of tired lasciviousness that had to be organic. For long moments, he'd put his lips against the chrome grid, and a voice like glue emerged from the loudspeakers, *I'm a respectable man* . . . ; I thought it would be a better deal to have a rubber doll with the mike concealed inside it, that way the singer could grab it in his arms and get as hot as he wanted while he was singing. But that wouldn't work for the tangos, better the chrome truncheon with the little skull glittering on top, and the frozen spasmodic smile of the gridwork.

It seems right for me to say here that I come to this dance hall to see the monsters, I know of no other place where you get so many of them at one time. They heave into sight around eleven in the evening, coming down from obscure sections of the city, deliberate and sure, by ones and by twos, the women almost dwarves and very dark, the guys like Javanese or Indians from the north bound into tight black suits or suits with checks, the hard hair painfully plastered down, little drops of brilliantine catching blue and pink reflections, the women with enormously high hairdos which make them look even more like dwarves, tough, laborious hairdos of the sort that let you know there's nothing left but weariness and pride. The men nowadays wear their hair loose and high in the middle, enormous, faggoty foxtails which have nothing to do with the brutal faces below them, or with the expression of aggressiveness, ready and waiting its hour, or the efficient torsos set on slender waists. They recognize and admire each other in silence and without letting on, it's their dance and their meeting, their big night out. (For the files: where they come from, what professions they pretend to during the day, what condition of servitude insulates and conceals them.) They come to this place, then, grave monsters twine with one another in grave esteem, one number after the other they twirl slowly without speaking, many with their eyes closed, enjoying at last complete parity and fulfillment. In the intervals they recover, at the tables they're arrogant and the women talk in shrieks so that they'll be looked at, then the gorillas grow more fierce and I've seen one let go with a flat of the hand that spun the face and half the hairdo of a crosseyed girl in white who was drinking anise. Furthermore there's the smell; one could not conceive of the monsters without that smell of damp powder against the skin, of rotten fruit, one thinks of them washing up hastily, the sour washcloth over the face and under the armpits, then what really matters, lotions, hairspray, powder on all their faces, a whitish crust, and under it the dusky patches shining through. They use peroxide too, dark girls raising a rigid ear of corn over the heavy earth of their faces; they even practice blond expressions, wear green dresses, convince themselves that they are authentic, manage even to condescend and scorn the girls who keep their natural color. Looking sidewise at Mauro, I could spell out the difference in his face with its Italian features, the face of the Buenos Aires docks, with neither Negro or provincial mixture, and I remembered suddenly that Celina was much closer to the monsters, much nearer than Mauro and I. I think that Kasidis had chosen her for the darker part of his clientele, whatever few of them enlivened his cabaret. I'd never been to Kasidis' when Celina was still there, but I went down afterwards one night to get to know the place she'd worked in before Mauro dragged her out of there, and I saw nothing but white girls, blondes, brunettes or redheads, but white.

"I feel like a tango now," Mauro complained. Finishing his fourth shot, he was a little drunk. I was thinking of Celina, she'd have been so much at home here, exactly where Mauro had never brought her. Anita Lozano was accepting the loud applause of the audience as she waved hello from the bandstand, I'd heard her sing at the Novelty when she'd been at the top of the bill; she was old and skinny now, but still had voice enough to do a tango, even better as a matter of fact, she had a way of singing it dirty, and the hoarse voice helped some, especially if the lyrics really had to be belted out. When she'd been drinking, Celina had a voice like that, and suddenly I realized that the Santa Fe was Celina, the almost insupportable presence of Celina.

It'd been a mistake for her to go off with Mauro. She put up with it because she loved him and he had dragged her out of Kasidis' greasy squalor, the promiscuity and the shots of amber-colored sugar-water amid the preliminary stumbling of knees against knees and the heavy breathing of the customers. But if she hadn't had to work in the dance halls, Celina would have enjoyed staying there. You could tell by her hips and her mouth, she was built for the tango, from top to bottom, born to make that scene. Which was why Mauro had to take her to dances, I've seen her transfigured just walking in, just the first lungful of hot air and the sound of accordions. At this moment, stuck and no way out at the Santa Fe, I could measure her magnificence, her courage in repaying Mauro with a few years in the kitchen and sugar with the *mate* in the patio. She had renounced her dance-hall heaven, her fiery vocation, anise and creole waltzing. As though condemning herself knowingly for Mauro and Mauro's life, intruding hardly at all on his life, just that he should take her out to a party once in a while.

Now Mauro was going past with a good grip on a colored girl taller than the others, with a shape nicer than most and good-looking besides. I had to laugh at his instinctive and at the same time deliberate choice, the chick was the one least like the monsters. Then the idea recurred to me, Celina in some way had been a monster like the others, except that elsewhere than here and during the day, it was not as apparent. I wondered if Mauro would have noticed it; I was a little afraid that he would blame me for dragging him to a joint where memories sprouted from everything like the hair on your arms.

There was no applause this time, and he came over with the girl who, outside of her tango, seemed suddenly to have grown stupid and open-mouthed as a fish.

"I want you to meet a friend of mine," he said to her.

We muttered "Enchanted to meetcha," coastal style, and without further ado we bought her a drink. I was happy to see Mauro getting into the swing of things, I even exchanged a few words with the woman, whose name was Emma, a name that doesn't fit skinny girls very well. Mauro seemed pretty well turned on and talked of orchestras with the short sententious phrases I admired him for. Emma rambled on with the names of singers and memories of Villa Crespo and El Talar. At that point, Anita Lozano announced an old tango, and there were cheers and applause from the monsters, the pimps especially stood by her to a man. Mauro was not so clobbered as to forget everything, and when the piece opened with a gut-twisting few bars from the accordions he shot me a look like a punch, he was remembering. I also, I saw myself at the thing for the Giants, Mauro and Celina holding one another tight, this same tango, she hummed it all night long, even in the taxi coming home.

"Are we gonna dance?" Emma said, sucking noisily on her grenadine.

Mauro didn't even look at her. It seems to me that at that moment we overtook one another in the depths. Now (now when I'm writing) I see a single image from my twenty years at the Barracas Sporting Club, I dive into the pool and at the bottom I come face-to-face with another swimmer, we touch bottom simultaneously and see each other imperfectly through the sour green water. Mauro pushed his chair back and braced himself with an elbow on the table. Same as me, he was looking at the dance floor, and between us sat Emma, confused and humiliated, though she tried to cover it up by eating the french fries. Now Anita began to sing breaking the beat, the couples danced nearly without moving from where they were and you could see that they were listening to the lyrics with desire and misery mixed, and all the dulled pleasure of cheap night life. Faces were turned toward the stand and you could see them, even twirling, fixed on Anita bent intimately over the microphone. Some of them moved their lips reciting the words, some of them with stupid smiles that seemed to come from behind themselves, and when she finished with her *you were so much, you were so much mine,/and now I look around for you and cannot find/you*, and the accordions came up simultaneously and full strength, the reply was a fresh violence in the dancing, lateral swoops and figure-eights interlarded mid-floor.

A lot of people were sweating, one chick who would have chewed off the second button on my jacket brushed against the table and I could see the sweat oozing from the roots of her hair and running down the back of her neck where a roll of fat made a tiny whiter rivulet. There was smoke pouring into the room from the next patio where they were scoffing down charcoal-broiled meat and dancing *rancheras*, the cigarette smoke and the barbecue laid down a low cloud which distorted the faces and the cheap paintings on the wall opposite. I think the four shots I'd drunk helped somewhat from inside, and Mauro was holding up his chin with the back of his hand, staring fixedly in front of him. The focus of our attention was not the tango which went on and on up there, once or twice I saw Mauro throw a glance toward the stand where Anita was going through the motions of wielding a baton, but then he turned back and fastened his eyes on the couples. I don't know how to say this, it seems to me I was following the direction of his look, and at the same time I was directing his; without looking at one another we realized (it seems to me that Mauro realized) we were both seeing the same spot, we would fall on the identical couple, seeing the same head of hair and trousers. I heard Emma saying something, some excuse, and the section of table between Mauro and myself was left somewhat clearer; still we did not look at one another. A moment of immense happiness seemed to have descended upon the dance floor, I breathed deeply as if to participate in it, and I think I heard Mauro do the same. The smoke was so thick that the faces on the other half of the floor were blurred, so much so that the line of chairs for those who were sitting it out could not be seen, what with the bodies in between and the haze. *You were so much mine*, weird how Anita's voice cracked over the speakers, again the dancers (always moving) grew immobile, and Celina who was on the right side of the floor, moving out of the smoke and whirling obedient to the lead of her partner, stopped for a moment in profile toward me, then her back, again, the other profile, then raised her face to listen to the music. I say: Celina; but it was a vision, a knowledge without understanding it, how, at that moment, understand it, sure, Celina there without being there. Suddenly the table shook, I realized that it was Mauro's arm that was shaking, or mine, but we were not afraid, it was something closer to dread and happiness and stomach-shakes. It was stupid, really, a feeling of something apart which would not allow us to leave, to recover ourselves. Celina was still there, not seeing us, drinking in the tango with all of her face changed and muddied by the yellow light of the smoke. Any one of the dark girls could have looked more like Celina than she did at that moment, happiness transfigured her face in a hideous way; I would not have been able to tolerate Celina as I saw her at that moment, in that tango. I had enough intelligence left to gauge the devastation of her happiness, her face enraptured and stupid in her paradise finally gained; had it not been for the work and the customers, she could have had that at Kasidis' place. There was nothing to stop her now in her heaven, her own heaven, she gave herself with all of her flesh to that joy and again entered the pattern where Mauro could not follow her. It was her hard-won heaven, her tango played once more for her alone and for her equals, until the glass-smashing applause that followed Anita's solo, Celina from the back, Celina in profile, other couples and the smoke blocking her out.

I didn't want to look at Mauro; then I recovered myself and my famous cynicism was racking up the defenses at top speed. It all depended on how he would get through the thing, so that I stayed as I was, watching the floor empty little by little.

"Did you see that?" Mauro asked.

"Yes."

"You saw how much she looked like her?"

I didn't answer him, my relief was heavier than any pity I felt. He was on this side, the poor guy was on this side and would never come to believe what we had known together. I watched him get up and stagger across the floor like a drunk, looking for the woman who looked like Celina. I stayed quiet and took my time over a cigarette, watching him going and coming, this way and that, knowing he was wasting his time, that he would come back, tired and thirsty, not having found the gates of heaven among all that smoke and all those people.

BLOW-UP
. . . .

It'll never be known how this has to be told, in the first person or in the second, using the third person plural or continually inventing modes that will serve for nothing. If one might say: I will see the moon rose, or: we hurt me at the back of my eyes, and especially: you the blond woman was the clouds that race before my your his our yours their faces. What the hell.

Seated ready to tell it, if one might go to drink a bock over there, and the typewriter continue by itself (because I use the machine), that would be perfection. And that's not just a manner of speaking. Perfection, yes, because here is the aperture which must be counted also as a machine (of another sort, a Contax 1.1.2) and it is possible that one machine may know more about another machine than I, you, she—the blond—and the clouds. But I have the dumb luck to know that if I go this Remington will sit turned to stone on top of the table with the air of being twice as quiet that mobile things have when they are not moving. So, I have to write. One of us all has to write, if this is going to get told. Better that it be me who am dead, for I'm less compromised than the rest; I who see only the clouds and can think without being distracted, write without being distracted (there goes another, with a grey edge) and remember without being distracted, I who am dead (and I'm alive, I'm not trying to fool anybody, you'll see when we get to the moment, because I have to begin some way and I've begun with this period, the last one back, the one at the beginning, which in the end is the best of the periods when you want to tell something).

All of a sudden I wonder why I have to tell this, but if one begins to wonder why he does all he does do, if one wonders why he accepts an invitation to lunch (now a pigeon's flying by and it seems to me a sparrow), or why when someone has told us a good joke immediately there starts up something like a tickling in the stomach and we are not at peace until we've gone into the office across the hall and told the joke over again; then it feels good immediately, one is fine, happy, and can get back to work. For I imagine that no one has explained this, that really the best thing is to put aside all decorum and tell it, because, after all's done, nobody is ashamed of breathing or of putting on his shoes; they're things that you do, and when something weird happens, when you find a spider in your shoe or if you take a breath and feel like a broken window, then you have to tell what's happening, tell it to the guys at the office or to the doctor. Oh, doctor, every time I take a breath . . . . Always tell it, always get rid of that tickle in the stomach that bothers you.

And now that we're finally going to tell it, let's put things a little bit in order, we'd be walking down the staircase in this house as far as Sunday, November 7, just a month back. One goes down five floors and stands then in the Sunday in the sun one would not have suspected of Paris in November, with a large appetite to walk around, to see things, to take photos (because we were photographers, I'm a photographer). I know that the most difficult thing is going to be finding a way to tell it, and I'm not afraid of repeating myself. It's going to be difficult because nobody really knows who it is telling it, if I am I or what actually occurred or what I'm seeing (clouds, and once in a while a pigeon) or if, simply, I'm telling a truth which is only my truth, and then is the truth only for my stomach, for this impulse to go running out and to finish up in some manner with, this, whatever it is.

We're going to tell it slowly, what happens in the middle of what I'm writing is coming already. If they replace me, if, so soon, I don't know what to say, if the clouds stop coming and something else starts (because it's impossible that this keep coming, clouds passing continually and occasionally a pigeon), if something out of all this . . . And after the "if" what am I going to put if I'm going to close the sentence structure correctly? But if I begin to ask questions, I'll never tell anything, maybe to tell would be like an answer, at least for someone who's reading it.

Roberto Michel, French-Chilean, translator and in his spare time an amateur photographer, left number 11, rue Monsieur-le-Prince Sunday November 7 of the current year (now there're two small ones passing, with silver linings). He had spent three weeks working on the French version of a treatise on challenges and appeals by José

Norberto Allende, professor at the University of Santiago. It's rare that there's wind in Paris, and even less seldom a wind like this that swirled around corners and rose up to whip at old wooden venetian blinds behind which astonished ladies commented variously on how unreliable the weather had been these last few years. But the sun was out also, riding the wind and friend of the cats, so there was nothing that would keep me from taking a walk along the docks of the Seine and taking photos of the Conservatoire and Sainte-Chapelle. It was hardly ten o'clock, and I figured that by eleven the light would be good, the best you can get in the fall; to kill some time I detoured around by the Isle Saint-Louis and started to walk along the quai d'Anjou, I stared for a bit at the hôtel de Lauzun, I recited bits from Apollinaire which always get into my head whenever I pass in front of the hôtel de Lauzun (and at that I ought to be remembering the other poet, but Michel is an obstinate beggar), and when the wind stopped all at once and the sun came out at least twice as hard (I mean warmer, but really it's the same thing), I sat down on the parapet and felt terribly happy in the Sunday morning.

One of the many ways of contesting level-zero, and one of the best, is to take photographs, an activity in which one should start becoming an adept very early in life, teach it to children since it requires discipline, aesthetic education, a good eye and steady fingers. I'm not talking about waylaying the lie like any old reporter, snapping the stupid silhouette of the VIP leaving number 10 Downing Street, but in all ways when one is walking about with a camera, one has almost a duty to be attentive, to not lose that abrupt and happy rebound of sun's rays off an old stone, or the pigtails-flying run of a small girl going home with a loaf of bread or a bottle of milk. Michel knew that the photographer always worked as a permutation of his personal way of seeing the world as other than the camera insidiously imposed upon it (now a large cloud is going by, almost black), but he lacked no confidence in himself, knowing that he had only to go out without the Contax to recover the keynote of distraction, the sight without a frame around it, light without the diaphragm aperture or 1/250 sec. Right now (what a word, *now*, what a dumb lie) I was able to sit quietly on the railing overlooking the river watching the red and black motorboats passing below without it occurring to me to think photographically of the scenes, nothing more than letting myself go in the letting go of objects, running immobile in the stream of time. And then the wind was not blowing.

After, I wandered down the quai de Bourbon until getting to the end of the isle where the intimate square was (intimate because it was small, not that it was hidden, it offered its whole breast to the river and the sky), I enjoyed it, a lot. Nothing there but a couple and, of course, pigeons; maybe even some of those which are flying past now so that I'm seeing them. A leap up and I settled on the wall, and let myself turn about and be caught and fixed by the sun, giving it my face and ears and hands (I kept my gloves in my pocket). I had no desire to shoot pictures, and lit a cigarette to be doing something; I think it was that moment when the match was about to touch the tobacco that I saw the young boy for the first time.

What I'd thought was a couple seemed much more now a boy with his mother, although at the same time I realized that it was not a kid and his mother, and that it was a couple in the sense that we always allegate to couples when we see them leaning up against the parapets or embracing on the benches in the squares. As I had nothing else to do, I had more than enough time to wonder why the boy was so nervous, like a young colt or a hare, sticking his hands into his pockets, taking them out immediately, one after the other, running his fingers through his hair, changing his stance, and especially why was he afraid, well, you could guess that from every gesture, a fear suffocated by his shyness, an impulse to step backwards which he telegraphed, his body standing as if it were on the edge of flight, holding itself back in a final, pitiful decorum.

All this was so clear, ten feet away—and we were alone against the parapet at the tip of the island—that at the beginning the boy's fright didn't let me see the blond very well. Now, thinking back on it, I see her much better at that first second when I read her face (she'd turned around suddenly, swinging like a metal weathercock, and the eyes, the eyes were there), when I vaguely understood what might have been occurring to the boy and figured it would be worth the trouble to stay and watch (the wind was blowing their words away and they were speaking in a low murmur). I think that I know how to look, if it's something I know, and also that every looking oozes with mendacity, because it's that which expels us furthest outside ourselves, without the least guarantee, whereas to smell, or (but Michel rambles on to himself easily enough, there's no need to let him harangue on this way). In any case, if the likely inaccuracy can be seen beforehand, it becomes possible again to look; perhaps it suffices to choose between looking and the reality looked at, to strip things of all their unnecessary clothing. And surely all that is difficult besides.

As for the boy I remember the image before his actual body (that will clear itself up later), while now I am sure that I remember the woman's body much better than the image. She was thin and willowy, two unfair words to describe what she was, and was wearing an almost-black fur coat, almost long, almost handsome. All the morning's wind (now it was hardly a breeze and it wasn't cold) had blown through her blond hair which pared away her

white, bleak face—two unfair words—and put the world
at her feet and horribly alone in front of her dark eyes, her
eyes fell on things like two eagles, two leaps into nothingness, two puffs of green slime. I'm not describing anything, it's more a matter of trying to understand it. And I
said two puffs of green slime.

Let's be fair, the boy was well enough dressed and was
sporting yellow gloves which I would have sworn belonged
to his older brother, a student of law or sociology; it was
pleasant to see the fingers of the gloves sticking out of his
jacket pocket. For a long time I didn't see his face, barely
a profile, not stupid—a terrified bird, a Fra Filippo angel,
rice pudding with milk—and the back of an adolescent
who wants to take up judo and has had a scuffle or two in
defense of an idea or his sister. Turning fourteen, perhaps
fifteen, one would guess that he was dressed and fed by
his parents but without a nickel in his pocket, having to
debate with his buddies before making up his mind to buy
a coffee, a cognac, a pack of cigarettes. He'd walk through
the streets thinking of the girls in his class, about how
good it would be to go to the movies and see the latest film,
or to buy novels or neckties or bottles of liquor with green
and white labels on them. At home (it would be a respectable home, lunch at noon and romantic landscapes on
the walls, with a dark entryway and a mahogany um-
brella stand inside the door) there'd be the slow rain of
time, for studying, for being mama's hope, for looking like
dad, for writing to his aunt in Avignon. So that there was
a lot of walking the streets, the whole of the river for him
(but without a nickel) and the mysterious city of fifteen-
year-olds with its signs in doorways, its terrifying cats, a
paper of fried potatoes for thirty francs, the pornographic
magazine folded four ways, a solitude like the emptiness
of his pockets, the eagerness for so much that was incom-

prehensible but illumined by a total love, by the availability analogous to the wind and the streets.

This biography was of the boy and of any boy whatsoever, but this particular one now, you could see he was insular, surrounded solely by the blond's presence as she continued talking with him. (I'm tired of insisting, but two long ragged ones just went by. That morning I don't think I looked at the sky once, because what was happening with the boy and the woman appeared so soon I could do nothing but look at them and wait, look at them and . . .) To cut it short, the boy was agitated and one could guess without too much trouble what had just occurred a few minutes before, at most half-an-hour. The boy had come onto the tip of the island, seen the woman and thought her marvelous. The woman was waiting for that because she was there waiting for that, or maybe the boy arrived before her and she saw him from one of the balconies or from a car and got out to meet him, starting the conversation with whatever, from the beginning she was sure that he was going to be afraid and want to run off, and that, naturally, he'd stay, stiff and sullen, pretending experience and the pleasure of the adventure. The rest was easy because it was happening ten feet away from me, and anyone could have gauged the stages of the game, the derisive, competitive fencing; its major attraction was not that it was happening but in foreseeing its denouement. The boy would try to end it by pretending a date, an obligation, whatever, and would go stumbling off disconcerted, wishing he were walking with some assurance, but naked under the mocking glance which would follow him until he was out of sight. Or rather, he would stay there, fascinated or simply incapable of taking the initiative, and the woman would begin to touch his face gently, muss his hair, still talking to him voicelessly, and soon would take him by the arm to lead him off, unless he, with an uneasiness beginning to tinge the edge of desire, even his stake in the adventure, would rouse himself to put his arm around her waist and to kiss her. Any of this could have happened, though it did not, and perversely Michel waited, sitting on the railing, making the settings almost without looking at the camera, ready to take a picturesque shot of a corner of the island with an uncommon couple talking and looking at one another.

Strange how the scene (almost nothing: two figures there mismatched in their youth) was taking on a disquieting aura. I thought it was I imposing it, and that my photo, if I shot it, would reconstitute things in their true stupidity. I would have liked to know what he was thinking, a man in a grey hat sitting at the wheel of a car parked on the dock which led up to the footbridge, and whether he was reading the paper or asleep. I had just discovered him because people inside a parked car have a tendency to disappear, they get lost in that wretched, private cage stripped of the beauty that motion and danger give it. And nevertheless, the car had been there the whole time, forming part (or deforming that part) of the isle. A car: like saying a lighted streetlamp, a park bench. Never like saying wind, sunlight, those elements always new to the skin and the eyes, and also the boy and the woman, unique, put there to change the island, to show it to me in another way. Finally, it may have been that the man with the newspaper also became aware of what was happening and would, like me, feel that malicious sensation of waiting for everything to happen. Now the woman had swung around smoothly, putting the young boy between herself and the wall, I saw them almost in profile, and he was taller, though not much taller, and yet she dominated him, it seemed like she was hovering over him (her laugh, all at once, a whip of feathers), crushing him just by being there, smiling, one hand taking a stroll through the air. Why wait any longer? Aperture at sixteen, a sighting which would not include the horrible black car, but yes, that tree, necessary to break up too much grey space . . .

I raised the camera, pretended to study a focus which did not include them, and waited and watched closely, sure that I would finally catch the revealing expression, one that would sum it all up, life that is rhythmed by movement but which a stiff image destroys, taking time in cross section, if we do not choose the essential imperceptible fraction of it. I did not have to wait long. The woman was getting on with the job of handcuffing the boy smoothly, stripping from him what was left of his freedom a hair at a time, in an incredibly slow and delicious torture. I imagined the possible endings (now a small fluffy cloud appears, almost alone in the sky), I saw their arrival at the house (a basement apartment probably, which she would have filled with large cushions and cats) and conjectured the boy's terror and his desperate decision to play it cool and to be led off pretending there was nothing new in it for him. Closing my eyes, if I did in fact close my eyes, I set the scene: the teasing kisses, the woman mildly repelling the hands which were trying to undress her, like in novels, on a bed that would have a lilac-colored comforter, on the other hand she taking off his clothes, plainly mother and son under a milky yellow light, and everything would end up as usual, perhaps, but maybe everything would go otherwise, and the initiation of the adolescent would not happen, she would not let it happen, after a long prologue wherein the awkwardnesses, the exasperating caresses, the running of hands over bodies would be resolved in who knows what, in a separate and solitary pleasure, in a petulant denial mixed with the art of tiring and disconcerting so much poor innocence. It might go like that, it might very well go like that; that woman was not looking for the boy as a lover, and at the same time she was dominating him toward some end impossible to understand if you do not imagine it as a cruel game, the desire to desire without satisfaction, to excite herself for someone else, someone who in no way could be that kid.

Michel is guilty of making literature, of indulging in fabricated unrealities. Nothing pleases him more than to imagine exceptions to the rule, individuals outside the species, not-always-repugnant monsters. But that woman invited speculation, perhaps giving clues enough for the fantasy to hit the bullseye. Before she left, and now that she would fill my imaginings for several days, for I'm given to ruminating, I decided not to lose a moment more. I got it all into the view-finder (with the tree, the railing, the eleven-o'clock sun) and took the shot. In time to realize that they both had noticed and stood there looking at me, the boy surprised and as though questioning, but she was irritated, her face and body flat-footedly hostile, feeling robbed, ignominiously recorded on a small chemical image.

I might be able to tell it in much greater detail but it's not worth the trouble. The woman said that no one had the right to take a picture without permission, and demanded that I hand her over the film. All this in a dry, clear voice with a good Parisian accent, which rose in color and tone with every phrase. For my part, it hardly mattered whether she got the roll of film or not, but anyone who knows me will tell you, if you want anything from me, ask nicely. With the result that I restricted myself to formulating the opinion that not only was photography in public places not prohibited, but it was looked upon with decided favor, both private and official. And while that was getting said, I noticed on the sly how the boy was falling back, sort of actively backing up though without moving, and all at once (it seemed almost incredible) he turned and broke into a run, the poor kid, thinking that he was walking off and in fact in full flight, running past the side of the car, disappearing like a gossamer filament of angel-spit in the morning air.

But filaments of angel-spittle are also called devil-spit, and Michel had to endure rather particular curses, to hear himself called meddler and imbecile, taking great pains meanwhile to smile and to abate with simple movements of his head such a hard sell. As I was beginning to get tired, I heard the car door slam. The man in the grey hat was there, looking at us. It was only at that point that I realized he was playing a part in the comedy.

He began to walk toward us, carrying in his hand the paper he had been pretending to read. What I remember best is the grimace that twisted his mouth askew, it covered his face with wrinkles, changed somewhat both in location and shape because his lips trembled and the grimace went from one side of his mouth to the other as though it were on wheels, independent and involuntary. But the rest stayed fixed, a flour-powdered clown or bloodless man, dull dry skin, eyes deepset, the nostrils black and prominently visible, blacker than the eyebrows or hair or the black necktie. Walking cautiously as though the pavement hurt his feet; I saw patent-leather shoes with such thin soles that he must have felt every roughness in the pavement. I don't know why I got down off the railing, nor very well why I decided to not give them the photo, to refuse that demand in which I guessed at their fear and cowardice. The clown and the woman consulted one another in silence: we made a perfect and unbearable triangle, something I felt compelled to break with a crack of a whip. I laughed in their faces and began to walk off, a little more slowly, I imagine, than the boy. At the level of the first houses, beside the iron footbridge, I turned around to look at them. They were not moving, but the man had dropped his newspaper; it seemed to me that the woman, her back to the parapet, ran her hands over the stone with the classical and absurd gesture of someone pursued looking for a way out.

What happened after that happened here, almost just now, in a room on the fifth floor. Several days went by before Michel developed the photos he'd taken on Sunday; his shots of the Conservatoire and of Sainte-Chapelle were all they should be. Then he found two or three proof-shots he'd forgotten, a poor attempt to catch a cat perched astonishingly on the roof of a rambling public urinal, and also the shot of the blond and the kid. The negative was so good that he made an enlargement; the enlargement was so good that he made one very much larger, almost the size of a poster. It did not occur to him (now one wonders and wonders) that only the shots of the Conservatoire were worth so much work. Of the whole series, the snapshot of the tip of the island was the only one which interested him; he tacked up the enlargement on one wall of the room, and the first day he spent some time looking at it and remembering, that gloomy operation of comparing the memory with the gone reality; a frozen memory, like any photo, where nothing is missing, not even, and especially, nothingness, the true solidifier of the scene. There was the woman, there was the boy, the tree rigid above their heads, the sky as sharp as the stone of the parapet, clouds and stones melded into a single substance and inseparable (now one with sharp edges is going by, like a thunderhead). The first two days I accepted what I had done, from the photo itself to the enlargement on the wall, and didn't even question that every once in a while I would interrupt my translation of José Norberto Allende's treatise to encounter once more the woman's face, the dark splotches on the railing. I'm such a jerk; it had never

occurred to me that when we look at a photo from the
front, the eyes reproduce exactly the position and the vision of the lens; it's these things that are taken for granted
and it never occurs to anyone to think about them. From
my chair, with the typewriter directly in front of me, I
looked at the photo ten feet away, and then it occurred to
me that I had hung it exactly at the point of view of the
lens. It looked very good that way; no doubt, it was the
best way to appreciate a photo, though the angle from the
diagonal doubtless has its pleasures and might even di-
vulge different aspects. Every few minutes, for example
when I was unable to find the way to say in good French
what José Norberto Allende was saying in very good Spanish, I raised my eyes and looked at the photo; sometimes
the woman would catch my eye, sometimes the boy, sometimes the pavement where a dry leaf had fallen admirably
situated to heighten a lateral section. Then I rested a bit
from my labors, and I enclosed myself again happily in
that morning in which the photo was drenched, I recalled
ironically the angry picture of the woman demanding I
give her the photograph, the boy's pathetic and ridiculous
flight, the entrance on the scene of the man with the white
face. Basically, I was satisfied with myself; my part had
not been too brilliant, and since the French have been
given the gift of the sharp response, I did not see very well
why I'd chosen to leave without a complete demonstration
of the rights, privileges and prerogatives of citizens. The
important thing, the really important thing was having
helped the kid to escape in time (this in case my theoriz-
ing was correct, which was not sufficiently proven, but the
running away itself seemed to show it so). Out of plain
meddling, I had given him the opportunity finally to take
advantage of his fright to do something useful; now he
would be regretting it, feeling his honor impaired, his
manhood diminished. That was better than the attentions

of a woman capable of looking as she had looked at him on that island. Michel is something of a puritan at times, he believes that one should not seduce someone from a position of strength. In the last analysis, taking that photo had been a good act.

Well, it wasn't because of the good act that I looked at it between paragraphs while I was working. At that moment I didn't know the reason, the reason I had tacked the enlargement onto the wall; maybe all fatal acts happen that way, and that is the condition of their fulfillment. I don't think the almost-furtive trembling of the leaves on the tree alarmed me, I was working on a sentence and rounded it out successfully. Habits are like immense herbariums, in the end an enlargement of 32 x 28 looks like a movie screen, where, on the tip of the island, a woman is speaking with a boy and a tree is shaking its dry leaves over their heads.

But her hands were just too much. I had just translated: "In that case, the second key resides in the intrinsic nature of difficulties which societies . . ." —when I saw the woman's hand beginning to stir slowly, finger by finger. There was nothing left of me, a phrase in French which I would never have to finish, a typewriter on the floor, a chair that squeaked and shook, fog. The kid had ducked his head like boxers do when they've done all they can and are waiting for the final blow to fall; he had turned up the collar of his overcoat and seemed more a prisoner than ever, the perfect victim helping promote the catastrophe. Now the woman was talking into his ear, and her hand opened again to lay itself against his cheekbone, to caress and caress it, burning it, taking her time. The kid was less startled than he was suspicious, once or twice he poked his head over the woman's shoulder and she continued talking, saying something that made him look back every few minutes toward that area where Michel knew the car was parked and the man in the grey hat, carefully eliminated from the photo but present in the boy's eyes (how doubt that now) in the words of the woman, in the woman's hands, in the vicarious presence of the woman. When I saw the man come up, stop near them and look at them, his hands in his pockets and a stance somewhere between disgusted and demanding, the master who is about to whistle in his dog after a frolic in the square, I understood, if that was to understand, what had to happen now, what had to have happened then, what would have to happen at that moment, among these people, just where I had poked my nose in to upset an established order, interfering innocently in that which had not happened, but which was now going to happen, now was going to be fulfilled. And what I had imagined earlier was much less horrible than the reality, that woman, who was not there by herself, she was not caressing or propositioning or encouraging for her own pleasure, to lead the angel away with his tousled hair and play the tease with his terror and his eager grace. The real boss was waiting there, smiling petulantly, already certain of the business; he was not the first to send a woman in the vanguard, to bring him the prisoners manacled with flowers. The rest of it would be so simple, the car, some house or another, drinks, stimulating engravings, tardy tears, the awakening in hell. And there was nothing I could do, this time I could do absolutely nothing. My strength had been a photograph, that, there, where they were taking their revenge on me, demonstrating clearly what was going to happen. The photo had been taken, the time had run out, gone; we were so far from one another, the abusive act had certainly already taken place, the tears already shed, and the rest conjecture and sorrow. All at once the order was inverted, they were alive, moving, they were deciding and had decided, they were going to their future; and I on this side, prisoner of another time, in a room on the fifth floor, to not know who they were, that woman, that man, and that boy, to be only the lens of my camera, something fixed, rigid, incapable of intervention. It was horrible, their mocking me, deciding it before my impotent eye, mocking me, for the boy again was looking at the flour-faced clown and I had to accept the fact that he was going to say yes, that the proposition carried money with it or a gimmick, and I couldn't yell for him to run, or even open the road to him again with a new photo, a small and almost meek intervention which would ruin the frame-work of drool and perfume. Everything was going to re-solve itself right there, at that moment; there was like an immense silence which had nothing to do with physical silence. It was stretching it out, setting itself up. I think I screamed, I screamed terribly, and that at that exact sec-ond I realized that I was beginning to move toward them, four inches, a step, another step, the tree swung its branches rhythmically in the foreground, a place where the railing was tarnished emerged from the frame, the woman's face turned toward me as though surprised, was enlarging, and then I turned a bit, I mean that the camera turned a little, and without losing sight of the woman, I began to close in on the man who was looking at me with the black holes he had in place of eyes, surprised and an-gered both, he looked, wanting to nail me onto the air, and at that instant I happened to see something like a large bird outside the focus that was flying in a single swoop in front of the picture, and I leaned up against the wall of my room and was happy because the boy had just man-aged to escape, I saw him running off, in focus again, sprinting with his hair flying in the wind, learning finally to fly across the island, to arrive at the footbridge, return to the city. For the second time he'd escaped them, for the second time I was helping him to escape, returning him to his precarious paradise. Out of breath, I stood in front of them; no need to step closer, the game was played out. Of the woman you could see just maybe a shoulder and a bit of the hair, brutally cut off by the frame of the picture; but the man was directly center, his mouth half open, you could see a shaking black tongue, and he lifted his hands slowly, bringing them into the foreground, an instant still in perfect focus, and then all of him a lump that blotted out the island, the tree, and I shut my eyes, I didn't want to see any more, and I covered my face and broke into tears like an idiot.

Now there's a big white cloud, as on all these days, all this untellable time. What remains to be said is always a cloud, two clouds, or long hours of a sky perfectly clear, a very clean, clear rectangle tacked up with pins on the wall of my room. That was what I saw when I opened my eyes and dried them with my fingers: the clear sky, and then a cloud that drifted in from the left, passed gracefully and slowly across and disappeared on the right. And then another, and for a change sometimes, everything gets grey, all one enormous cloud, and suddenly the splotches of rain cracking down, for a long spell you can see it raining over the picture, like a spell of weeping reversed, and little by little, the frame becomes clear, perhaps the sun comes out, and again the clouds begin to come, two at a time, three at a time. And the pigeons once in a while, and a sparrow or two.

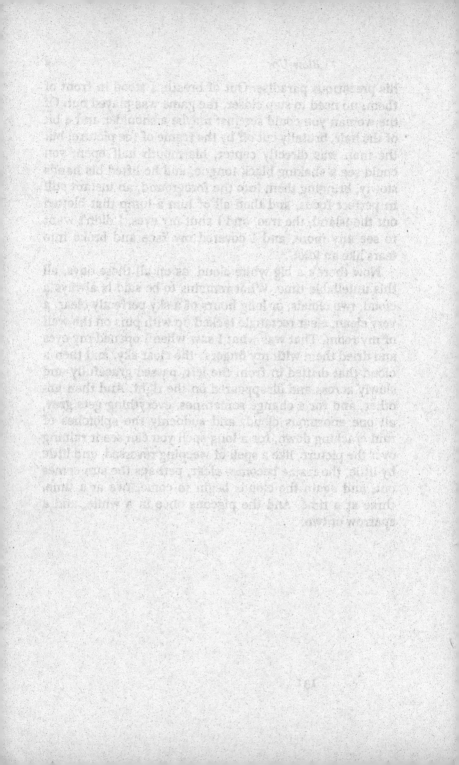

THREE

END OF THE GAME

· · · · · · · · · · · · · · · · ·

Letitia, Holanda and I used to play by the Argentine Central tracks during the hot weather, hoping that Mama and Aunt Ruth would go up to their siesta so that we could get out past the white gate. After washing the dishes, Mama and Aunt Ruth were always tired, especially when Holanda and I were drying, because it was then that there were arguments, spoons on the floor, secret words that only we understood, and in general, an atmosphere in which the smell of grease, José's yowling, and the dimness of the kitchen would end up in an incredible fight and the subsequent commotion. Holanda specialized in rigging this sort of brawl, for example, letting an already clean glass slip into the pan of dirty water, or casually dropping a remark to the effect that the Loza house had two maids to do all the work. I had other systems: I liked to suggest to Aunt Ruth that she was going to get an allergy rash on her hands if she kept scrubbing the pots instead of doing the cups and plates once in a while, which were exactly what Mama liked to wash, and over which they would confront one another soundlessly in a war of advantage to get the easy item. The heroic expedient, in case the bits of advice and the drawn-out family recollections began to bore us, was to upset some boiling water on the cat's back. Now that's a big lie about a scalded cat, it really is, except that you have to take the reference to cold water literally; because José never backed away from hot water, almost insinuating himself under it, poor animal, when we spilled a half-cup of it somewhere around 220° F., or less, a good deal less, probably, because his hair never fell out. The whole point was to get Troy burning, and in the confusion, crowned by a splendid G-flat from Aunt Ruth and Mama's sprint for the whipstick, Holanda and I would take no time at all to get lost in the long porch, toward the empty rooms off the back, where Letitia would be waiting for us, reading Ponson de Terrail, or some other equally inexplicable book.

Normally, Mama chased us a good part of the way, but her desire to bust in our skulls evaporated soon enough, and finally (we had barred the door and were begging for mercy in emotion-filled and very theatrical voices), she got tired and went off, repeating the same sentence: "Those ruffians'll end up on the street."

Where we ended up was by the Argentine Central tracks, when the house had settled down and was silent, and we saw the cat stretched out under the lemon tree to take its siesta also, a rest buzzing with fragrances and wasps. We'd open the white gate slowly, and when we shut it again with a slam like a blast of wind, it was a freedom which took us by the hands, seized the whole of our bodies and tumbled us out. Then we ran, trying to get the speed to scramble up the low embankment of the right-of-way, and there spread out upon the world, we silently surveyed our kingdom.

Our kingdom was this: a long curve of the tracks ended its bend just opposite the back section of the house. There was just the gravel incline, the crossties, and the double line of track; some dumb sparse grass among the rubble where mica, quartz and feldspar—the components of granite—sparkled like real diamonds in the two o'clock afternoon sun. When we stooped down to touch the rails (not wasting time because it would have been dangerous to spend much time there, not so much from the trains as for fear of being seen from the house), the heat off the stone roadbed flushed our faces, and facing into the wind from the river there was a damp heat against our cheeks and ears. We liked to bend our legs and squat down, rise, squat again, move from one kind of hot zone to the other, watching each other's faces to measure the perspiration— a minute or two later we would be sopping with it. And we were always quiet, looking down the track into the distance, or at the river on the other side, that stretch of coffee-and-cream river.

After this first inspection of the kingdom, we'd scramble down the bank and flop in the meager shadow of the willows next the wall enclosing the house where the white gate was. This was the capital city of the kingdom, the wilderness city and the headquarters of our game. Letitia was the first to start the game; she was the luckiest and the most privileged of the three of us. Letitia didn't have to dry dishes or make the beds, she could laze away the day reading or pasting up pictures, and at night they let her stay up later if she asked to, not counting having a room to herself, special hot broth when she wanted it, and all kinds of other advantages. Little by little she had taken more and more advantage of these privileges, and had been presiding over the game since the summer before, I think really she was presiding over the whole kingdom; in any case she was quicker at saying things, and Holanda and I accepted them without protest, happy almost. It's likely that Mama's long lectures on how we ought to behave toward Letitia had had their effect, or simply that we loved her enough and it didn't bother us that she was boss. A pity that she didn't have the looks for the boss, she was the shortest of the three of us and very skinny. Holanda was skinny, and I never weighed over 110, but Letitia was scragglier than we were, and even worse, that kind of skinniness you can see from a distance in the neck and ears. Maybe it was the stiffness of her back that made her look so thin, for instance she could hardly move her head from side to side, she was like a folded-up ironing board, one of those kind they had in the Loza house, with a cover of white material. Like an ironing board with the wide part up, leaning closed against the wall. And she led us.

The best satisfaction was to imagine that someday Mama or Aunt Ruth would find out about the game. If they managed to find out about the game there would be an unbelievable mess. The G-flat and fainting fits, incredible protests of devotion and sacrifice ill-rewarded, and a string of words threatening the more celebrated punishments, closing the bid with a dire prediction of our fates, which consisted of the three of us ending up on the street. This final prediction always left us somewhat perplexed, because to end up in the street always seemed fairly normal to us.

First Letitia had us draw lots. We used to use pebbles hidden in the hand, count to twenty-one, any way at all. If we used the count-to-twenty-one system, we would pretend two or three more girls and include them in the counting to prevent cheating. If one of them came out 21, we dropped her from the group and started drawing again, until one of us won. Then Holanda and I lifted the stone and we got out the ornament-box. Suppose Holanda had won, Letitia and I chose the ornaments. The game took two forms: Statues and Attitudes. Attitudes did not require ornaments but an awful lot of expressiveness, for Envy you could show your teeth, make fists and hold them in a position so as to seem cringing. For Charity the ideal was an angelic face, eyes turned up to the sky, while the hands offered something—a rag, a ball, a branch of willow—to a poor invisible orphan. Shame and Fear were easy to do; Spite and Jealousy required a more conscientious study. The Statues were determined, almost all of them, by the choice of ornaments, and here absolute liberty reigned. So that a statue would come out of it, one had to think carefully of every detail in the costume. It was a rule of the game that the one chosen could not take part in the selection; the two remaining argued out the business at hand and then fitted the ornaments on. The winner had to invent her statue taking into account what they'd dressed her in, and in this way the game was much more complicated and exciting because sometimes there were counterplots, and the victim would find herself rigged out in adornments which were completely hopeless; so it was up to her to be quick then in composing a good statue. Usually when the game called for Attitudes, the winner came up pretty well outfitted, but there were times when the Statues were horrible failures.

Well, the story I'm telling, lord knows when it began, but things changed the day the first note fell from the train. Naturally the Attitudes and Statues were not for our own consumption, we'd have gotten bored immediately. The rules were that the winner had to station herself at the foot of the embankment, leaving the shade of the willow trees, and wait for the train from Tigre that passed at 2:08. At that height above Palermo the trains went by pretty fast and we weren't bashful doing the Statue or the Attitude. We hardly saw the people in the train windows, but with time, we got a bit more expert, and we knew that some of the passengers were expecting to see us. One man with white hair and tortoise-shell glasses used to stick his head out the window and wave at the Statue or the Attitude with a handkerchief. Boys sitting on the steps of the coaches on their way back from school shouted things as the train went by, but some of them remained serious and watching us. In actual fact, the Statue or the Attitude saw nothing at all, because she had to concentrate so hard on holding herself stock-still, but the other two under the willows would analyze in excruciating detail the great success produced, or the audience indifference. It was a Wednesday when the note dropped as the second coach went by. It fell very near Holanda (she did Malicious Gossip that day) and ricocheted toward me. The small piece of paper was tightly folded up and had been shoved through a metal nut. In a man's handwriting, and pretty bad too, it said: "The Statues very pretty. I ride in the third window of the second coach. Ariel B." For all the trouble of stuffing it through the nut and tossing it, it seemed to us a little dry, but it delighted us. We chose lots to see who would keep it, and I won. The next day nobody wanted to play because we all wanted to see what Ariel B. was like, but we were afraid he would misinterpret our interruption, so finally we chose lots and Letitia won. Holanda and I were very happy because Letitia did Statues very well, poor thing. The paralysis wasn't noticeable when she was still, and she was capable of gestures of enormous nobility. With Attitudes she always chose Generosity, Piety, Sacrifice and Renunciation. With Statues she tried for the style of the Venus in the parlor which Aunt Ruth called the Venus de Nilo. For that reason we chose ornaments especially so that Ariel would be very impressed. We hung a piece of green velvet on her like a tunic, and a crown of willow on her hair. As we were wearing short sleeves, the Greek effect was terrific. Letitia practiced a little in the shade, and we decided that we'd show ourselves also and wave at Ariel, discreetly, but very friendly.

Letitia was magnificent, when the train came she didn't budge a finger. Since she couldn't turn her head, she threw it backward, bringing her arms against her body almost as though she were missing them; except for the green tunic, it was like looking at the Venus de Nilo. In the third window we saw a boy with blond curly hair and light eyes, who smiled brightly when he saw that Holanda and I were waving at him. The train was gone in a second, but it was 4:30 and we were still discussing whether he was wearing a dark suit, a red tie, and if he were really nice or a creep. On Thursday I did an Attitude, Dejection, and we got another note which read: "The three of you I like very much. Ariel." Now he stuck his head and one arm out the window and laughed and waved at us. We figured him to be eighteen (we were sure he was no older than sixteen), and we decided that he was coming back every day from some English school, we couldn't stand the idea of any of the regular peanut factories. You could see that Ariel was super.

As it happened, Holanda had the terrific luck to win three days running. She surpassed herself, doing the attitudes Reproach and Robbery, and a very difficult Statue of The Ballerina, balancing on one foot from the time the train hit the curve. The next day I won, and the day after that too; when I was doing Horror, a note from Ariel almost caught me on the nose; at first we didn't understand it: "The prettiest is the laziest." Letitia was the last to understand it; we saw that she blushed and went off by herself, and Holanda and I looked at each other, just a little furious. The first judicial opinion it occurred to us to hand down was that Ariel was an idiot, but we couldn't tell Letitia that, poor angel, with the disadvantage she had to put up with. She said nothing, but it seemed to be understood that the paper was hers, and she kept it. We were sort of quiet going back to the house that day, and didn't get together that night. Letitia was very happy at the supper table, her eyes shining, and Mama looked at Aunt Ruth a couple of times as evidence of her own high spirits. In those days they were trying out a new strengthening treatment for Letitia, and considering how she looked, it was miraculous how well she was feeling.

Before we went to sleep, Holanda and I talked about the business. The note from Ariel didn't bother us so much, thrown from a train going its own way, that's how it is, but it seemed to us that Letitia from her privileged position was taking too much advantage of us. She knew we weren't going to say anything to her, and in a household where there's someone with some physical defect and a lot of pride, everyone pretends to ignore it starting with the one who's sick, or better yet, they pretend they don't know that the other one knows. But you don't have to exaggerate it either, and the way Letitia was acting at the table, or the way she kept the note, was just too much. That night I went back to having nightmares about trains, it was morning and I was walking on enormous railroad beaches covered with rails filled with switches, seeing in the distance the red glows of locomotives approaching, anxiously trying to calculate if the train was going to pass to my left and threatened at the same time by the arrival of an express back of me or—what was even worse—that one of the trains would switch off onto one of the sidings and run

directly over me. But I forgot it by morning because Letitia was all full of aches and we had to help her get
dressed. It seemed to us that she was a little sorry for the
business yesterday and we were very nice to her, telling
her that's what happens with walking too much and that
maybe it would be better for her to stay in her room reading. She said nothing but came to the table for breakfast,
and when Mama asked, she said she was fine and her
back hardly hurt at all. She stated it firmly and looked at
us.

That afternoon I won, but at that moment, I don't know
what came over me, I told Letitia that I'd give her my
place, naturally without telling her why. That this guy
clearly preferred her and would look at her until his eyes
fell out. The game drew to Statues, and we selected simple
items so as not to complicate life, and she invented a sort
of Chinese Princess, with a shy air, looking at the ground,
and the hands placed together as Chinese princesses are
wont to do. When the train passed, Holanda was lying on
her back under the willows, but I watched and saw that
Ariel had eyes only for Letitia. He kept looking at her until
the train disappeared around the curve, and Letitia stood
there motionless and didn't know that he had just looked
at her that way. But when it came to resting under the
trees again, we saw that she knew all right, and that she'd
have been pleased to keep the costume on all afternoon
and all night.

Wednesday we drew between Holanda and me, because
Letitia said it was only fair she be left out. Holanda won,
darn her luck, but Ariel's letter fell next to me. When I
picked it up I had the impulse to give it to Letitia who
didn't say a word, but I thought, then, that neither was it a
matter of catering to everybody's wishes, and I opened it
slowly. Ariel announced that the next day he was going to
get off at the nearby station and that he would come by

the embankment to chat for a while. It was all terribly written, but the final phrase was handsomely put: "Warmest regards to the three Statues." The signature looked like a scrawl though we remarked on its personality.

While we were taking the ornaments off Holanda, Letitia looked at me once or twice. I'd read them the message and no one had made any comments, which was very upsetting because finally, at last, Ariel was going to come and one had to think about this new development and come to some decision. If they found out about it at the house, or if by accident one of the Loza girls, those envious little runts, came to spy on us, there was going to be one incredible mess. Furthermore, it was extremely unlike us to remain silent over a thing like this; we hardly looked at one another, putting the ornaments away and going back through the white gate to the house.

Aunt Ruth asked Holanda and me to wash the cat, and she took Letitia off for the evening treatment and finally we could get our feelings off our chests. It seemed super that Ariel was going to come, we'd never had a friend like that, our cousin Tito we didn't count, a dumbbell who cut out paper dolls and believed in first communion. We were extremely nervous in our expectation and José, poor angel, got the short end of it. Holanda was the braver of the two and brought up the subject of Letitia. I didn't know what to think, on the one hand it seemed ghastly to me that Ariel should find out, but also it was only fair that things clear themselves up, no one had to out and out put herself on the line for someone else. What I really would have wanted was that Letitia not suffer; she had enough to put up with and now the new treatment and all those things.

That night Mama was amazed to see us so quiet and said what a miracle, and had the cat got our tongues, then looked at Aunt Ruth and both of them thought for sure we'd been raising hell of some kind and were conscience-stricken. Letitia ate very little and said that she hurt and would they let her go to her room to read Rocambole. Though she didn't much want to, Holanda gave her a hand, and I sat down and started some knitting, something I do only when I'm nervous. Twice I thought to go down to Letitia's room, I couldn't figure out what the two of them were doing there alone, but then Holanda came back with a mysterious air of importance and sat next to me not saying a word until Mama and Aunt Ruth cleared the table. "She doesn't want to go tomorrow. She wrote a letter and said that if he asks a lot of questions we should give it to him." Half-opening the pocket of her blouse she showed me the lilac-tinted envelope. Then they called us in to dry the dishes, and that night we fell asleep almost immediately, exhausted by all the high-pitched emotion and from washing José.

The next day it was my turn to do the marketing and I didn't see Letitia all morning, she stayed in her room. Before they called us to lunch I went in for a moment and found her sitting at the window with a pile of pillows and a new Rocambole novel. You could see she felt terrible, but she started to laugh and told me about a bee that couldn't find its way out and about a funny dream she had had. I said it was a pity she wasn't coming out to the willows, but I found it difficult to put it nicely. "If you want, we can explain to Ariel that you feel upset," I suggested, but she said no and shut up like a clam. I insisted for a little while, really, that she should come, and finally got terribly gushy and told her she shouldn't be afraid, giving as an example that true affection knows no barriers and other fat ideas we'd gotten from *The Treasure of Youth*, but it got harder and harder to say anything to her because she was looking out the window and looked as if she were going to cry. Finally I left, saying that Mama needed me. Lunch lasted for days, and Holanda got a slap from Aunt Ruth for having spattered some tomato sauce from the spaghetti onto the tablecloth. I don't even remember doing the dishes, right away we were out under the willows hugging one another, very happy, and not jealous of one another in the slightest. Holanda explained to me everything we had to say about our studies so that Ariel would be impressed, because high school students despised girls who'd only been through grade school and studied just home ec and knew how to do raised needlework. When the train went past at 2:08, Ariel waved his arms enthusiastically, and we waved a welcome to him with our embossed handkerchiefs. Some twenty minutes later we saw him arrive by the embankment; he was taller than we had thought and dressed all in grey.

I don't even remember what we talked about at first; he was somewhat shy in spite of having come and the notes and everything, and said a lot of considerate things. Almost immediately he praised our Statues and Attitudes and asked our names, and why had the third one not come. Holanda explained that Letitia had not been able to come, and he said that that was a pity and that he thought Letitia was an exquisite name. Then he told us stuff about the Industrial High School, it was not the English school, unhappily, and wanted to know if we would show him the ornaments. Holanda lifted the stone and we let him see the things. He seemed to be very interested in them, and at different times he would take one of the ornaments and say, "Letitia wore this one day," or "This was for the Oriental statue," what he meant was the Chinese Princess. We sat in the shade under a willow and he was happy but distracted, and you could see that he was only being polite. Holanda looked at me two or three times when the conversation lapsed into silence, and that made both of us feel awful, made us want to get out of it, or wish that Ariel had never come at all. He asked again if Letitia were ill and Holanda looked at me and I thought she was going to tell him, but instead she answered that Letitia had not been able to come. Ariel drew geometric figures in the dust with a stick and occasionally looked at the white gate and we knew what he was thinking, and because of that Holanda was right to pull out the lilac envelope and hand it up to him, and he stood there surprised with the envelope in his hand; then he blushed while we explained to him that Letitia had sent it to him, and he put the letter in an inside jacket pocket, not wanting to read it in front of us. Almost immediately he said that it had been a great pleasure for him and that he was delighted to have come, but his hand was soft and unpleasant in a way it'd have been better for the interview to end right away, although later we could only think of his grey eyes and the sad way he had of smiling. We also agreed on how he had said good-bye: "Until always," a form we'd never heard at home and which seemed to us so godlike and poetic. We told all this to Letitia who was waiting for us under the lemon tree in the patio, and I would have liked to have asked her what she had said in the letter, but I don't know what, it was because she'd sealed the envelope before giving it to Holanda, so I didn't say anything about that and only told her what Ariel was like and how many times he'd asked for her. This was not at all an easy thing to do because it was a nice thing and a terrible thing at the same time; we noticed that Letitia was feeling very happy and at the same time she was almost crying, and we found ourselves saying that Aunt Ruth wanted us now and we left her looking at the wasps in the lemon tree.

When we were going to sleep that night, Holanda said to me, "The game's finished from tomorrow on, you'll see." But she was wrong though not by much, and the next day

Letitia gave us the regular signal when dessert came around. We went out to wash the dishes somewhat astonished, and a bit sore, because that was sheer sauciness on Letitia's part and not the right thing to do. She was waiting for us at the gate, and we almost died of fright when we got to the willows for she brought out of her pocket Mama's pearl collar and all her rings, even Aunt Ruth's big one with the ruby. If the Loza girls were spying on us and saw us with the jewels, sure as anything Mama would learn about it right away and kill us, the nasty little creeps. But Letitia wasn't scared and said if anything happened she was the only one responsible. "I would like you to leave it to me today," she added without looking at us. We got the ornaments out right away, all of a sudden we wanted to be very kind to Letitia and give her all the pleasure, although at the bottom of everything we were still feeling a little spiteful. The game came out Statues, and we chose lovely things that would go well with the jewels, lots of peacock feathers to set in the hair, and a fur that from a distance looked like silver fox, and a pink veil that she put on like a turban. We saw that she was thinking, trying the Statue out, but without moving, and when the train appeared on the curve she placed herself at the foot of the incline with all the jewels sparkling in the sun. She lifted her arms as if she were going to do an Attitude instead of a Statue, her hands pointed at the sky with her head thrown back (the only direction she could, poor thing) and bent her body backwards so far it scared us. To us it seemed terrific, the most regal statue she'd ever done; then we saw Ariel looking at her, hung halfway out the window he looked just at her, turning his head and looking at her without seeing us, until the train carried him out of sight all at once. I don't know why, the two of us started running at the same time to catch Letitia who was standing there, still with her eyes closed and enormous tears all down her face. She pushed us back, not angrily, but we helped her stuff the jewels in her pocket, and she went back to the house alone while we put the ornaments away in their box for the last time. We knew almost what was going to happen, but just the same we went out to the willows the next day, just the two of us, after Aunt Ruth imposed absolute silence so as not to disturb Letitia who hurt and who wanted to sleep. When the train came by, it was no surprise to see the third window empty, and while we were grinning at one another, somewhere between relief and being furious, we imagined Ariel riding on the other side of the coach, not moving in his seat, looking off toward the river with his grey eyes.

AT YOUR SERVICE

For some time now it's been a problem lighting the fire. The matches are not as good as they used to be, now you have to hold them head down and hope that the flame has some force to it; the kindling arrives damp, and no matter how often I tell Frederic to bring me dry logs, they always smell wet and do not take well. Since my hands started shaking, everything is more of a problem. Before, I could make a bed in two seconds, and the sheets would look and feel as though they'd just been ironed. Now I have to make my way around and around the bed, and madame Beauchamp gets irritable and says that if they're paying me by the hour it's not to waste time smoothing out one wrinkle here and another there. And all that fuss because my hands shake, and because the sheets today are not like they used to be, not so solid and heavy. Doctor Lebrun says there's nothing wrong, only I have to be very careful, not to catch cold and to go to bed early. "And that glass of wine every now and then, eh, madame Francinet? It would be better if we eliminated that, and the pernod before lunch also." Doctor Lebrun is a young doctor and his ideas are very good for young people. In my day, nobody would have said that wine was bad for one. But after that, I don't drink, not what you'd call drinking, like that Germaine on the third floor, or that animal Felix, the carpenter. I don't know why that reminds me now, that poor monsieur Bébé, the night he made me drink a glass of whiskey. Monsieur Bébé! Monsieur Bébé! In the kitchen at madame Rosay's apartment the night of the party. I used to go out a lot then, still even while I was working house to house. Mr. Renfeld's place was one, at the sisters' who taught piano and violin, a lot of places, all of them very nice houses. Now I can hardly make it three times a week at madame Beauchamp's, and it looks like that's not going to last long. My hands shake so badly, and madame Beauchamp gets irritable with me. These days, madame Rosay would never give me a recommendation, nor would madame Rosay come herself looking for me, now monsieur Bébé would not talk with me in the kitchen. No, especially not monsieur Bébé.

When madame Rosay came to my house it was already afternoon, and she didn't stay more than a few minutes. To be frank, my house consists of a single room, but I have a kitchen in the back and what I have left over of the furniture from when George died and I had to sell everything, it seems to me I have the right to call it my house. In any case, there're three chairs, and madame Rosay removed her gloves, sat down and said that the room was small but pleasant. I wasn't very impressed with madame Rosay, though I would have preferred to have been better dressed. She took me by surprise, and I had on the green skirt that the sisters had given me. Madame Rosay was not looking at anything, I mean that she looked and immediately looked away, as though to disengage herself from what she'd just seen. Her nose wrinkled a little; probably the onion smell bothered her (I love onions) or the smell of cat-piss. Poor Minouche. But I was pleased that madame Rosay should have come, and told her so.

"Ah yes, madame Francinet. I also am very happy to have found you, I'm so busy . . ." She screwed up her nose as if housework smelled bad. "I would like to ask you to . . . that is to say that madame Beauchamp thought that perhaps you might have Sunday night free."

"Well, naturally," I said. "What can you do on Sunday after attending mass? I go to Gustave's for a while, and then . . ."

"Of course," madame Rosay said. "If you're free Sunday, I'd like you to help me around the house. We're giving a party."

"A party? Congratulations, madame Rosay." But that seemed to offend her somehow and she got up suddenly.

"You would help in the kitchen, there's a good deal to do there. If you can come at seven, my butler will give you the necessary instructions."

"Naturally, madame Rosay."

"This is my address," and she gave me a cream-colored calling card. "Will five hundred francs be all right?"

"Five hundred francs."

"We'll say six hundred. You'll be free at midnight and there'll be time to catch the last metro. Madame Beauchamp told me that you are to be trusted."

"Oh, madame Rosay!"

When she was gone I near had to laugh, thinking that I'd almost offered her a cup of tea (I would have had to look for a cup that wasn't chipped). Sometimes I don't pay attention to who it is I'm talking to. Only when I go to a lady's house I hold my tongue and talk like a maid. It must be because I'm nobody's maid in my own house, or because it feels as though I were still living in our little three-room backyard house, when George and I were working in the factory and never lacked for anything. Perhaps by dint of scolding at poor Minouche, who makes pee-pee under the stove, it seems to me I am also a lady like madame Rosay.

Just as I was going to go into the house, I almost lost the heel off one shoe. Right away I said, "Good luck come, hum, hum, wanton whoreson devil begone." And I pushed the bell.

A gentleman with grey side-whiskers like in the theater came out and told me to come in. It was a very, very large apartment that smelled like floorwax. The gentleman with the side-whiskers was the butler and smelled of benzoin.

"At last," he said and hurried to make me follow him down a hallway that led to the servant's quarters. "The next time you'll call at the door on the left."

"Madame Rosay didn't tell me anything."

"The lady doesn't have to think about those things. Alice, this is madame Francinet. You'll give her one of your aprons."

Alice brought me to her room on the other side of the kitchen (and what a kitchen) and gave me an apron that was too big for me. It looked like madame Rosay had given her the job of explaining everything to me, but at the beginning the business about the dogs seemed to be a mistake and I stood looking at Alice, Alice had a wart right under her nose. In crossing the kitchen everything in

sight was so lavish and shiny that just the idea of being
there that night shining up the crystal and preparing the
trays of hors d'oeuvres that they eat in such homes,
seemed to me it was better than going to the theater or to
the country. Probably that was why, at the beginning, I
didn't understand the business about the dogs, and I stood
there looking at Alice.

"Mmm, yeah," Alice said, she was from Brittany and
you couldn't miss it. "The missus said so."

"But why me? That gentleman with the whiskers,
couldn't he take care of the dogs?"

"Mr. Rodolos is the head butler," Alice said, with holy
veneration.

"Well, if not him, then anyone. I don't understand why
me."

Alice suddenly grew insolent.

"And why not, madame . . . ?"

"Francinet, at your service."

". . . madame Francinet? It's not strenuous work.
Fido is the worst, Miss Lucienne has spoiled him terribly . . ."

She went on explaining to me, all friendly again, like
jello.

"Cube sugar every minute and holding it in her lap.
Monsieur Bébé ruins him too, whenever he comes, he pets
and fondles him a lot, you know . . . But Médor is very
good, and Fifine won't budge out of her corner."

"In that case," I said, so my astonishment wouldn't
show, "there are a lot of dogs."

"Mmm, sure, a lot of them."

"In an apartment!" I said, I was indignant and couldn't
hide it. "I don't know what you think about it, madame . . ."

"Mademoiselle."

"Pardon me. But in my day, mademoiselle, the dogs

lived in the dog kennels, and well might I say so, because my late husband and I had a house next to a gentleman's villa where . . . ." But Alice did not let me finish the explanation. Not that she would say anything, but you could see that she was impatient and that's something I notice very quick in people. I stopped, and she began to tell me how madame Rosay adored dogs, and that her husband put up with all her tastes. And, too, there was their daughter, who had inherited the same leanings.

"The young lady is crazy about Fido, and sure as anything, she'll buy a female of the same breed so they can have puppies. Now there're no more than six: Médor, Fifine, Fido, Tiny, Chow, and Hannibal. Fido is the worst, Miss Lucienne has spoiled him terribly. Don't you hear him? Absolutely sure that's him barking in the reception hall."

"And where will I have to stay to take care of them?" I asked with an unprejudiced air, so that Alice shouldn't think that I felt offended.

"Mr. Rodolos will take you to the dogs' room."

"Unhuh, so the dogs have their own room?" I was as natural as possible. It was not Alice's fault, really, but the truth of the matter is I would have liked to have boxed her ears a couple of times, then and there.

"Of course they have their own room," Alice said. "Madame wants the dogs to sleep each one on his own mattress, and they've fixed up a room for just them. We've already brought up a chair so you can sit and take care of them."

I fixed the apron as best I could and we went back to the kitchen. Just at that moment another door swung open and in came madame Rosay. She had on a blue dressing gown trimmed in white fur and her face full of creams. She looked like a piece of pastry, if you'll pardon me for saying so. But she was very friendly and you could see that my arrival was a relief to her.

"Ah, madame Francinet. Alice will already have explained to you what your duties are. Perhaps later you'll be able to help out with some other light duty, drying glasses or something similar, but the main thing is to keep my darlings quiet. They are luscious dears, but they don't know how to behave together, and especially not all by themselves, and I cannot *tolerate* the idea that Fido might bite poor little Chow, or that Médor . . ." she lowered her voice and came a little closer. "Besides, you must watch Tiny very closely, she's a Pomeranian with lovely eyes. It seems to me that . . . well, the moment is coming when . . . and I wouldn't want Médor or Fido . . . do you understand? Tomorrow I'll take her out to our estate, but until then I want her watched very closely. And I wouldn't know where else to keep her except with the others in their room. The poor darling, so delicate! I couldn't stand having her away from me all night. They won't give you any trouble, you'll see. On the contrary, you're going to have a good time, you'll see how intelligent they are. I shall come up now and then to see how everything's going."

I realized that was more of a warning than a friendly offer, but madame Rosay continued smiling under the flower-scented cream.

"My daughter Lucienne will come up also, naturally. She can't be without her Fido. She even sleeps with him, can you imagine . . ." But this last part she was saying to someone she'd just thought of, for at the same time she turned around to leave and I didn't see her again. Alice, leaning against the table, was looking at me with an idiotic expression. It's not that I despise people, but she was looking at me with that idiot expression.

"What time is the party?" I asked, realizing that without thinking I was continuing to speak in madame Rosay's tone of voice, her way of putting questions a little to one side of a person, as though she were asking them of a coatrack or a doorway.

"It's going to begin now," Alice said, and Mr. Rodolos, who was coming in at that moment brushing a speck of dust from his black suit, agreed to this with an air of importance.

"Yes, no time to waste," he said, with a hand-sign to Alice to get busy with several lovely silver trays. "Monsieur Fréjus and monsieur Bébé are already here, and they want cocktails."

"They always come so early, those two," said Alice. "And they drink, too . . . I explained everything to madame Francinet, and madame Rosay told her what had to be done."

"Ah, perfect. It would be best, then, that I take her up to the room where she'll be staying. Then I'll go bring the dogs up; the master and monsieur Bébé are playing with them in the salon."

"Miss Lucienne had Fido with her in her room," Alice said.

"Yes, she'll bring him to madame Francinet herself. All right now, if you would like to come with me . . ."

So then I found myself sitting in an old, high-backed chair, right in the exact center of an enormous room, the floor filled with mattresses, and where they had a little doghouse with a straw roof, just like an African hut, and according to Mr. Rodolos' explanation, it was a caprice of Miss Lucienne's for her Fido. The six mattresses were thrown down every which way, and there were bowls with food and water. The only light in the room was a bulb hanging just over my head that gave off a very weak light. I mentioned it to Mr. Rodolos, and that I was afraid of falling asleep with nobody there but the dogs.

"Oh no, you won't fall asleep, madame Francinet," he replied. "The dogs are very affectionate but they're spoiled, and you'll have to pay some attention to them the whole while. Wait here a moment."

When he shut the door and left me alone, sitting in the middle of this funny room, with the smell of dogs (well, it was a clean smell) and all the mattresses on the floor, I felt a little strange myself because it was almost like dreaming, especially with the yellow light over my head and the silence. Of course, the time would pass quickly, and it wouldn't be too disagreeable, but every minute I felt as though something were wrong. Not exactly that they'd called on me for this without telling me in advance, but something strange about having to do this work, or maybe I really thought that it just wasn't right. The floor gleamed with a real luster, and the dogs, you could tell that they did their business somewhere else, because there was no smell except of their own which isn't terrible once you've been there a little while. But the worst thing was sitting there alone and waiting, and I was almost happy when Miss Lucienne came in carrying Fido in her arms, an awful Pekingese (I can't stand Pekingeses), and Mr. Rodolos arrived yelling at and calling to the other five dogs until they were all in the room. Miss Lucienne was lovely, all in white, and had platinum hair that fell to her shoulders. She kissed and fondled Fido for a long spell, paying no attention to the others, who were drinking water or playing, and then she brought him over to me and looked at me for the first time.

"You're the one who's going to take care of them?" Her voice was a little shrill, but you can't deny that she was very pretty.

"I am madame Francinet, at your service," I said greeting her.

"Fido is very delicate. Take him. Yes, in your arms. He's not going to dirty you. I bathe him myself every morning.

As I told you, very delicate. Don't let him mix with *them*.
Give him water once in a while."

The dog stayed quiet in my lap, but at the same time, I
was a bit disgusted. A great Dane with black spots came
over and began to smell him, as dogs do, and Miss Lucienne let out a screech and gave him a kick with the
point of her shoe. Mr. Rodolos never moved from the
doorway, he looked used to the whole thing.

"You see, you see," Miss Lucienne screeched. "That's
what I don't want to happen, and you must not permit it.
Mama has explained that already, isn't that right? You
will not move from here until the party's over. And if Fido
feels badly or begins to cry, knock on the door and *that*
will let me know."

She went out without looking at me again, after taking
the Pekingese up in her arms again and kissing him until
the dog began to whine. Mr. Rodolos stayed around for a
moment.

"The dogs are not ill-behaved, madame Francinet," he
said. "In any case, if there is any problem, knock on the
door and I'll come. Take it easy," he added, as though it
had occurred to him at the last moment, and he closed the
door very carefully. I wondered if he'd locked it from the
outside, but I resisted the temptation to get up and go see;
I think I would have felt much worse if I found out he
had.

As a matter of fact, it wasn't difficult taking care of the
dogs. They didn't fight, and it was far from sure that what
madame Rosay had said about Tiny was true, at least it
didn't seem to have started yet. Naturally, as soon as the
door was shut, I let the nasty little Pekingese loose and let
him jump around peacefully with the others. He was the
worst, asking for a quarrel the whole time, but they didn't
do anything to him, they even seemed to be inviting him

to play. They drank a little once in a while, or ate the rich meat in the bowls. God help me for saying it, but it almost made me hungry to see what good meat there was in the bowls.

At times, from far away, you could hear somebody laughing and I don't know whether it was because I was informed that they were going to have music (Alice had said so in the kitchen), but I seemed to hear a piano, although perhaps it was in another apartment. Time dragged and it seemed very long, especially on account of the single light hanging from the ceiling, so yellow it was. Four of the dogs fell asleep right away, and Fido and Fifine (I'm not sure it was Fifine but it seemed to me it must have been she) played on for a while biting each other's ears, and ended up lapping a lot of water and lying down one against the other on a mattress. Sometimes I thought I heard steps outside, and ran to take up Fido in my arms, so that if Miss Lucienne should walk in . . . But no one came and much time passed, until I began to fall asleep in the chair, and almost would have liked to put out the light and really fall asleep on one of the empty mattresses.

I shan't say I wasn't happy when Alice came to get me. Alice's face had a very high color and one could see that she was still excited by the party and all they'd said in the kitchen among all the other maids and Mr. Rodolos.

"You're a marvel, madame Francinet," she said. "The missus is sure to be delighted and'll call you every time there's a party. The last one who came couldn't manage to keep them quiet, until Miss Lucienne had to stop dancing and come tend to them. Look at how they're sleeping!"

"The guests've gone already?" I asked, a little embarrassed at her praise.

"The guests, yes, but there are others're more at home, more like family here, and they always stay on a little while. Everybody's drunk a lot, you can be sure. Even the master, who never drinks at home, came into the kitchen very cheerful and joked with Ginette and me over how well the meal had been served, and gave us a hundred francs each. They'll give you a tip too, I think. They're still dancing, Miss Lucienne with her boyfriend, and monsieur Bébé and his friends are playing masquerade."

"Then will I have to stay?"

"No, the missus said that when the deputy and the others had left, the dogs should be let out. They love to play with them in the salon. I'll carry Fido and all you have to do is come with me to the kitchen."

I followed her, extremely tired and groggy with sleep, but very curious to see something of the party, if it were only the glasses and plates in the kitchen. And I saw them, for there were mountains of them piled everywhere, and bottles of champagne and whiskey, some still had a whisker to drink in them. In the kitchen they had tubes with a blue light and I was almost blinded by so many white cabinets, so many shelves, the plates and casseroles shining off them. Ginette was a tiny redhead who was also very excited and greeted Alice with little laughs and making faces. She seemed shameless enough, as so many of them are these days.

"Still going on?" Alice asked her, looking toward the door.

"Oh, yes," Ginette said, wiggling her hips. "Is that the lady who was taking care of the dogs?"

I was sleepy and thirsty, but they didn't offer me anything, not even a place to sit down. They were too enthused by the party, by everything they'd seen while they were serving table or taking coats in the entryway. A bell rang and Alice, who still had the Pekingese in her arms, went out on the run. Mr. Rodolos came in and past without seeing me, and was surrounded immediately by the five dogs leaping about and playing. I saw that he had a handful of lumps of sugar and that he was parceling them out so that the dogs would follow him to the salon. I leaned up against the large central table trying not to look much at Ginette, and hardly had Alice returned when she continued gabbling about monsieur Bébé and the disguises, about monsieur Fréjus, of the pianist who seemed to be tubercular, and how Miss Lucienne had had a dispute with her father. Alice seized one of the half-empty bottles and brought it to her lips with such vulgarity that it left me very upset, so much I didn't know where to look; but even worse was that then she passed it to the little redhead, who finished it off. The two of them laughed as if they also had had a lot to drink during the party. That was perhaps the reason that they didn't think of me, that I was hungry and above all else, thirsty. Surely, if they'd been in their right minds, they would have noticed. People are not bad, and they are discourteous often because they really don't know what they're doing; the same thing happens on the bus, or in stores, or in offices.

The bell rang again, and the two girls hurried out. You could hear great peals of laughter, and once in a while the piano. I didn't understand why they were making me wait; all they had to do was pay me and let me go. I sat down in a chair and put my elbows on the table. My eyes were dropping with sleep and I guess I didn't notice that someone had just entered the kitchen. First I heard a noise of glasses clinking together and a very soft whistle. I thought that it was Ginette and turned around to ask her what they were going to do with me.

"Oh, excuse me, sir!" I said getting up. "I didn't know it was you here."

"Not here, I'm not here," said the gentleman, who was very young. "Loulou, come see!"

He was staggering slightly, holding on to one of the

shelves. He'd filled one glass with a whitish drink, and was looking at its transparency as if mistrusting it. Loulou, who'd been called, did not show up, so the young man came over toward me and said I should sit down. He was blond, very pale, and had on a white suit. When I noticed that he was dressed in white in the middle of winter, I wondered if I was dreaming. This is not a way of speaking, when I see something strange I always ask myself if I am dreaming, in capital letters. It's not impossible, because sometimes I dream some strange things. But the gentleman was there, smiling away with an air of fatigue, almost of boredom. I felt bad to see how pale he was.

"You must be the one who takes care of the dogs," he said, and set right away to drinking.

"I am madame Francinet, at your service," I said. He was so pleasant and didn't make me feel afraid at all. Rather, he made me want to be useful to him in some way, to have some sort of courtesy in dealing with him. Now again he was looking at the half-open door.

"Loulou! Are you coming? There's vodka out here. Why, have you been crying, madame Francinet?"

"Oh, no, sir. I must have been yawning a little just before you came out. I'm a little tired and the light in the room up . . . in the other room, was not very good. When one yawns . . . "

" . . . the eyes water," he said. He had perfect teeth, and the whitest hands I've ever seen on a man. He stood up all at once, he went to meet the young man who was staggering in.

"This lady," he explained to him, "is the one who has liberated us all evening from those nasty animals. Loulou, say good evening."

I stood up and gave another greeting. But the gentleman called Loulou did not even look at me. He'd found a bottle of champagne in the refrigerator and was trying to uncork it. The young man in white went over to help him, and the two of them fell to laughing and struggling with the bottle. When you laugh you lose your strength, so neither of them could manage the uncorking. Then they wanted to do it together and threw themselves into line on either side and ended up leaning against one another, getting happier all the time, but without being able to open the bottle. Monsieur Loulou was saying, "Bébé, Bébé, please, let's go home now . . ." and monsieur Bébé was laughing harder all the time and pushed him away playfully until at last he uncorked it and let a great jet of foam spurt all over monsieur Loulou's face, who let out a string of swear-words and rubbed his eyes, running back and forth from one side of the room to the other.

"The poor dear, he's too drunk," monsieur Bébé said, putting his hands on his back and trying to push him out of the kitchen. "Go keep poor Nina company, she's very unhappy . . ." and he laughed, but without meaning it.

Then he came back in, and I found him nicer than ever. He had a nervous tic that made him raise one eyebrow. He repeated it three or four times, looking at me.

"Poor madame Francinet," he said, touching my head very softly. "They've left her all alone, and for sure they haven't given her anything to drink."

"They'll come soon to tell me that I can go home, sir," I answered. It didn't annoy me that he'd have taken the liberty of touching me on the head.

"That you can go, that you can go . . . Why does anyone have to give you permission to do anything?" monsieur Bébé asked, sitting down opposite me. He'd picked up his glass again, but set it down on the table and went to get a clean one and filled it with a tea-colored drink.

"Madame Francinet, we are going to drink together," he said, handing me the glass. "You like whiskey, of course."

"Heavens, sir," I said, frightened. "Outside of wine, and

a little pernod at Gustave's place on Saturdays, I don't know anything about drinking."

"You've never tasted whiskey, really?" he asked in astonishment. "One swallow, not more, try, you'll see how good it is. Come, madame Francinet, cheer up. The first swallow is the one that counts . . ." And he began to recite a poem, what, I don't remember, where it says something about seafarers from some strange place. I took a swallow of the whiskey and found it so aromatic that I took another, and then another. Monsieur Bébé was sipping his vodka and watching me fascinated.

"It's a pleasure to be with you, madame Francinet," he said. "Luckily you are not young, with you one can be a friend . . . One has only to look at you to see how good-hearted you are, like an aunt from the provinces, one whom one can cater to, but without risk, without risk . . . Look, for example, Nina has an aunt in Poitou who sends him chickens, baskets of vegetables, even honey . . . isn't that wonderful?"

"It certainly is, sir," I said, letting him pour me another little glass since it gave him so much pleasure. "It's always nice to have someone to look after you, especially when you're so young. When you get old there's nothing else to do but to think of oneself, because the rest . . . Here I take care of myself, for example. When my George died . . ."

"Have another small one, madame Francinet. Nina's aunt lives way down there, and she does nothing, she has nothing else to do besides send chickens . . . There's no risk in telling family stories . . ."

I was so dizzy already I didn't even care what might happen if Mr. Rodolos came in and surprised me sitting in the kitchen talking with one of the guests. It was a tremendous pleasure for me to look at monsieur Bébé, to hear his laugh, it was so sharp, probably because of the drinking. And it pleased him that I was watching him, although he seemed a little uncomfortable at first but then he only smiled and drank, looking back at me all the time. I know that he was terribly drunk because Alice had told me that they'd drunk an awful lot, and besides, the way monsieur Bébé's eyes shone so. If he hadn't been drunk, what would he have been doing in the kitchen with an old woman like me? But the others were drunk too, and yet monsieur Bébé was the only one who was keeping me company, the only one who'd given me a drink and patted me on the head, though maybe he shouldn't have done that. But because of that I felt very pleased with monsieur Bébé, and looked at him more and more, and he liked it, people looking at him, because once or twice he turned his profile and he had a very handsome nose, like a statue's. He was, all of him, like a statue, especially with his white suit. Even what he was drinking was white, and he was so pale that I was a little afraid for him. You could see he lived a shut-in life, like so many young men these days. I would have liked to tell him so, but who was I to give advice to a gentleman like him, and furthermore I had no time to then because there was a knock on the door and monsieur Loulou came in dragging the great Dane along behind him with a sort of curtain that'd been twisted to make a kind of rope. He'd drunk a good deal more than monsieur Bébé and nearly fell when the great Dane ran around him and tangled the curtain around his legs. There were voices in the hallway and a gentleman with grey hair appeared, he must have been monsieur Rosay, and right after him madame Rosay all flushed and excited and a thin young man with such black hair, blacker than I'd ever seen before. All of them were trying to help monsieur Loulou, who was getting more and more tangled up with the great Dane and the curtain, all the while laughing and joking at the top of his lungs. No one paid any attention to me, until madame Rosay saw me finally and became serious. I couldn't hear what she said to the grey-haired gentleman, who then looked at my glass (it was empty, but there was the bottle next to it), and monsieur Rosay looked at monsieur Bébé and made an indignant face while monsieur Bébé winked at him and threw himself back in his chair laughing to beat the band. I was very mixed up, it seemed to me that I ought to stand up, that would be better, and greet everyone with a curtsy, and then go to one side and wait. Madame Rosay had left the kitchen and an instant later Alice and Mr. Rodolos came in, they came over and indicated that I should follow them. I curtsied to everyone there, but I don't think anyone saw me because they were all trying to quiet monsieur Loulou down, he'd suddenly burst into tears and was saying incomprehensible things waving his hands at monsieur Bébé. The last thing I remember was monsieur Bébé's laugh, throwing his chair back and laughing.

Alice waited until I'd taken the apron off, and Mr. Rodolos handed me six hundred francs. In the street it was snowing, and the subway had stopped running some time back. I had to walk for over an hour to get back home, but the whiskey kept me warm, and remembering so many nice things, and how much fun I'd had in the kitchen at the end of the party.

Time flies, as Gustave says. You think it's Monday and it's Thursday already. Autumn ends and suddenly you're in the middle of next summer. Every time Robert shows up to ask me if the chimney doesn't have to be cleaned (he's a very good man, Robert, and charges me half of what he charges the other tenants), I turn around twice and see that winter's here already. So, I don't rightly remember how much time had passed until I saw monsieur Rosay again. He came at nightfall, almost at the same

time as madame Rosay had the first time. He also began
by saying that he'd come because madame Beauchamp
had recommended me, and sat down in the chair rather
confusedly. No one sits comfortably in my house, not even
me when there are visitors who are not good friends. I begin to rub my hands together as if they were dirty, and
begin to realize only afterwards that other people are going to think they really are dirty, and I don't know where
to put them. It wasn't so bad, monsieur Rosay was as upset as I was, although he hid it better. He used his cane to
tap slowly on the floor, frightening Minouche a great deal,
and as if to avoid my eyes, looked around constantly. I
didn't know what saint to call on, because it was the first
time that a gentleman had been so upset in front of me,
and I didn't know what to do in a case like that except to
offer him a cup of tea.

"No, no thanks," he said impatiently. "I've come at the
request of my wife . . . You remember me, surely."

"Oh, go on, monsieur Rosay. That night of the party
when there were so many distinguished guests . . ."

"That's right. The party. Exactly . . . I mean, this has
nothing to do with the party, but that was a time you were
very helpful to us, madame . . ."

"Francinet, at your service."

"Madame Francinet, of course. My wife thought . . .
Look, it's something somewhat delicate. But I wish, above
all else, to reassure you, what I am going to propose to
you is not . . . how do they say . . . illegal."

"Illegal, monsieur Rosay?"

"Oh, you know, these days . . . But I repeat: it has to
do with something very delicate, but basically perfectly
correct. My wife has been informed of all the details and
has given her consent. I say this to you to reassure you."

"If madame Rosay is in favor, for me it's like communion bread," I said, so he would feel more at home, al-

though I didn't know a great deal about madame Rosay and furthermore she struck me as unsympathetic.

"In short, the situation is, madame . . . Francinet, that's it, madame Francinet. One of our friends . . . perhaps it would be better to say one of our acquaintances, has just passed away under very particular circumstances."

"Oh, monsieur Rosay! I'm so sorry."

"Thank you," said monsieur Rosay, and made a very strange face, almost as though he were going to yell in rage or break into tears. The face of a really crazy person, it made me afraid. Luckily, the door was ajar and Fresnay's shop is next door.

"This gentleman . . . well, a very well known fashion designer . . . lived alone, that is, estranged from his family, do you understand? He had no one besides his friends, well, his clients, you understand, that doesn't count in these cases. Well then, for a series of reasons which would take too long to explain, his friends have been thinking about the details of the burial, and . . . "

How beautifully he spoke! He picked every word, beating the floor slowly with his cane, and without looking at me. It was like listening to the news on the radio, only that monsieur Rosay spoke more slowly, aside from which you could see he wasn't reading a script. The effect was much better. I felt so much admiration that I lost my suspicion and brought my chair a little closer. I felt a sort of warmth in my stomach feeling that such an important gentleman had come to ask a service of me whatever it might be. And I was frightened to death and rubbed my hands without knowing what to do.

"It seemed to us," monsieur Rosay went on, "that a ceremony to which only his friends would be invited, a few . . . anyway, it would not have the magnitude requisite in the case of this gentleman . . . nor would it translate

the consternation"—that's what he said—"which his loss
has produced . . . Do you understand? It seemed to us
that if you would function with your presence at the wake,
and naturally at the burial. . . let's say in the capacity
of a relative very close to the deceased . . . do you see
what I mean to say? A very close relative . . . let's say
an aunt . . . I would even venture to suggest . . ."

"Yes, monsieur Rosay?" I said at the height of wonder.

"Well, it all depends upon you, and certainly you are
. . . But if you would receive an adequate recompense
. . . after all it's not a matter of your taking the trouble
for nothing . . . In that case, isn't it so, madame Francinet? . . . if the remuneration would be suitable to
you . . . you understand . . . let's say the mother of
the deceased . . . Let me explain carefully . . . The
mother who has just arrived from Normandy, having
been apprised of her son's death, has come to accompany
him to the cemetery . . . No, no, before saying anything . . . My wife thought that perhaps you would
agree to help us out of friendship . . . and for my part,
my friends and I have agreed to offer you ten thousand—
would that be all right, madame Francinet?—ten thousand francs for your assistance . . . Three thousand at
this moment and the rest when we leave the cemetery,
after the . . ."

I opened my mouth, only because it had fallen open on
me all by itself, but monsieur Rosay didn't let me say anything. He was very flushed and was speaking rapidly, as if
he wished to finish it as soon as possible.

"If you accept, madame Francinet . . . as all of us
hope you will, it's understood that we rely on your assistance, and we are not asking of you anything . . . irregular, to put it that way, in that case my wife and her maid
will be here within half an hour, with appropriate cloth-

ing . . . and the car, naturally, to take you to the house
. . . of course it will be necessary that you . . . how
shall I say . . . that you become used to the idea of
what's involved . . . the deceased's mother . . . My
wife will give you the necessary information and you,
naturally, will have to give the impression, once in the
house . . . You understand . . . Grief, ah, desperation
. . . This has to do chiefly with the clients," he added.
"In front of us it will be enough to keep silent."

I don't know how it happened but a bundle of bank
notes, very new ones, appeared in his hand, and may I
drop dead this very moment if I know how, suddenly I felt
them in my hand, and monsieur Rosay got up and left
murmuring and forgetting to close the door like everyone
who leaves my house.

May God pardon me this and so many other things, I
know. It wasn't right, but monsieur Rosay had assured me
that it was not illegal, and that in that fashion it would
lend a very substantial assistance (I believe that those
were his very words). It wasn't right that I pretend to pass
for the mother of the gentleman who had died, and who
was a fashion designer, because there are things that just
ought not to be done, not to trick anyone. But he had to
think of the clients, and if the mother wasn't at the burial,
or at least an aunt or a sister, the ceremony would not
have the significance or give the feeling of grief generated
by the loss. Monsieur Rosay had just finished saying these
exact words, and he knew better than I. It wasn't right for
me to do this, but God knows I hardly earn three thousand
francs a month, breaking my back at madame Beau-
champs's house and other places, and now I was going to
get ten thousand for nothing more than crying a little, to
lament the death of this gentleman who was going to be
my son until they buried him.

The house was located near Saint-Cloud, and they drove me there in a car the like of which I've never seen except from the outside. Madame Rosay and the maid had dressed me, and I knew that the deceased was named monsieur Linard, his given name Octave, and that he was the only son of his aged mother who lived in Normandy and had just arrived on the five o'clock train. The aged mother was me, but I was so excited and mixed up that I heard very little of all they told me and what madame Rosay advised me. I remember that in the car she entreated me many times (she entreated me, I won't gainsay it, she had changed a lot since the night of the party) to not be too exaggerated in my grief, and told me it would be better to give the impression of being terribly fatigued and on the edge of an attack.

"Unfortunately I shall not be able to be next to you," she said as we were already arriving. "But act as I have indicated to you, and aside from that my husband will take care of everything that's necessary. But please, *please*, madame Francinet, above all when you see newspapermen, and ladies, especially the reporters . . ."

"Won't you be there, madame Rosay?" I asked, really amazed.

"No. You can't understand, it would be something to explain. My husband will be there, he has some interests in monsieur Linard's business . . . Naturally, he will be there out of respect . . . a business matter and a humane one . . . But I shall not go in, it wouldn't be appropriate for me to . . . Don't worry about that."

I saw monsieur Rosay and various other gentlemen in the doorway. They were coming over and madame Rosay gave me a last piece of advice, then threw herself back in the seat so they shouldn't see her. I let monsieur Rosay open the car door, then I got out into the street, crying at the top of my lungs while monsieur Rosay was hugging me and leading me inside, followed by some of the other gentlemen. I couldn't see much of the house because I was wearing a shawl which almost covered my eyes, and besides I was crying so hard that I couldn't manage to see anything, but you could tell it was luxurious by the odor and also by the thickness of the carpets. Monsieur Rosay was murmuring consolations, and his voice sounded as though he were crying too. In a very, very large salon where the chandeliers had fringes, there were several gentlemen who were looking at me with a lot of compassion and sympathy, and I'm sure they would have come to console me if monsieur Rosay had not hurried me forward, holding me across the shoulders. I managed to see a young man on a sofa who had his eyes closed and a glass in one hand. Hearing me come in, he didn't even move, even though I was crying very hard just then. They opened another door and two gentlemen came out carrying their handkerchiefs. Monsieur Rosay gave me a little shove, and I went into a room, tottering, and let myself be led over to where the dead man was, and I saw the dead man who was my son, I saw the profile of monsieur Bébé, more blond and white than ever now that he was dead.

I think I grabbed hold of the edge of the bed, because monsieur Rosay and several other gentlemen leaped over and came around me and held me up, while I was looking at the handsome face of dead monsieur Bébé, his long black eyelashes and his nose like wax, and I couldn't believe that he was monsieur Linard, the gentleman who was a fashion designer and had just died, I couldn't convince myself that this corpse there in front of me was monsieur Bébé. Without knowing, I swear, I had begun to cry for real, grabbing hold of the edge of the big deluxe bed of carved oak, remembering how monsieur Bébé had patted my head the night of the party, and had poured me a glass of whiskey, talking to me and paying attention to me while the others were having fun. When monsieur Rosay murmured something like, "Speak to him, say son, son . . ." I had no trouble lying at all, and I think that crying for him made me feel a lot better, as if it were a reward for being so afraid as I'd been up to that moment. Nothing seemed strange to me now, and when I raised my eyes and at one side of the bed I saw monsieur Loulou with his eyes all red and his mouth trembling, I started to cry at the top of my lungs looking him right in the face, and he was crying as well in spite of his surprise, he was crying because I was crying, and was filled with surprise at realizing that I was crying like him, really crying, because we both loved monsieur Bébé, and we almost challenged one another from opposite sides of the bed, almost as if, without rhyme or reason, monsieur Bébé might laugh and make jokes like when he was alive, sitting at the kitchen table and laughing at all of us.

They led me back to a sofa in the big salon with chandeliers, and a lady there who'd pulled a bottle of smelling salts out of her purse, and a servant pushed a small table on wheels over next to me that had a tray with hot coffee and a glass of water on it. Monsieur Rosay was much more at ease now that he saw I was capable of doing what they'd asked me. I saw that when he went off to speak with some other gentlemen, and there was a long period when no one came into or left the salon. On the sofa opposite me, the young man I'd seen when I came in was still sitting there and crying with his face in his hands. Every now and then he'd take out his handkerchief and blow his nose. Monsieur Loulou appeared in the doorway and looked at him a minute before coming over and sitting down beside him. I felt so sorry for both of them, you could see they'd been very good friends of monsieur Bébé, and they were so young, and felt it so greatly. Monsieur Rosay also watched them from one corner of the room,

where he was standing talking in a low voice to two ladies
who were already standing up to leave. And so the moments passed until monsieur Loulou jumped up with a
shriek, and drew away from the other young man who
was looking at him furiously, and I heard monsieur Loulou say something like, "Nothing at all was ever of any
importance to you, Nina," and I remembered that there
was someone called Nina who had an aunt in Poitou who
sent him chickens and vegetables. Monsieur Loulou
shrugged his shoulders and went on to say that Nina was
a liar, and at last he went off making faces and gestures of
annoyance. Then monsieur Nina stood up also, and both
of them were almost running to the room where monsieur
Bébé was laid out, and I heard them arguing, but right
away monsieur Rosay went in to make them be quiet, and
I couldn't hear anything else until monsieur Loulou came
back to sit on the sofa, with a soaked handkerchief in his
hand. Just behind the sofa there was a window which
opened on an inside court. I think that of all the things
there were in that room, I remember the window best
(and also the chandeliers, they were so elegant), because
toward the end of the night I saw the sky changing color
little by little and growing more and more grey and finally
pink, just before the sun came up. And all that time I was
sitting thinking of monsieur Bébé, and suddenly I wasn't
able to restrain myself and I cried, although only monsieur Rosay and monsieur Loulou were there, because
monsieur Nina had left or was in another part of the
house. And so the night passed, and at times I couldn't
help thinking about monsieur Bébé so young, and I began
crying again, though also it was a little bit because I was
tired; then monsieur Rosay came over to sit beside me
with a very strange look on his face, and said that it was
not necessary for me to continue to pretend, and that I
should ready myself for when the time came for the burial

and the people and the newspaper reporters would arrive. But it's difficult at times to know when one is crying for true or not, and I begged monsieur Rosay to let me sit wake on monsieur Bébé. He seemed very surprised that I didn't want to go to sleep a bit, and different times he suggested that he should take me to a bedroom, but finally he was convinced and left me alone. I took advantage of a few minutes when he'd gone out, probably to the bathroom, and I went into the other room where monsieur Bébé was.

I had thought I would be alone with him there, but there was monsieur Nina looking at him, stationed at the foot of the bed. As we did not know one another (I mean to say that he knew that I was the lady who was passing as monsieur Bébé's mother, but we had not seen one another before this), we looked at one another suspiciously, though he didn't say anything when I approached and stood beside monsieur Bébé. We stood there for a while, and I saw that the tears were running down his cheeks and that they'd made like a furrow near his nose.

"You were there also the night of the party," I said, hoping to distract him. "Monsieur Bébé . . . monsieur Linard said that you were very unhappy and asked monsieur Loulou to go out and keep you company."

Monsieur Nina looked at me without understanding. He shook his head, and I smiled at him so as to cheer him up.

"The night of the party at monsieur Rosay's house," I said. "Monsieur Linard came out to the kitchen and gave me some whiskey."

"Whiskey?"

"Yes. He was the only one all night who offered me something to drink . . . And monsieur Loulou was opening a bottle of champagne, and then monsieur Linard let fly a jet of foam in his face and . . ."

"Oh, be quiet, be quiet," murmured monsieur Nina. "Don't mention that . . . Bébé was crazy, really crazy . . ."

"And you were sad because of that?" I asked, so as to say something, but now he didn't hear me, he was looking at monsieur Bébé as if to ask him something, his mouth moved repeating over and over again the same thing until I couldn't watch him any longer. Monsieur Nina wasn't such a nice boy as monsieur Bébé or monsieur Loulou, and to me he seemed very small, although people in black are always smaller, as Gustave says. I would have wanted to console monsieur Nina, he was so despondent, but at that moment monsieur Rosay came in and motioned for me to go back to the salon.

"It's getting to be morning now, madame Francinet," he said. His face was getting green, the poor fellow. "You ought to rest for a bit. You're not going to be able to stand the fatigue, and pretty soon people are going to start arriving. The burial is going to be at nine-thirty."

In fact I was dropping from weariness, and it would be better if I slept for an hour. It's incredible how one hour of sleep refreshes me. So I let monsieur Rosay take my arm and lead me out, and when we were crossing the salon with the chandeliers, the window was already a pale pink, and I felt cold in spite of the fire in the fireplace. Monsieur Rosay let go of me at that moment all at once, and stood looking at the doorway that led to the entrance hall. A man with a scarf knotted around his neck had come in, and for a second I was frightened thinking that maybe we had been discovered (although there was nothing illegal) and that the man with the scarf was a brother or something like that of monsieur Bébé's. But that was impossible, he had such a coarse air about him, as if Pierre or Gustave might have been brothers of someone as refined as monsieur Bébé. Behind the man with the scarf I sud-

denly saw monsieur Loulou looking as though he were
scared, but at the same time it seemed to me he looked
satisfied that something was about to happen. Then monsieur Rosay motioned me to stay where I was and took two
or three steps toward the man with the scarf, without
much wanting to, I thought.

"You're coming? . . ." he started by saying, in the
same tone of voice he used to talk with me, which at bottom was not at all friendly.

"Where is Bébé?" asked the man with a voice that
showed he had been drinking or shouting. Monsieur
Rosay made a vague gesture, wanting to keep him from
entering, but the man came forward and swept him aside
with just a look. I was very surprised at such rudeness at
such a sad moment, but monsieur Loulou, who'd been
standing in the doorway (I think it was he who'd let the
man in), broke into peals of laughter, and then monsieur
Rosay went over and began slapping him as you would a
boy, just like you would slap a boy. I didn't hear very well
what they were saying, but monsieur Loulou seemed
happy in spite of having his ears boxed, and said something like, "Now he'll see . . . now he'll see, that
whore . . ." although I don't like to repeat his words, and
he said it several times until suddenly he burst into tears
and put his hands to his face, while monsieur Rosay was
pushing and pulling him toward the sofa where he stayed,
sobbing and crying, and everybody had forgotten about
me, as usual.

Monsieur Rosay seemed very nervous and couldn't
make up his mind to go into the dead man's room, but a
moment later you could hear monsieur Nina's voice arguing about something, and monsieur Rosay made up his
mind and ran to the doorway just as monsieur Nina came
sailing out protesting, and I would have sworn that the
man with the scarf had given him a good shove to throw

him out. Monsieur Rosay backed off, looking at monsieur Nina, and both of them began to speak in low voices but even so it came out shrill, and monsieur Nina wept in despair and made such a face that I felt very sorry for him. Finally, he calmed down a little and monsieur Rosay led him over to the sofa where monsieur Loulou was, who began to laugh again (that's how it was, they could as soon laugh as cry), but monsieur Nina made a disdainful face and went over to sit on the other sofa near the fireplace. I stayed in one corner of the room, waiting for the ladies and reporters to arrive, as madame Rosay had instructed me, and finally the sun was shining directly into the panes of the window and a servant in livery showed in two very elegant gentlemen and a lady, who looked first at monsieur Nina thinking that perhaps he was family, then they looked at me, and I had my face in my hands but I could see very well from between my fingers. These gentlemen and others who came in later passed through to see monsieur Bébé, and later they gathered together in the salon, and some of them came over to where I was, accompanied by monsieur Rosay, and gave me condolences and pressed my hand very feelingly. The ladies also were very friendly, one of them especially, very young and pretty, who sat down beside me for a moment and said that monsieur Linard had been a great artist and that his death was an irreparable misfortune. I said yes to everyone and I was really crying, although I should have been pretending all the time, but it affected me to think of monsieur Bébé inside there, so handsome and so young, and of what a great artist he had been. The young lady kept patting my hands and telling me that no one would ever forget monsieur Linard, and that she was sure that monsieur Rosay would take care of the fashion house just as monsieur Linard had always wanted, that his style would never be lost, and many other things I don't remember but always filled with praise for monsieur Bébé. And then monsieur Rosay came looking for me, and after looking at everyone around me so that they would understand what was about to happen, he told me in a low voice that it was time to say goodbye to my son, because they were going to seal the casket soon. I had a terrible fright come over me, thinking that now I had to do the hardest scene, but he held me up and helped me to sit up, and we went into the room; there was only the man with the scarf at the foot of the bed, looking at monsieur Bébé, and monsieur Rosay gestured toward him pleadingly as though to have him understand that he ought to leave me alone with my son, but the man answered with a wry face and shrugged his shoulders and didn't budge. Monsieur Rosay didn't know what to do, and went back to looking at the man as though imploring him to leave, for other gentlemen who must have been the reporters were just entering the room behind us, and really the man was very disrespectful there with that scarf and his way of looking at monsieur Rosay as if it were to insult him. I couldn't hold back any longer, I was afraid of them all, I was sure that something terrible was going to happen, and even though monsieur Rosay was paying no attention to me and was still making gestures at the man to convince him to leave, I went over to monsieur Bébé and began to cry and wail, and then monsieur Rosay held me back because really I would have wanted to kiss monsieur Bébé on the forehead, for me he was still the best of them all, but he didn't let me go and begged me to calm myself, and finally made me go back to the salon, consoling me while he was squeezing my arm until it hurt, but as for that, no one could feel it but me and it meant nothing to me. Then I was on the sofa and the waiter brought some water and two ladies were fanning me with their handkerchiefs, but there was a large crowd in the other room, and new people came in and gathered around me so I couldn't see what was happening. Among those who had just arrived was the priest, and I was very happy that he had come to accompany monsieur Bébé. It would soon be time to leave for the cemetery, and it was good that the priest was going to come with us, with the mother and the friends of monsieur Bébé. Certainly they, too, would be happy that he was coming along, especially monsieur Rosay who was so upset, all the fault of the man in the scarf, and that he was so careful that everything be correct and as it ought to be, so that people should know how good the dead man had been and how much everyone loved monsieur Bébé.

THE PURSUER
· · · · · · · · · · ·

In memoriam Ch. P.

Be thou faithful unto death
Apocalypse 2:10

O make me a mask
Dylan Thomas

Dédée had called me in the afternoon saying that Johnny wasn't very well, and I'd gone to the hotel right away. Johnny and Dédée have been living in a hotel in the rue Lagrange for a few days now, they have a room on the fourth floor. All I have to do is see the door to the room to realize that Johnny's in worse shape than usual; the window opens onto an almost black courtyard, and at one in the afternoon you have to keep the light on if you want to read the newspaper or see someone else's face. It's not that cold out, but I found Johnny wrapped up in a blanket, and squeezed into a raunchy chair that's shedding yellowed hunks of old burlap all over the place. Dédée's gotten older, and the red dress doesn't suit her at all: it's a dress for working under spotlights; in that hotel room it turns into a repulsive kind of coagulation.

"Faithful old buddy Bruno, regular as bad breath," Johnny said by way of hello, bringing his knees up until his chin was resting on them. Dédée reached me a chair and I pulled out a pack of Gauloises. I'd brought a bottle of rum too, had it in the overcoat pocket, but I didn't want to bring it out until I had some idea of how things were going. I think the lightbulb was the worst irritation, its eye pulled out and hanging suspended from a long cord dirtied by flies. After looking at it once or twice, and putting my hand up to shade my eyes, I asked Dédée if we couldn't put out the damned light and wouldn't the light from the window be okay. Johnny followed my words and gestures with a large, distracted attention, like a cat who is looking fixedly, but you know it's something else completely; that it is something else. Finally Dédée got up and turned off the light. Under what was left, some mishmosh of black and grey, we recognized one another better. Johnny had pulled one of his big hands out from under the blanket and I felt the limber warmth of his skin. Then Dédée said she'd make us some nescafé. I was happy to know that at least they had a tin of nescafé. I always know, whatever the score is, when somebody has a can of nescafé it's not fatal yet; they can still hold out.

"We haven't seen one another for a while," I said to Johnny. "It's been a month at least."

"You got nothin' to do but tell time," he answered. He was in a bad mood. "The first, the two, the three, the twenty-one. You, you put a number on everything. An' that's cool. You wanna know why she's sore? 'Cause I lost the horn. She's right, after all."

"Lost it, but how could you lose it?" I asked, realizing at the same moment that that was just what you couldn't ask Johnny.

"In the metro," Johnny said. "I shoved it under the seat so it'd be safe. It was great to ride that way, knowing I had it good and safe down there between my legs."

"He finally missed it when he was coming up the stairs in the hotel," Dédée said, her voice a little hoarse. "And I had to go running out like a nut to report it to the metro lost-and-found and to the police." By the silence that followed I figured out that it'd been a waste of time. But Johnny began to laugh like his old self, a deep laugh back of the lips and teeth.

"Some poor devil's probably trying to get some sound out of it," he said. "It was one of the worst horns I ever had; you know that Doc Rodriguez played it? Blew all the soul out of it. As an instrument, it wasn't awful, but Rodriguez could ruin a Stradivarius just by tuning it."

"And you can't get ahold of another?"

"That's what we're trying to find out," Dédée said. "It might be Rory Friend has one. The awful thing is that Johnny's contract . . ."

"The contract," Johnny mimicked. "What's this with the contract? I gotta play and that's it, and I haven't got a horn or any bread to buy one with, and the boys are in the same shape I am."

This last was not the truth, and the three of us knew it. Nobody would risk lending Johnny an instrument, because he lost it or ruined it right off. He lost Louis Rolling's sax in Bordeaux, the sax Dédée bought him when he had that contract for a tour in England he broke into three pieces, whacking it against a wall and trampling on it. Nobody knew how many instruments had already been lost, pawned, or smashed up. And on all of them he played like I imagine only a god can play an alto sax, given that they quit using lyres and flutes.

"When do you start, Johnny?"

"I dunno. Today, I think, huh De?"

"No, day after tomorrow."

"Everybody knows the dates except me," Johnny grumbled, covering himself up to the ears in his blanket. "I'd've sworn it was tonight, and this afternoon we had to go in to rehearse."

"It amounts to the same thing," Dédée said. "The thing is that you haven't got a horn."

"What do you mean, the same thing? It isn't the same thing. Day after tomorrow is the day after tomorrow, and tomorrow is much later than today. And today is later than right now, because here we are yakking with our old buddy Bruno, and I'd feel a lot better if I could forget about time and have something hot to drink."

"I'll boil some water, hold on for a little."

"I was not referring to boiling water," Johnny said. So I pulled out the bottle of rum, and it was as though we'd turned the light on; Johnny opened his mouth wide, astonished, and his teeth shone, until even Dédée had to smile at seeing him, so surprised and happy. Rum and nescafé isn't really terrible, and all three of us felt a lot better after the second swallow and a cigarette. Then I noticed that Johnny was withdrawing little by little and kept on referring to time, a subject which is a preoccupation of his ever since I've known him. I've seen very few men as occupied as he is with everything having to do with time. It's a mania of his, the worst of his manias, of which he has plenty. But he explains and develops it with a charm hard to resist. I remember a rehearsal before a recording session in Cincinnati, long before he came to Paris, in forty-nine or fifty. Johnny was in great shape in those days and I'd gone to the rehearsal just to talk to him and also to Miles Davis. Everybody wanted to play, they were happy, and well-dressed (this occurs to me maybe by contrast with how Johnny goes around now, dirty and messed up), they were playing for the pleasure of it, without the slightest impatience, and the sound technician was making happy signs from behind his glass window, like a satisfied baboon. And just at that moment when Johnny was like gone in his joy, suddenly he stopped playing and threw a punch at I don't know who and said, "I'm playing this tomorrow," and the boys stopped short, two or three of them went on for a few measures, like a train slowly coming to a halt, and Johnny was hitting himself in the forehead and repeating, "I already played this tomorrow, it's horrible, Miles, I already played this tomorrow," and they couldn't get him out of that, and everything was lousy from then on, Johnny was playing without any spirit and wanted to leave (to shoot up again, the sound technician said, mad as hell), and when I saw him go out, reeling and his face like ashes, I wondered how much longer that business could go on.

"I think I'll call Dr. Bernard," Dédée said, looking at Johnny out of the corner of her eye, he was taking his rum in small sips. "You've got a fever and you're not eating anything."

"Dr. Bernard is a sad-assed idiot," Johnny said, licking his glass. "He's going to give me aspirin and then he'll tell me how very much he digs jazz, for example Ray Noble. Got the idea, Bruno? If I had the horn I'd give him some music that'd send him back down the four flights with his ass bumping on every step."

"It won't do you any harm to take some aspirin in any case," I said, looking out of the corner of my eye at Dédée. "If you want, I'll telephone when I leave so Dédée won't

have to go down. But look, this contract . . . If you have
to start day after tomorrow, I think something can be
done. Also I can try to get a sax from Rory Friend. And at
worst . . . The whole thing is you have to take it easier,
Johnny."

"Not today," Johnny said, looking at the rum bottle.
"Tomorrow, when I have the horn. So don't you talk about
that now. Bruno, every time I notice that time . . . I
think the music always helps me understand this business
a little better. Well, not understand, because the truth of
the matter is, I don't understand anything. The only thing
I do is notice that there is something. Like those dreams,
I'm not sure, where you begin to figure that everything is
going to smash up now, and you're a little afraid just to be
ready for it; but at the same time nothing's certain, and
maybe it'll flip over like a pancake and all of a sudden,
there you are, sleeping with a beautiful chick and everything's cool."

Dédée's washing the cups and glasses in one corner of
the room. I noticed they don't even have running water in
the place; I see a stand with pink flowers, and a washbasin which makes me think of an embalmed animal.
And Johnny goes on talking with his mouth half stopped
up by the bottle, and he looks stuffed too, with his knees
up under his chin and his black smooth face which the
rum and the fever are beginning to sweat up a little.

"I read some things about all that, Bruno. It's weird,
and really awful complicated . . . I think the music
helps, you know. Not to understand, because the truth is I
don't understand anything." He knocks on his head with a
closed fist. His head sounds like a coconut.

"Got nothing inside here, Bruno, what they call, nothing. It doesn't think and don't understand nothing. I've
never missed it, tell you the truth. I begin to understand

from the eyes down, and the lower it goes the better I understand. But that's not really understanding, oh, I'm with you there."

"You're going to get your fever up," Dédée muttered from the back of the place.

"Oh, shut up. It's true, Bruno. I never thought of nothing, only all at once I realize what I thought of, but that's not funny, right? How's it funny to realize that you've thought of something? Because it's all the same thing whether you think, or someone else. I am not I, me. I just use what I think, but always afterwards, and that's what I can't stand. Oh it's hard, it's so hard . . . Not even a slug left?"

I'd poured him the last drops of rum just as Dédée came back to turn on the light; you could hardly see in the place. Johnny's sweating, but keeps wrapped up in the blanket, and from time to time he starts shaking and the chair legs chatter on the floor.

"I remember when I was just a kid, almost as soon as I'd learned to play sax. There was always a helluva fight going on at home, and all they ever talked about was debts and mortgages. You know what a mortgage is? It must be something terrible, because the old lady blew her wig every time the old man mentioned mortgage, and they'd end up in a fistfight. I was thirteen then . . . but you already heard all that."

Damned right I'd heard it; and damned right I'd tried to write it well and truly in my biography of Johnny.

"Because of the way things were at home, time never stopped, dig? From one fistfight to the next, almost not stopping for meals. And to top it all off, religion, aw, you can't imagine. When the boss got me a sax, you'd have laughed yourself to death if you'd seen it, then I think I noticed the thing right off. Music got me out of time, but that's only a way of putting it. If you want to know what I think, really, I believe that music put me *into* time. But then you have to believe that this time had nothing to do with . . . well, with us, as they say."

For some time now I've recognized Johnny's hallucinations, all those that constitute his own life, I listen to him attentively, but without bothering too much about what he's saying. On the other hand, I was wondering where he'd made a connection in Paris. I'd have to ask Dédée, ignoring her possible complicity. Johnny isn't going to be able to stand this much longer. Heroin and poverty just don't get along very well together. I'm thinking of the music being lost, the dozens of sides Johnny would be able to cut, leaving that presence, that astonishing step forward where he had it over any other musician. "I'm playing that tomorrow" suddenly fills me with a very clear sense of it, because Johnny is always blowing tomorrow, and the rest of them are chasing his tail, in this today he just jumps over, effortlessly, with the first notes of his music.

I'm sensitive enough a jazz critic when it comes to understanding my limitations, and I realize that what I'm thinking is on a lower level than where poor Johnny is trying to move forward with his decapitated sentences, his sighs, his impatient angers and his tears. He gives a damn where I think everything ought to go easy, and he's never come on smug that his music is much farther out than his contemporaries are playing. It drags me to think that he's at the beginning of his sax-work, and I'm going along and have to stick it out to the end. He's the mouth and I'm the ear, so as not to say that he's the mouth and I'm the . . . Every critic, yeah, is the sad-assed end of something that starts as taste, like the pleasure of biting into something and chewing on it. And the mouth moves again, relishing it, Johnny's big tongue sucks back a little string of saliva from the lips. The hands make a little picture in the air.

"Bruno, maybe someday you'll write . . . Not for me, dig, what the hell does it matter to me. But it has to be beautiful, I feel it's gotta be beautiful. I was telling you how when I was a kid learning to play, I noticed that time changed. I told that to Jim once and he said that everybody in the world feels the same way and when he gets lost in it . . . He said that, when somebody gets lost in it . . . Hell no, I don't get lost when I'm playing. Only the place changes. It's like in an elevator, you're in an elevator talking with people, you don't feel anything strange, meanwhile you've passed the first floor, the tenth, the twenty-first, and the city's down there below you, and you're finishing the sentence you began when you stepped into it, and between the first words and the last ones, there're fifty-two floors. I realized that when I started to play I was stepping into an elevator, but the elevator was time, if I can put it that way. Now realize that I haven't forgotten the mortgage or the religion. Like it's the mortgage and the religion are a suit I'm not wearing at the moment; I know that the suit's in the closet, but at that moment you can't tell me that that suit exists. The suit exists when I put it on, and the mortgage and religion existed when I got finished playing and the old lady came in with her hair, dangling big hunks of hair all over me and complaining I'm busting her ears with that goddamned music."

Dédée had brought another cup of nescafé, but Johnny was looking with misery at his empty glass.

"This time business is complicated, it grabs me. I'm beginning to notice, little by little, that time is not like a bag that keeps filling up. What I mean is, even though the contents change, in the bag there's never more than a certain amount, and that's it. You see my suitcase, Bruno? It holds two suits and two pairs of shoes. Now, imagine that you empty it, okay? And afterwards you're going to put back the two suits and the two pairs of shoes, and then you realize that only one suit and one pair of shoes fit in there. But that's not the best of it. The best is when you realize you can put a whole store full of suits and shoes in there, in that suitcase, hundreds and hundreds of suits, like I get into the music when I'm blowing sometimes. Music, and what I'm thinking about when I ride the metro."

"When you ride the metro."

"Oh yeah, that, now there's the thing," Johnny said, getting crafty. "The metro is a great invention, Bruno. Riding the metro you notice everything that might end up in the suitcase. Maybe I didn't lose the horn in the metro, maybe . . ."

He breaks into laughter, coughs, and Dédée looks at him uneasily. But he's making gestures, laughing and coughing at the same time, shivering away under the blanket like a chimpanzee. His eyes are running and he's drinking the tears, laughing the whole time.

"Don't confuse the two things," he says after a spell. "I lost it and that's it. But the metro was helpful, it made me notice the suitcase bit. Look, this bit of things being elastic is very weird, I feel it everyplace I go. It's all elastic, baby. Things that look solid have an elasticity . . ."

He's thinking, concentrating.

". . . a sort of delayed stretch," he concludes surprisingly. I make a gesture of admiring approval. Bravo, Johnny. The man who claims he's not capable of thinking. Wow. And now I'm really interested in what he's going to say, and he notices that and looks at me more cunning than ever.

"You think I'll be able to come by another horn so I can play day after tomorrow, Bruno?"

"Sure, but you'll have to take care of it."

"Sure, I'll have to take care of it."

"A month's contract," explains poor Dédée. "Two weeks in Rémy's club, two concerts and the record dates. We could clean up."

"A month's contract," Johnny imitates her with broad gestures. "Rémy's club, two concerts, and the record dates. Be-bata-bop bop bop, chrrr. What I got is a thirst, a thirst, a thirst. And I feel like smoking, like smoking. More'n anything else, I feel like a smoke."

I offer him my pack of Gauloises, though I know perfectly well that he's thinking of pot. It's already dark out, people are beginning to come and go in the hallway, conversations in Arabic, singing. Dédée's left, probably to buy something to eat for that night. I feel Johnny's hand on my knee.

"She's a good chick, you know? But I've had enough. It's some time now I'm not in love with her, and I can't stand her. She still excites me, she knows how to make love like . . ." he brought his forefinger and middle finger together, Italian-fashion. "But I gotta split, go back to New York. Everything else aside, I gotta get back to New York, Bruno."

"What for? There you were worse off than you are here. I'm not talking about work but about your own life. Here, it looks like you have more friends."

"Sure, there's you, and the marquesa, and the guys at the club . . . Did you ever make love with the marquesa, Bruno?"

"No."

"Well, it's something that . . . But I was talking about the metro, and I don't know, how did we change the subject? The metro is a great invention, Bruno. One day I began to feel something in the metro, then I forgot . . . Then it happened again, two or three days later. And finally I realized. It's easy to explain, you dig, but it's easy because it's not the right answer. The right answer simply can't be explained. You have to take the metro and wait until it happens to you, though it seems to me that that only would happen to me. It's a little like that, see. But honestly, you never made love with the marquesa? You have to ask her to get up on that gilt footstool that she has in the corner of her bedroom, next to that pretty lamp and then . . . Oh shit, she's back already."

Dédée comes in with a package and looks at Johnny.

"Your fever's higher. I telephoned the doctor already, he's going to come at ten. He says you should stay quiet."

"Okay, okay, but first I'm going to tell Bruno about the subway. The other day I noticed what was happening. I started to think about my old lady, then about Lan and the guys, an' whup, it was me walking through my old neighborhood again, and I saw the kids' faces, the ones from then. It wasn't thinking, it seems to me I told you a lot of times, I never think; I'm like standing on a corner watching what I think go by, but I'm not thinking what I see. You dig? Jim says that we're all the same, that in general (as they say) one doesn't think on his own. Let's say that's so, the thing is I'd took the metro at Saint-Michel, and right away I began to think about Lan and the guys, and to see the old neighborhood. I'd hardly sat down and I began to think about them. But at the same time I realized that I was in the metro, and I saw that in a minute or two we had got to Odéon, and that people were getting on and off. Then I went on thinking about Lan, and I saw my old lady when she was coming back from doing the shopping, and I began to see them all around, to be with them in a very beautiful way, I hadn't felt that way in a long time. Memories are always a drag, but this time I liked thinking about the guys and seeing them. If I start telling you everything I saw you're not going to believe it because I would take a long time doing it. And that would be if I economized on details. For example, just to tell you one thing, I saw Lan in a green suit that she wore when she came to Club 33 where I was playing with Hamp. I was seeing the suit with some ribbons, a loop, a sort of trim down the side and a collar . . . Not at the same time, though, really, I was walking around Lan's suit and looking at it pretty slow. Then I looked at Lan's face and at the boys' faces, and then I remembered Mike who lived in the next room, and how Mike had told me a story about some wild horses in Colorado, once he worked on a ranch, and talked about the balls it took for cowboys to break wild horses . . ."

"Johnny," Dédée said from her far corner.

"Now figure I've told you only a little piece of everything that I was thinking and seeing. How much'll that take, what I'm telling you, this little piece?"

"I don't know, let's say about two minutes."

"Let's say about two minutes," Johnny mimicked. "Two minutes and I've told you just a little bitty piece, no more. If I were to tell you everything I saw the boys doing, and how Hamp played *Save it, pretty mama*, and listened to every note, you dig, every note, and Hamp's not one of them who gets tired, if I told you I heard an endless harangue of my old lady's, she was saying something about cabbages, if I remember, she was asking pardon for my old man and for me, and was saying something about some heads of cabbage . . . Okay, if I told you all that in detail, that'd take more than two minutes, huh, Bruno?"

"If you really heard and saw all that, it'd take a good quarter-hour," I said, laughing to myself.

"It'd take a good quarter-hour, huh, Bruno. Then tell me how it can be that I feel suddenly the metro stop and I come away from my old lady and Lan and all that, and I see that we're at Saint-Germain-des-Prés, which is just a minute and a half from Odéon."

I never pay too much attention to the things Johnny says, but now, with his way of staring at me, I felt cold.

"Hardly a minute and a half in your time, in her time," Johnny said nastily. "And also the metro's time and my watch's, damn them both. Then how could I have been thinking a quarter of an hour, huh, Bruno? How can you think a quarter of an hour in a minute and a half? That day I swear I hadn't smoked even a roach, not a crumb," he finished like a boy excusing himself. "And then it happened to me again, now it's beginning to happen to me everyplace. But," he added astutely, "I can only notice in the metro, because to ride the metro is like being put in a clock. The stations are minutes, dig, it's that time of yours, now's time; but I know there's another, and I've been thinking, thinking . . ."

He covers his face with his hands and shakes. I wish I'd gone already, and I don't know how to get out now without Johnny resenting it, he's terribly touchy with his friends. If he goes on this way he's going to make a mess of himself, at least with Dédée he's not going to talk about things like that.

"Bruno, if I could only live all the time like in those moments, or like when I'm playing and the time changes then too . . . Now you know what can happen in a minute and a half . . . Then a man, not just me but her and you and all the boys, they could live hundreds of years, if we could find the way we could live a thousand times faster than we're living because of the damned clocks, that mania for minutes and for the day after tomorrow . . ."

I smile the best I can, understanding fuzzily that he's right, but what he suspects and the hunch I have about what he suspects is going to be deleted as soon as I'm in the street and've gotten back into my everyday life. At that moment I'm sure that what Johnny's saying doesn't just come from his being half-crazy, that he's escaping from reality; I'm sure that, in the exchange, what he thinks leaves him with a kind of parody which he changes into a hope. Everything Johnny says to me at such moments (and it's been five years now Johnny's been saying things like this to me and to people) you can't just listen and promise yourself to think about it later. You hardly get down into the street, the memory of it barely exists and no Johnny repeating the words, everything turns into a pot-dream, a monotonous gesticulating (because there're others who say things like that, every minute you hear similar testimony) and after the wonder of it's gone you get an irritation, and for me at least it feels as though Johnny's been pulling my leg. But this always happens the next day, not when Johnny's talking to me about it, because then I feel that there's something that I'd like to admit at some point, a light that's looking to be lit, or better yet, as though it were necessary to break something, split it from top to bottom like a log, setting a wedge in and hammering it until the job's done. And Johnny hasn't got the strength to hammer anything in, and me, I don't know where the hammer is to tap in the wedge, which I can't imagine either.

So finally I left the place, but before I left one of those things that have to happen happened—if not that, then something else—and it was when I was saying goodbye to Dédée and had my back turned to Johnny that I felt something was happening, I saw it in Dédée's eyes and swung around quickly (because maybe I'm a little afraid of Johnny, this angel who's like my brother, this brother who's like my angel) and I saw Johnny had thrown off the blanket around him in one motion, and I saw him sitting in the easy-chair completely nude, his legs pulled up and the knees underneath his chin, shivering but laughing to himself, naked from top to bottom in that grimy chair.

"It's beginning to get warm," Johnny said. "Bruno, look what a pretty scar I got between my ribs."

"Cover yourself," Dédée ordered him, embarrassed and not knowing what to say. We know one another well enough and a naked man is a naked man, that's all, but anyway Dédée was scandalized and I didn't know how to not give the impression that what Johnny was doing had shocked me. And he knew it and laughed uproariously, mouth wide open, obscenely keeping his legs up so that his prick hung down over the edge of the chair like a monkey in the zoo, and the skin of his thighs had some weird blemishes which disgusted me completely. Then Dédée grabbed the blanket and wrapped it tightly around him, while Johnny was laughing and seemed very cheerful. I said goodbye hesitatingly, promised to come back the next day, and Dédée accompanied me to the landing, closing the door so Johnny couldn't hear what she was going to say to me.

"He's been like this since we got back from the Belgian tour. He'd played very well everyplace, and I was so happy."

"I wonder where he got the heroin from," I said, looking her right in the eye.

"Don't know. He'd been drinking wine and cognac almost constantly. He's been shooting up too, but less than there . . ."

There was Baltimore and New York, three months in Bellevue psychiatric, and a long stretch in Camarillo.

"Did Johnny play really well in Belgium, Dédée?"

"Yes, Bruno, better than ever, seems to me. The people went off their heads, and the guys in the band told me so, too, a number of times. Then all at once some weird things were happening, like always with Johnny, but luckily never in front of an audience. I thought . . . but you see now, he's worse than ever."

"Worse than in New York? You didn't know him those years."

Dédée's not stupid, but no woman likes you to talk about her man before she knew him, aside from the fact that now she has to put up with him and whatever "before" was is just words. I don't know how to say it to her, I don't even trust her fully, but finally I decide.

"I guess you're short of cash."

"We've got that contract beginning day after tomorrow," said Dédée.

"You think he's going to be able to record and do the gig with an audience too?"

"Oh, sure." Dédée seemed a bit surprised. "Johnny can play better than ever if Dr. Bernard can get rid of that flu. The problem is the horn."

"I'll take care of that. Here, take this, Dédée. Only . . . Maybe better Johnny doesn't know about it."

"Bruno . . ."

I made a motion with my hand and began to go down the stairway, I'd cut off the predictable words, the hopeless gratitude. Separated from her by four or five steps, made it easier for me to say it to her.

"He can't shoot up before the first concert, not for anything in the world. You can let him smoke a little, but no money for the other thing."

Dédée didn't answer at all, though I saw how her hands were twisting and twisting the bills as though she were trying to make them disappear. At least I was sure that Dédée wasn't on drugs. If she went along with it, it was only out of love or fear. If Johnny gets down on his knees, like I saw once in Chicago, and begs her with tears . . . But that's a chance, like everything else with Johnny, and for the moment they'd have enough money to eat, and for medicines. In the street I turned up the collar on my raincoat because it was beginning to drizzle, and took a breath so deep that my lungs hurt; Paris smelled clean, like fresh bread. Only then I noticed how Johnny's place had

smelled, of Johnny's body sweating under the blanket. I
went into a café for a shot of cognac and to wash my
mouth out, maybe also the memory that insisted and insisted in Johnny's words, his stories, his way of seeing
what I didn't see and, at bottom, didn't want to see. I began to think of the day after tomorrow and it was like
tranquillity descending, like a bridge stretching beautifully from the zinc counter into the future.

When one is not too sure of anything, the best thing to
do is to make obligations for oneself that'll act as pon-
toons. Two or three days later I thought that I had an obligation to find out if the marquesa was helping Johnny
Carter score for heroin, and I went to her studio down in
Montparnasse. The marquesa is really a marquesa, she's
got mountains of money from the marquis, though it's
been some time they've been divorced because of dope and
other, similar, reasons. Her friendship with Johnny dates
from New York, probably from the year when Johnny got
famous overnight simply because someone had given him
the chance to get four or five guys together who dug his
style, and Johnny could work comfortably for the first
time, and what he blew left everyone in a state of shock.
This is not the place to be a jazz critic, and anyone who's
interested can read my book on Johnny and the new post-
war style, but I can say that forty-eight—let's say until
fifty—was like an explosion in music, but a cold, silent
explosion, an explosion where everything remained in its
place and there were no screams or debris flying, but the
crust of habit splintered into a million pieces until its de-
fenders (in the bands and among the public) made hip-
ness a question of self-esteem over something which
didn't feel to them as it had before. Because after Johnny's
step with the alto sax you couldn't keep on listening to
earlier musicians and think that they were the end; one

must submit and apply that sort of disguised resignation which is called the historical sense, and say that any one of those musicians had been stupendous, and kept on being so, in his moment. Johnny had passed over jazz like a hand turning a page, that was it.

The marquesa had the ears of a greyhound for everything that might be music, she'd always admired Johnny and his friends in the group enormously. I imagine she must have "loaned" them no small amount of dollars in the Club 33 days, when the majority of critics were screaming bloody murder at Johnny's recordings, and were criticizing his jazz by worse-than-rotten criteria. Probably also, in that period, the marquesa began sleeping with Johnny from time to time, and shooting up with him. I saw them together often before recording sessions or during intermissions at concerts, and Johnny seemed enormously happy at the marquesa's side, even though Lan and the kids were waiting for him on another floor or at his house. But Johnny never had the vaguest idea of what it is to wait for anything, he couldn't even imagine that anyone was somewhere waiting for him. Even to his way of dropping Lan, which tells it like it really is with him. I saw the postcard that he sent from Rome after being gone for four months (after climbing onto a plane with two other musicians, Lan knowing nothing about it). The postcard showed Romulus and Remus, which had always been a big joke with Johnny (one of his numbers has that title), said: "Waking alone in a multitude of loves," which is part of a first line of a Dylan Thomas poem, Johnny was reading Dylan all the time then; Johnny's agents in the States agreed to deduct a part of their percentages and give it to Lan, who, for her part, understood quickly enough that it hadn't been such a bad piece of business to have gotten loose from Johnny. Some-

body told me that the marquesa had given Lan money too,
without Lan knowing where it had come from. Which
didn't surprise me at all, because the marquesa was ab-
surdly generous and understood the world, a little like
those omelets she makes at her studio when the boys begin to arrive in droves, and which begins to take on the
aspect of a kind of permanent omelet that you throw
different things into and you go on cutting out hunks and
offering them in place of what's really missing.

I found the marquesa with Marcel Gavoty and Art Boucaya, and they happened just at that moment to be talking
about the sides Johnny had recorded the previous afternoon. They fell all over me as if I were the archangel himself arriving, the marquesa necked with me until it was
beginning to get tedious, and the boys applauded the per-
formance, bassist and baritone sax. I had to take refuge
behind an easy-chair and stand them off as best I could,
all because they'd learned that I'd provided the magnificent sax with which Johnny had cut four or five of the
best. The marquesa said immediately that Johnny was a
dirty rat, and how they'd had a fight (she didn't say over
what) and that the dirty rat knew very well that all he had
to do was beg her pardon properly and there would have
been a check immediately to buy a new horn. Naturally
Johnny hadn't wanted to beg her pardon since his return
to Paris—the fight appears to have taken place in London,
two months back—and so nobody'd known that he lost his
goddamned horn in the metro, etcetera. When the marquesa started yakking you wondered if Dizzy's style hadn't
glued up her diction, it was such an interminable series of
variations in the most unexpected registers, until the end
when the marquesa slapped her thighs mightily, opened
her mouth wide and began to laugh as if someone were
tickling her to death. Then Art Boucaya took advantage of

the break to give me details of the session the day before, which I'd missed on account of my wife having pneumonia.

"Tica can tell you," Art said, pointing to the marquesa who was still squirming about with laughter. "Bruno, you can't imagine what it was like until you hear the discs. If God was anywhere yesterday, I think it was in that damned recording studio where it was as hot as ten thousand devils, by the way. You remember *Willow Tree*, Marcel?"

"Sure, I remember," Marcel said. "The fuck's asking me if I remember. I'm tattooed from head to foot with *Willow Tree*."

Tica brought us highballs and we got ourselves comfortable to chat. Actually we talked very little about the recording session, because any musician knows you can't talk about things like that, but what little they did say restored my hope and I thought maybe my horn would bring Johnny some good luck. Anyway, there was no lack of anecdotes which stomped that hope a bit, for example, Johnny had taken his shoes off between one cutting and the next and walked around the studio barefoot. On the other hand, he'd made up with the marquesa and promised to come to her place to have a drink before the concert tonight.

"Do you know the girl Johnny has now?" Tica wanted to know. I gave the most succinct possible description of the French girl, but Marcel filled it in with all sorts of nuances and allusions which amused the marquesa very much. There was not the slightest reference to drugs, though I'm so up tight that it seemed to me I could smell pot in Tica's studio, besides which Tica laughed in a way I've noted in Johnny at times, and in Art, which gives the teahead away. I wondered how Johnny would have gotten heroin, though, if he'd had a fight with the marquesa; my confidence in Dédée hit the ground floor, if really I'd ever had any confidence in her. They're all the same, at bottom.

I was a little envious of the equality that brought them closer together, which turned them into accomplices so easily; from my puritanical world—I don't need to admit it, anyone who knows me knows that I'm horrified by vice —I see them as sick angels, irritating in their irresponsibility, but ultimately valuable to the community because of, say, Johnny's records, the marquesa's generosity. But I'm not telling it all and I want to force myself to say it out: I envy them, I envy Johnny, that Johnny on the other side, even though nobody knows exactly what that is, the other side. I envy everything except his anguish, something no one can fail to understand, but even in his pain he's got to have some kind of in to things that's denied me. I envy Johnny and at the same time I get sore as hell watching him destroy himself, misusing his gifts, and the stupid accumulation of nonsense the pressure of his life requires. I think that if Johnny could straighten out his life, not even sacrificing anything, not even heroin, if he could pilot that plane he's been flying blind for the last five years better, maybe he'd end up worse, maybe go crazy altogether, or die, but not without having played it to the depth, what he's looking for in those sad *a posteriori* monologues, in his retelling of great, fascinating experiences which, however, stop right there, in the middle of the road. And all this I back up with my own cowardice, and maybe basically I want Johnny to wind up all at once like a nova that explodes into a thousand pieces and turns astronomers into idiots for a whole week, and then one can go off to sleep and tomorrow is another day.

It felt as though Johnny had surmised everything I'd been thinking, because he gave me a big hello when he came in, and almost immediately came over and sat beside me, after kissing the marquesa and whirling her around in the air, and exchanging with Art and her a complicated onomatopoetic ritual which made everybody feel great.

"Bruno," Johnny said, settling down on the best sofa, "that's a beautiful piece of equipment, and they tell me I was dragging it up out of my balls yesterday. Tica was crying electric-light bulbs, and I don't think it was because she owed bread to her dressmaker, huh, Tica?"

I wanted to know more about the session, but Johnny was satisfied with this bit of braggadocio. Almost immediately he turned to Marcel and started coming on about that night's program and how well both of them looked in their brand-new grey suits in which they were going to appear at the theater. Johnny was really in great shape, and you could see he hadn't used a needle overmuch in days; he has to take exactly the right amount to put him in the mood to play. And just as I was thinking that, Johnny dropped his hand on my shoulder and leaned over:

"Dédée told me I was very rough with you the other afternoon."

"Aw, you don't even remember."

"Sure. I remember very well. You want my opinion, actually I was terrific. You ought to have been happy I put on that act with you; I don't do that with anybody, believe me. It just shows how much I appreciate you. We have to go someplace soon where we can talk over a pile of things. Here . . ." He stuck out his lower lip contemptuously, laughed, shrugged his shoulders, it looked like he was dancing on the couch. "Good old Bruno. Dédée told me I acted very bad, honestly."

"You had the flu. You better now?"

"It wasn't flu. The doc arrived and right away began telling me how he liked jazz enormously, and that one night I'd have to come to his house and listen to records. Dédée told me that you gave her money."

"So you could get through all right until you get paid. How do you feel about tonight?"

"Good, shit, I feel like playing, I'd play right now if I had the horn, but Dédée insisted she'd bring it to the theater herself. It's a great horn, yesterday it felt like I was making love when I was playing it. You should have seen Tica's face when I finished. Were you jealous, Tica?"

They began to laugh like hell again, and Johnny thought it an opportune moment to race across the studio with great leaps of happiness, and between him and Art they started dancing without the music, raising and lowering their eyebrows to set the beat. It's impossible to get impatient with either Johnny or Art; it'd be like getting annoyed with the wind for blowing your hair into a mess. Tica, Marcel and I, in low voices, traded our conceptions of what was going to happen that night. Marcel is certain that Johnny's going to repeat his terrific success of 1951, when he first came to Paris. After yesterday's job, he's sure everything is going to be A-okay. I'd like to feel as confident as he does, but anyway there's nothing I can do except sit in one of the front rows and listen to the concert. At least I have the assurance that Johnny isn't out of it like that night in Baltimore. When I mentioned this to Tica, she grabbed my hand like she was going to fall into the water. Art and Johnny had gone over to the piano, and Art was showing him a new tune, Johnny was moving his head and humming. Both of them in their new grey suits were elegant as hell, although Johnny's shape was spoiled a bit by the fat he'd been laying on these days.

We talked with Tica about that night in Baltimore, when Johnny had his first big crisis. I looked Tica right in the eye as we were talking, because I wanted to be sure she understood what I was talking about, and that she shouldn't give in to him this time. If Johnny managed to drink too much cognac, or smoke some tea, or go off on shit, the concert would flop and everything fall on its ass. Paris isn't a casino in the provinces, and everybody has his eye on Johnny. And while I'm thinking that, I can't help having a bad taste in my mouth, anger, not against Johnny nor the things that happen to him; rather against the people who hang around him, myself, the marquesa and Marcel, for example. Basically we're a bunch of egotists; under the pretext of watching out for Johnny what we're doing is protecting our idea of him, getting ourselves ready for the pleasure Johnny's going to give us, to reflect the brilliance from the statue we've erected among us all and defend it till the last gasp. If Johnny zonked, it would be bad for my book (the translation into English or Italian was coming out any minute), and part of my concern for Johnny was put together from such things. Art and Marcel needed him to help them earn bread, and the marquesa, well, dig what the marquesa saw in Johnny besides his talent. All this has nothing to do with the other Johnny, and suddenly I realized that maybe that was what Johnny was trying to tell me when he yanked off the blanket and left himself as naked as a worm, Johnny with no horn, Johnny with no money and no clothes, Johnny obsessed by something that his intelligence was not equal to comprehending, but which floats slowly into his music, caresses his skin, perhaps is readying for an unpredictable leap which we will never understand.

And when one thinks things out that way, one really ends up with a bad taste in the mouth, and all the sincerity in the world won't equalize the sudden discovery that next to Johnny Carter one is a piss-poor piece of shit, that now he's come to have a drink of cognac and is looking at me from the sofa with an amused expression. Now it's time for us to go to the Pleyel Hall. That the music at least will save the rest of the night, and fulfill basically one of its worst missions, to lay down a good smokescreen in front of the mirror, to clear us off the map for a couple of hours.

As is natural, I'll write a review of tonight's concert tomorrow for *Jazz*. But now at intermission, with this shorthand scrawl on my knee, I don't feel exactly like talking like a critic, no comparative criticisms. I know very well that, for me, Johnny has ceased being a jazzman and that his musical genius is a façade, something that everyone can manage to understand eventually and admire, but which conceals something else, and that other thing is the only one I ought to care for, maybe because it's the only thing really important to Johnny himself.

It's easy to say it, while I'm still in Johnny's music. When you cool off . . . Why can't I do like him, why can't I beat my head against the wall? Pickily enough, I prefer the words to the reality that I'm trying to describe, I protect myself, shielded by considerations and conjectures that are nothing other than a stupid dialectic. I think I understand why prayer demands instinctively that one fall on one's knees. The change of position is a symbol of the change in the tone of voice, in what the voice is about to articulate, in the diction itself. When I reach the point of specifying the insight into that change, things which seemed to have been arbitrary a second before are filled with a feeling of depth, simplify themselves in an extraordinary manner and at the same time go still deeper. Neither Marcel nor Art noticed yesterday that Johnny was not crazy to take his shoes off at the recording session. At that moment, Johnny had to touch the floor with his own skin, to fasten himself to the earth so that his music was a reaffirmation, not a flight. Because I feel this also in

Johnny, he never runs from anything, he doesn't shoot up to get out of it like most junkies, he doesn't blow horn to squat behind a ditch of music, he doesn't spend weeks in psychiatric clinics to feel protected from the pressures he can't put up with. Even his style, the most authentic thing he has, that style which deserves all the absurd names it's ever gotten, and doesn't need any of them, proves that Johnny's art is neither a substitute nor a finished thing. Johnny abandoned the language of *That Old Fashioned Love* more or less current ten years ago, because that violently erotic language was too passive for him. In his case he preferred desire rather than pleasure and it hung him up, because desire necessitated his advancing, experimenting, denying in advance the easy rushing around of traditional jazz. For that reason, I don't think Johnny was terribly fond of the blues, where masochism and nostalgia . . . But I've spoken of all that in my book, showing how the denial of immediate satisfaction led Johnny to elaborate a language which he and other musicians are carrying today to its ultimate possibilities. This jazz cuts across all easy eroticism, all Wagnerian romanticism, so to speak, to settle firmly into what seems to be a very loose level where the music stands in absolute liberty, as when painting got away from the representational, it stayed clear by not being more than painting. But then, being master of a music not designed to facilitate orgasms or nostalgia, of a music which I should like to call metaphysical, Johnny seems to use that to explore himself, to bite into the reality that escapes every day. I see here the ultimate paradox of his style, his aggressive vigor. Incapable of satisfying itself, useful as a continual spur, an infinite construction, the pleasure of which is not in its highest pinnacle but in the exploratory repetitions, in the use of faculties which leave the suddenly human behind without losing humanity. And when Johnny, like tonight, loses himself in the continuous creation of his music, I know best of all that he's not losing himself in anything, nothing escapes him. To go to a date you can't get away from, even though you change the place you're going to meet each time. And as far as what is left behind, can be left, Johnny doesn't know or puts it down supremely. The marquesa, for example, thinks that Johnny's afraid of poverty, without knowing that the only thing Johnny can be afraid of is maybe not finding the pork chop on the end of the fork when it happens he would like to eat it, or not finding a bed when he's sleepy, or a hundred dollars in his wallet when it seems he ought to be the owner of a hundred dollars. Johnny doesn't move in a world of abstractions like we do; the reason for his music, that incredible music I've listened to tonight, has nothing to do with abstractions. But only he can make the inventory of what he's taken in while he was blowing, and more likely, he's already onto something else, losing that already in a new conjecture or a new doubt. His conquests are like a dream, when he wakes up he forgets them, when the applause brings him back from his spin, that man who goes so far out, living his quarter of an hour in a minute and a half.

It would be like living connected to a lightning rod in the middle of a thunderstorm and expecting that nothing's going to happen. Four or five days later I ran into Art Boucaya at the Dupont in the Latin Quarter, and he had no opportunity to make his expression blank as he gave me the bad news. For the first second I felt a kind of satisfaction which I find no other way of qualifying except to call it spiteful, because I knew perfectly well that the calm could not last long; but then I thought of the consequences and my fondness for Johnny, thinking of them, made my stomach churn; then I downed two cognacs while Art was telling me what had happened. In short, it seems that

Delaunay called a recording session to put out a new quintet under Johnny's name, with Art, Marcel Gavoty and a pair of very good sidemen from Paris on piano and drums. The thing was supposed to begin at three in the afternoon, and they were counting on having the whole day and part of the night for warmup and to cut a number of tunes. And what happened? It started when Johnny arrived at five, Delaunay was boiling already, then Johnny sat down on a chair and said he didn't feel very well and that the only reason he came was not to queer the day's work for the boys, but HE didn't feel up to playing.

"Between Marcel and me, we tried to convince him to lie down for a bit and rest, but he wouldn't do anything but talk about, I don't know, he'd found some fields with urns, and he gave us those goddamned urns for about a quarter of an hour. Finally, he started to haul out piles of leaves that he'd gathered in some park or another and had jammed into his pockets. The floor of the goddamned studio looked like a botanical garden, the studio personnel were tromping around looking as mean as dogs, and all this without laying anything down on the acetate; just imagine the engineer sitting in his booth for three hours smoking, and in Paris that's a helluva lot for an engineer.

"Finally Marcel convinced Johnny it'd be better to try something, the two of them started to play and we moved in after a bit, better that than sitting around getting tired of doing nothing. After a while I noticed that Johnny was having a kind of contraction in his right arm, and when he began to blow it was terrible to watch, I'm not shitting you. His face all grey, you dig, and every once in a while a chill'd shake him; and I didn't catch that moment when it got him on the floor. After a few tries he lets loose with a yell, looks at each of us one by one, slowly, and asks us what the hell we're waiting for, begin *Amorous*. You know, that tune of Alamo's. Well, Delaunay signals the engineer, we all start out the best possible, and Johnny opens his legs, stands up as though he were going to sleep in a boat rocking away, and lets loose with a sound I swear I'd never heard before or since. That goes on for three minutes, then all of a sudden he lets go with a blast, could of split the fuckin' celestial harmonies, and he goes off into one corner leaving the rest of us blowing away in the middle of the take, which we finish up best we can.

"But now the worst part, when we get finished, the first thing Johnny says was that it was all awful, that it came out like a piece of shit, and that the recording was not worth a damn. Naturally, neither we nor Delaunay paid any attention because, in spite of the defects, Johnny's solo was worth any thousand of what you can hear today. Something all by itself, I can't explain it to you . . . You'll hear it, I guess. I don't imagine that either Delaunay or the technicians thought of wiping out the acetate. But Johnny insisted like a nut, he was gonna break the glass in the control booth if they didn't show him that the acetate had been wiped. Finally the engineer showed him something or other and convinced him, and then Johnny suggested we record *Streptomycin,* which came out much better, and at the same time much worse, I mean it's clean and full, but still it hasn't got that incredible thing Johnny blew on *Amorous.*"

Breathing hard, Art had finished his beer and looked at me, very depressed. I asked him what Johnny had done after that, and he told me that after boring them all to tears with his stories about the leaves and the fields full of urns, he had refused to play any more and went stumbling out of the studio. Marcel had taken his horn away from him so that he couldn't lose it or stomp on it again, and between him and one of the French sidemen, they'd gotten him back to the hotel.

What else was there to do except to go see him immediately? But what the hell, I left it for the next day. And the next morning I found Johnny in the Police Notices in *Figaro*, because Johnny'd set fire to the hotel room during the night and had escaped running naked down the halls. Both he and Dédée had gotten out unhurt, but Johnny's in the hospital under observation. I showed the news report to my wife so as to cheer her up in her convalescence, and dashed off immediately to the hospital where my press pass got me exactly nowhere. The most I managed to find out was that Johnny was delirious and had enough junk in him to drive ten people out of their heads. Poor Dédée had not been able to resist him, or to convince him to not shoot up; all Johnny's women ended up his accomplices, and I'm sure as can be that the marquesa was the one who got the junk for him.

Finally I ended up by going immediately to Delaunay's place to ask if I could hear *Amorous* as soon as possible. To see if *Amorous* would turn out to be Johnny's last will and testament. In which case, my professional duty would be . . .

But not yet, no. Five days later Dédée's phoned me saying that Johnny is much better and that he wants to see me. I'd rather not reproach her, first of all because I imagine it'd be a waste of time, and secondly because poor Dédée's voice sounds as though it were coming out of a cracked teakettle. I promised to go immediately, and said that perhaps when Johnny was better, we could organize a tour through the provinces, a lot of cities. I hung up when Dédée started crying into the phone.

Johnny's sitting up in bed, in a semi-private with two other patients who are sleeping, luckily. Before I can say anything to him, he's grabbed my head with both paws and kissed me on the forehead and cheeks numerous times. He's terribly emaciated, although he tells me that he's got a good appetite and that they give him plenty to eat. For the moment the thing that worries him most is whether the boys are bad-mouthing him, if his crisis has hurt anyone, things like that. It's almost useless to answer him, he knows well enough that the concerts have been canceled and that that hurt Art and Marcel and the others; but he asks me like he expected that something good had happened meanwhile, anything that would put things together again. And at the same time he isn't playing me a trick, because back of everything else is his supreme indifference; Johnny doesn't give a good goddamn if everything goes to hell, and I know him too well to pay any attention to his coming on.

"What do you want me to tell you, Johnny? Things could have worked out better, except you have this talent for fucking up."

"Okay, I don't deny that," Johnny said tiredly. "And all because of the urns."

I remembered Art's account of it and stood there looking at him.

"Fields filled with urns, Bruno. Piles of invisible urns buried in an immense field. I was wandering around there and once in a while I'd stumble across something. You'd say that I'd dreamt it, huh? It was just like that, believe it: every once in a while I'd stumble across an urn, until I realized that the whole field was full of urns, that there were miles and miles of them, and there were a dead man's ashes inside every urn. Then I remember I got down on my knees and began to dig up the ground with my nails until one of the urns appeared. Then I remember thinking, 'This one's going to be empty because it's the one for me.' But no, it was filled with a grey dust like I knew all the others were I hadn't seen yet. Then . . . then that was when we began to record *Amorous*, if I remember."

I glanced discreetly at the temperature chart. According to it, reasonably normal. A young intern showed up in the doorway, acknowledging me with a nod, and made a gesture indicating food to Johnny, an almost sporty gesture, a good kid, etc. But when Johnny didn't answer him, when the intern had left, not even entering the door, I saw Johnny's hands were clenched tight.

"They'll never understand," he said. "They're like a monkey with a feather duster, like the chicks in the Kansas City Conservatory who think they're playing Chopin, nothing less. Bruno, in Camarillo they put me in a room with another three people, and in the morning an intern came in all washed up and all rosy, he looked so good. He looked like the son of Tampax out of Kleenex, you believe it. A kind of specimen, an immense idiot that sat down on the edge of the bed and was going to cheer me up, I mean that was when I wanted to kill myself, and I hadn't thought of Lan or of anyone, I mean, forget it. And the worst was, the poor cat was offended because I wasn't paying attention to him. He seemed to think I should sit up in bed en-goddamn-chanted with his white skin and beautifully combed hair and his nails all trimmed, and that way I'd get better like the poor bastards who come to Lourdes and throw away the crutches and leave, really jumping . . .

"Bruno, this cat and all the cats at Camarillo were convinced. You know what I'm saying? What of? I swear I don't know, but they were convinced. Of what they were, I imagine, of what they were worth, of their having a diploma. No, it's not that. Some were modest and didn't think they were infallible. But even the most humble were sure. That made me jumpy, Bruno, *that they felt sure of themselves.* Sure of what, tell me what now, when a poor devil like me with more plagues than the devil under his skin had enough awareness to feel that everything was like a jelly, that everything was very shaky everywhere, you only had to concentrate a little, feel a little, be quiet for a little bit, to find the holes. In the door, in the bed: holes. In the hand, in the newspaper, in time, in the air: everything full of holes, everything spongy, like a colander straining itself . . . But they were American science, Bruno, dig? White coats were protecting them from the holes; didn't see anything, they accepted what had been seen by others, they imagined that they were living. And naturally they couldn't see the holes, and they were very sure of themselves, completely convinced of their prescriptions, their syringes, their goddamned psychoanalysis, their don't smoke and don't drink . . . Ah, the beautiful day when I was able to move my ass out of that place, get on the train, look out the window how everything was moving backward, I don't know, have you seen how the landscape breaks up when you see it moving away from you . . ."

We're smoking Gauloises. They've given Johnny permission to drink a little cognac and smoke eight or ten cigarettes a day. But you can see it's not *him*, just his body that's smoking, and he's somewhere else almost as if he'd refuse to climb out of the mine shaft. I'm wondering what he's seen, what he's felt these last few days. I don't want to get him excited, if he could speak for himself . . . We smoke silently, and occasionally he moves his arm and runs his fingers over my face as though he were identifying me. Then he plays with his wrist watch, he looks at it tenderly.

"What happens to them is that they get to think of themselves as wise," he said sharply. "They think it's wisdom because they've piled up a lot of books and eaten them. It makes me laugh, because really they're good kids and are really convinced that what they study and what they do are really very difficult and profound things. In the circus, Bruno, it's all the same, and between us it's the same. People figure that some things are the height of difficulty, and so they applaud trapeze artists, or me. I don't know what they're thinking about, do they imagine that you break yourself up to play well, or that the trapeze artist sprains tendons every time he takes a leap? The really difficult things are something else entirely, everything that people think they can do anytime. To look, for instance, or to understand a dog or a cat. Those are the difficult things, the big difficulties. Last night I happened to look in this little mirror, and I swear, it was so terribly difficult I almost threw myself out of bed. Imagine that you're looking at yourself; that alone is enough to freeze you up for half an hour. In reality, this guy's not me, the first second I felt very clearly that he wasn't me. I took it by surprise, obliquely, and I knew it wasn't me. I felt that, and when something like that's felt . . . But it's like at Atlantic City, on top of one wave the second one falls on you, and then another . . . You've hardly felt and already another one comes, the words come . . . No, not words, but what's in the words, a kind of glue, that slime. And the slime comes and covers you and convinces you that that's you in the mirror. Sure, but not to realize it. But sure, I am, with my hair, this scar. And people don't realize that the only thing that they accept is the slime, and that's why they think it's easy to look in a mirror. Or cut a hunk of bread with a knife. Have you ever cut a hunk of bread with a knife?"

"I'm in the habit of it," I said, amused.

"And you've stayed all that calm. Not me, Bruno, I can't. One night I shot all of it so far that the knife almost knocked the eye out of a Japanese at the next table. That was in Los Angeles, and there was such a fantastic brawl . . . When I explained to them, they dumped me. And it seemed to me so simple to explain it all to them. At that time I knew Dr. Christie. A terrific guy, and you know how I am about doctors . . ."

One hand waves through the air, touching it on all sides, laying it down as though marking its time. He smiles. I have the feeling that he's alone, completely alone. I feel hollow beside him. If it had occurred to Johnny to pass his hand through me I would have cut like butter, like smoke. Maybe that's why once in a while he grazes my face with his fingers, cautiously.

"You have the loaf of bread there, on the tablecloth," Johnny says looking down into the air. "It's solid, no denying it, toasted a lovely color, smells beautiful. Something that's not me, something apart, outside me. But if I touch it, if I move my fingers and grasp it, then something changes, don't you think so? The bread is outside me, but I touch it with my fingers, I feel it, I feel that that's the world, but if I can touch it and feel it, then you can't really say it's something else, or do you think you can say it's something else?"

"Oh baby, for thousands of years now, whole armies of greybeards have been beating their heads to solve that problem."

"There's some day in the bread," murmured Johnny, covering his face. "And I dared to touch it, to cut it in two, to put some in my mouth. Nothing happened, I know; that's what's terrible. Do you realize it's terrible that nothing happened? You cut the bread, you stick the knife into it, and everything goes on as before. I don't understand, Bruno."

Johnny's face was beginning to upset me, his excitement. Every time, it was getting more difficult to get him to talk about jazz, about his memories, his plans, to drag him back to reality. (To reality: I barely get that written down and it disgusts me. Johnny's right, reality can't be this way, it's impossible to be a jazz critic if there's any reality, because then someone's pulling your leg. But at the same time, as for Johnny, you can't go on buying it out of his bag or we'll all end up crazy.)

Then he fell asleep, or at least he's closed his eyes and is pretending to be asleep. Again I realize how difficult it is to tell where Johnny *is* from what he's doing. If he's asleep, if he's pretending to sleep, if he thinks he's asleep. One is much further away from Johnny than from any other friend. No one can be more vulgar, more common, more strung out by the circumstances of a miserable life; apparently accessible on all sides. Apparently, he's no exception. Anyone can be like Johnny if he just resigns himself to being a poor devil, sick, hung up on drugs, and without will power—and full of poetry and talent. Apparently. I, who've gone through life admiring geniuses, the Picassos, the Einsteins, the whole blessed list anyone could make up in a minute (and Gandhi, and Chaplin, and Stravinsky), like everyone else, I tend to think that these exceptions walk in the clouds somewhere, and there's no point in being surprised at anything they do. They're different, there's no other trip to take. On the other hand, the difference with Johnny is secret, irritating by its mystery, because there's no explanation for it. Johnny's no genius, he didn't discover anything, he plays jazz like several thousand other black and white men, though he's better than any of them, and you have to recognize that that depends somewhat on public taste, on the styles, in short, the times. Panassié, for example, has decided that Johnny is outright bad, and although we believe that if anyone's outright bad it's Panassié, in any case there's an area open to controversy. All this goes to prove is that Johnny is not from some other world, but the moment I think that, then I wonder if precisely so there is not in Johnny something of another world (he'd be the first to deny it). Likely he'd laugh his ass off if you told him so. I know fairly well what he thinks, which of these things he lives. I say: which of these things he lives, because Johnny . . . But I'm not going that far, what I would like to explain to myself is the distance between Johnny and ourselves that has no easy answer, is not based in explainable differences. And it seems to me that he's the first to pay for the consequences of that, that it affects him as much as it does us. I really feel like saying straight off that Johnny is some kind of angel come among men, until some elementary honesty forces me to swallow the sentence, turn it around nicely and realize that maybe what is really happening is that Johnny is a man among angels, one reality among the unrealities that are the rest of us. Maybe that's why Johnny touches my face with his fingers and makes me feel so unhappy, so transparent, so damned small, in spite of my good health, my house, my wife, my prestige. My prestige above all. Above all, my prestige.

But it turns out the same old way, I leave the hospital and hardly do I hit the street, check the time, remember what all I have to do, the omelet turns smoothly in the air and we're right side up again. Poor Johnny, he's so far out of it. (That's the way it is, the way it is. It's easier for me to believe that that's the way it really is, now I'm in the café and the visit to the hospital was two hours ago, with everything that I wrote up there forcing me, like a condemned prisoner, to be at least a little decent with my own self.)

Luckily, the business about the fire got fixed up okay, or it seemed reasonable to imagine that the marquesa did her best to see that the fire business would be fixed up okay. Dédée and Art Boucaya came looking for me at the paper, and the three of us went over to *Vix* to listen to the already

famous—still secret—recording of *Amorous*. Dédée told
me, not much caring to, in the taxi, how the marquesa
had gotten Johnny out of the trouble over the fire, that anyway there was nothing worse than a scorched mattress
and a terrible scare thrown into all the Algerians living in
the hotel in the rue Lagrange. The fine (already paid),
another hotel (already arranged for by Tica), and Johnny
is convalescing in an enormous bed, very pretty, drinking
milk out of a milkcan and reading *Paris Match* and *The
New Yorker*, once in a while changing off to his famous
(and scroungy) pocket notebook with Dylan Thomas
poems and penciled notations all through it.

After all this news and a cognac in the corner café, we
settled down in the audition room to listen to *Amorous*
and *Streptomycin*. Art had asked them to put out the
lights, and lay down on the floor to hear better. And then
Johnny came in and his music moved over our faces, he
came in there even though he was back in the hotel
propped up in bed, and scuttled us with his music for a
quarter of an hour. I understand why the idea that they
were going to release *Amorous* infuriated him, anyone
could hear its deficiencies, the breathing perfectly audible
at the ends of the phrase, and especially the final savage
drop, that short dull note which sounded to me like a
heart being broken, a knife biting into the bread (and he
was speaking about bread a few days back). But on the
other hand, and it would escape Johnny, there was what
seemed to us a terrible beauty, the anxiety looking for an
outlet in an improvisation full of flights in all directions,
of interrogation, of desperate gestures. Johnny can't
understand (because what for him is a calamity, for us
looks like a road, at least a road-sign, a direction) that
Amorous is going to stand as one of jazz's great moments.
The artist inside him is going to blow his stack every time
he hears this mockery of his desire, of everything that he'd

wanted to say while he was fighting, the saliva running out of his mouth along with the music, more than ever alone up against that he was pursuing, against what was trying to escape him while he was chasing it. That hard. Curious, it had been indispensable to listen to this, even though already everything was converging into this, this solo in *Amorous*, so that I realized that Johnny was no victim, not persecuted as everyone thought, as I'd even insisted upon in my biography of him (the English edition has just appeared and is bound to sell like Coca-Cola). I know now that's not the way it is, that Johnny pursues and is not pursued, that all the things happening in his life are the hunter's disasters, not the accidents of the harassed animal. No one can know what Johnny's after, but that's how it is, it's there, in *Amorous*, in the junk, in his absurd conversations on any subject, in his breakdowns, in the Dylan Thomas notebook, in the whole of the poor sonofabitch that Johnny is, which makes him larger than life, and changes him into a living weirdo, into a hunter with no arms and legs, into a rabbit running past a sleeping tiger's nose. And I find it absolutely necessary to say that, at bottom, *Amorous* made me want to go vomit, as if that might free me of him, of everything in him that was going up against me and against everybody, that shapeless black mass without feet or hands, that crazy chimp that puts his fingers on my face and looks at me tenderly.

Art and Dédée don't see (I think they don't want to see) more than the formal loveliness of *Amorous*. Dédée even liked *Streptomycin* better, where Johnny improvises with his usual ease and freedom, which the audience understands perfectly well and which to me sounds more like Johnny's distracted, he just lets the music run itself out, that he's on the other side. When we got into the street, I asked Dédée what their plans were, and she said that as soon as Johnny was out of the hotel (for the moment the police had him under surveillance), a new record company wanted to have him record anything he wanted to and it'd pay him very well. Art backed her up, said Johnny was full of terrific ideas, and that he and Marcel Gavoty were going to do this new bit with Johnny, though after the past few weeks you could see that Art wasn't banking on it, and privately I knew that he'd been having conversations with his agent about going back to New York as soon as possible. Something I more than understood, poor guy.

"Tica's doing very well," Dédée said bitterly. "Of course, it's easy for her. She always arrives at the last minute and all she has to do is open her handbag and it's all fixed up. On the other hand, I . . ."

Art and I looked at one another. What in hell could we say? Women spend their whole lives circling around Johnny and people like Johnny. It's not weird, it's not necessary to be a woman to feel attracted to Johnny. What's hard is to circle about him and not lose your distance, like a good satellite, like a good critic. Art wasn't in Baltimore at that time, but I remember from the times I knew Johnny when he was living with Lan and the kids. To look at Lan really hurt. But after dealing with Johnny for a while, after accepting little by little his music's influence, his dragged-out terrors, his inconceivable explanations of things that had never happened, his sudden fits of tenderness, then one understood why Lan wore that face and how it was impossible that she live with Johnny and have any other face at all. Tica's something else, she gets out from under by being promiscuous, by living the dolce vita, and besides she's got the dollar bill by the short hairs, and that's a better scene than owning a machine gun, at least if you believe what Art Boucaya says when he gets pissed off at Tica or when he's got a hangover.

"Come as soon as you can," Dédée said. "He'd like to talk with you."

●   222

I would have liked to lecture the hell out of him about the first (the cause of the fire, in which he was most certainly involved), but it would have been almost as hopeless to try to convince Johnny that he should become a useful citizen. For the moment everything's going well (it makes me uneasy) and it's strange that whenever everything goes well for Johnny, I feel immensely content. I'm not so innocent as to think this is merely a friendly reaction. It's more like a truce, a breather. I don't need to look for explanations when I can feel it as clearly as the nose on my face. It makes me sore to be the only person who feels this, who is hung with it the whole time. It makes me sore that Art Boucaya, Tica or Dédée don't realize that every time Johnny gets hurt, goes to jail, wants to kill himself, sets a mattress on fire or runs naked down the corridors of a hotel, he's paying off something for them, he's killing himself for them. Without knowing it, and not like he was making great speeches from the gallows or writing books denouncing the evils of mankind or playing the piano with the air of someone washing away the sins of the world. Without knowing it, poor saxophonist, as ridiculous as that word is, however little a thing it is, just one among so many other poor saxophonists.

What's terrible is if I go on like that, I'm going to end up writing more about myself than about Johnny. I'm beginning to compare myself to a preacher and that doesn't give me too big a laugh, I'm telling you. By the time I got home I was thinking cynically enough to restore my confidence, that in my book on Johnny I mention the pathological side of his personality only in passing and very discreetly. It didn't seem necessary to explain to people that Johnny thinks he's walking through fields full of urns, or that pictures move when he looks at them; junk-dreams, finally, which stop with the cure. But one could say that Johnny leaves these phantoms with me in pawn, lays them on me like putting a number of handkerchiefs in a pocket until the time comes to take them back. And I think I'm the only one who can stand them, who lives with them and is scared shitless of them; and nobody knows this, not even Johnny. One can't admit things like that to Johnny, as one might confess them to a really great man, a master before whom we humiliate ourselves so as to obtain some advice in exchange. What is this world I have to cart around like a burden? What kind of preacher am I? There's not the slightest bit of greatness in Johnny, I've known that since I've known him, since I began to admire him. And for a while now this hasn't surprised me, although at the beginning the lack of greatness upset me, perhaps because it's one quality one is not likely to apply to the first comer, and especially to jazzmen. I don't know why (I don't *know* why) I believed at one time that Johnny had a kind of greatness which he contradicts day after day (or which we contradict, it's not the same thing really; because, let's be honest, there is in Johnny the phantom of another who could be, and this other Johnny is very great indeed; one's attention is drawn to the phantom by the lack of that quality which nevertheless he evokes and contains negatively).

I say this because the tries Johnny has made to change his life, from his unsuccessful suicide to using junk, are ones you finally expect from someone with as little greatness as he. I think I admire him all the more for that, because he really is the chimpanzee who wants to learn to read, a poor guy who looks at all the walls around him, can't convince himself, and starts all over again.

Ah, but what if one day the chimp does begin to read, what a crack in the dam, what a commotion, every man for himself, head for the hills, and I first of all. It's terrible to see a man lacking all greatness beat his head against the wall that way. He is the critic of us all with his bones

cracking, he tears us to shreds with the opening notes of
his music. (Martyrs, heroes, fine, right: one is certain
with them. But Johnny!)

Sequences. I don't know how better to say it, it's like an
idea of what abruptly brings about terrible or idiotic sequences in a man's life, without his knowing what law
outside the categories labeled "law" decides that a certain
telephone call is going to be followed immediately by the
arrival of one's sister who lives in the Auvergne, or that
the milk is going to be upset into the fire, or that from a
balcony we're going to see a boy fall under an automobile.
As on football teams or boards of directors, it appears that
destiny always appoints a few substitutes when those
named to the positions fall out as if by themselves. And so
it's this morning, when I'm still happy knowing that
things are going better and more cheerfully with Johnny
Carter, there's an urgent telephone call for me at the
paper, and it's Tica calling, and the news is that Bee,
Johnny and Lan's youngest daughter, has just died in Chicago, and that naturally Johnny's off his head and it
would be good of me to drop by and give his friends a
hand.

I was back climbing the hotel stairs—and there have
been a lot of them during my friendship with Johnny—to
find Tica drinking tea, Dédée soaking a towel, and Art,
Delaunay, and Pepe Ramírez talking in low voices about
the latest news of Lester Young, Johnny very quiet on the
bed, a towel on his forehead, and wearing a perfectly tranquil and almost disdainful air. I immediately put my sym-
pathetic face back into my pocket, restricting myself to
squeezing Johnny's hand very hard, lighting a cigarette,
and waiting.

"Bruno, I hurt here," Johnny said after a while, touching his chest in the conventional location. "Bruno, she was

like a small white stone in my hand. I'm nothing but a pale horse with granulated eyelids whose eyes'll run forever."

All of this said solemnly, almost recited off, and Tica looking at Art, and both of them making gestures of tender forbearance, taking advantage of the fact that Johnny has his face covered with the towel and can't see them. Personally, I dislike cheap sentimentality and its whole vocabulary, but everything that Johnny had just said, aside from the impression that I'd read it somewhere, felt to me like a mask that he'd put on to speak through, that empty, that useless. Dédée had come over with another towel to replace the one plastered on there, and in the interval I caught a glimpse of Johnny's face uncovered and I saw an ashy greyness, the mouth twisted, and the eyes shut so tight they made wrinkles on his forehead. As always with Johnny, things had happened in a way other than what one had expected, and Pepe Ramírez who doesn't know him very well is still flipped out and I think from the scandal, because after a time Johnny sat up in bed and started slowly, chewing every word, and then blew it out like a trumpet solo, insulting everyone connected with recording *Amorous*, without looking at anyone but nailing us all down like bugs in a box with just the incredible obscenity of his words, and so for two full minutes he continued cursing everyone on *Amorous*, starting with Art and Delaunay, passing over me (but I . . .) and ending with Dédée, Christ omnipotent and the whore who without exception gave birth to us all. And this was profoundly, this and the small white stone, the funeral oration for Bee, dead from pneumonia in Chicago.

Two empty weeks will pass; piles of work, journalism, magazine articles, visits here and there—a good résumé of a critic's life, a man who only lives on borrowed time, borrowed everything, on novelties for the news-hungry and decisions not of one's making. I'm talking about what happened one night Tica, Baby Lennox and I were together in the Café de Flore humming *Out of Nowhere* very contentedly and talking about a piano solo of Bud Powell's which sounded particularly good to all three of us, especially to Baby Lennox who, on top of being otherwise spectacular, had done herself up à la Saint-Germain-des-Prés, and you should have seen how great it looked on her. Baby will see Johnny show up with the rapturous admiration of her twenty years, and Johnny look at her without seeing her and continue wide of us and sit alone at another table, dead drunk or asleep. I'll feel Tica's hand on my knee.

"You see, he started shoving needles in his arm again last night. Or this afternoon. Damn that woman . . ."

I answered grudgingly that Dédée was as guilty as anyone else, starting with her, she'd turned on with Johnny dozens of times and would continue to do so whenever she goddamn well felt like it. I'd feel an overwhelming impulse to go out and be by myself, as always when it's impossible to get close to Johnny, to be with him and beside him. I'll watch him making designs on the table with his finger, sit staring at the waiter who's asking him what he would like to drink, and finally Johnny'll draw a sort of arrow in the air and hold it up with both hands as though it weighed a ton, and people at other tables would begin to be discreetly amused, which is the normal reaction in the Flore. Then Tica will say, "Shit," and go over to Johnny's table, and after placing an order with the waiter, she'll begin to talk into Johnny's ear. Not to mention that Baby will hasten to confide in me her dearest hopes, but then I'll tell her vaguely that she has to leave Johnny alone and that nice girls are supposed to be in bed early, and if possible with a jazz critic. Baby will laugh amiably, her hand

227

stroking my hair, and then we'll sit quietly and watch the
chick go by who wears the white-leaded cape up over her
face and who has green eyeshadow and green lipstick
even. Baby will say it really doesn't look so bad on her, and
I'll ask her to sing me very quietly one of those blues that
have already made her famous in London and Stockholm.
And then we'll go back to *Out of Nowhere*, which is following us around tonight like a dog which would also be
the chick in the cape and green eyes.

Two of the guys from Johnny's new quintet will also
show up, and I'll take advantage of the moment to ask
how the gig went tonight; that way I'll find out that
Johnny was barely able to play anything, but that what he
had been able to play was worth the collected ideas and
works of a John Lewis, assuming that the last-named
could manage any idea whatsoever, like one of the boys
said, the only one he having always close at hand being to
push in enough notes to plug the hole, which is not the
same thing. Meanwhile I'll wonder how much of this is
Johnny going to be able to put up with, not to mention the
audience that believes in Johnny. The boys will not sit
down and have a beer, Baby and I'll be sitting there alone
again, and I'll end up by answering her questions and explain to Baby, who is really worthy of her nickname, why
Johnny is so sick and washed up, why the guys in the
quintet are getting more fed up every day, why one day
the whole shebang is going to blow up, in one of those
scenes that had already blown up San Francisco, Baltimore and New York half-a-dozen times.

Other musicians who work in the quarter'll come in,
and some'll go to Johnny's table to say hello to him, but
he'll look at them from far off like some idiot with wet
mild eyes, his mouth unable to keep back the saliva glis-
tening off his lips. It will be interesting to watch the double maneuvers of Tica and Baby, Tica having recourse to

228

her domination of men to keep them away from Johnny, turning them off with a quick explanation and a smile, Baby whispering her admiration of Johnny in my ear and how good it would be to get him off to a sanitorium for a cure, and all because she's jealous and would like to sleep with Johnny tonight even, something impossible furthermore as anyone can see and which pleases me considerably. For ever since I've known her, I've been thinking of how nice it would be to caress, to run my hand over Baby's thighs, and I'll be a step away from suggesting that we leave and have a drink someplace quieter (she won't care to, and at bottom, neither will I, because that other table will hold us there, attached and unhappy) until suddenly, no notice of what's coming, we'll see Johnny get up slowly, looking at us, recognizing us, coming toward us—I should say towards me, Baby doesn't count—and reaching the table he'll bend over a little naturally as if he were about to take a fried potato off the plate, and we'll see him go to his knees just in front of me, with all naturalness he'll get down on his knees in front of me and look me in the eye, and I'll see that he's crying and'll know without any say-so that Johnny is crying for little Bee.

My reaction is that human, I wanted to get Johnny up, keep him from making an ass of himself, and finally I make myself the ass, because there's absolutely nothing more ridiculous than a man trying to move another who is very well off where he is and comfortable and feels perfectly natural in that position, he likes it down there, so that the customers at the Flore, who never get upset over trifles, looked at me in a rather unfriendly fashion, none of them knowing, however, that the Negro on his knees there is Johnny Carter, they all look at me as if they were looking at someone climbing up on the altar to tug Christ down from his cross. Johnny was the first to reproach me, just weeping silently he raised his eyes and looked at me, and between that and the evident disapproval of the customers I was left with the sole option of sitting down again in front of Johnny, feeling worse than he did, wanting to be anywhere else in the world but in that chair face to face with Johnny on his knees.

The rest hadn't been so bad, though it's hard to tell how many centuries passed with no one moving, with the tears coursing down Johnny's face, with his eyes fixed on mine continuously, meanwhile I was trying to offer him a cigarette, to light one for myself, to make an understanding gesture toward Baby who, it seemed to me, was on the point of racing out or of breaking into tears herself. As usual, it was Tica who settled the problem, sitting herself down at our table in all her tranquillity, drawing a chair over next to Johnny and putting a hand on his shoulder, not pushing it, until finally Johnny rose a little and changed from that horror into the conventional attitude of a friend sitting down with us, it was a matter only of raising his knees a few centimeters and allowing the honorable comfort of a chair to be edged between his buttocks and the floor (I almost said "and the cross," really this is getting contagious). People had gotten tired of looking at Johnny, he'd gotten tired of crying, and we of sitting around like dogs. I suddenly understood the loving attitude some painters have for chairs, any one of the chairs in the Flore suddenly seemed to me a miraculous object, a flower, a perfume, the perfect instrument of order and uprightness for men in their city.

Johnny pulled out a handkerchief, made his apologies without undue stress, and Tica had a large coffee brought and gave it to him to drink. Baby was marvelous, all at once dropping her stupidity when it came to Johnny, she began to hum *Mamie's Blues* without giving the impression that she was doing it on purpose, and Johnny looked at her and smiled, and it felt to me that Tica and I at the same time thought that Bee's image was fading slowly at the back of Johnny's eyes, and that once again Johnny was willing to return to us for a spell, keep us company until the next flight. As usual, the moment of feeling like a dog had hardly passed, when my superiority to Johnny allowed me to be indulgent, talking a little with everyone without getting into areas rather too personal (it would have been horrible to see Johnny slip off the chair back onto his . . .), and luckily Tica and Baby were both acting like angels and the people at the Flore had been going and coming for at least the length of an hour, being replaced, until the customers at one in the morning didn't even realize that something had just happened, although really it hadn't been a big scene if you think of it rightly. Baby was the first to leave (Baby is a chick full of application, she'll be rehearsing with Fred Callender at nine in the morning for a recording session in the afternoon) and Tica had downed her third cognac and offered to take us home. When Johnny said no, he'd rather stay and bat the breeze with me, Tica thought that was fine and left, not without paying the rounds for us all, as befits a marquesa. And Johnny and I ordered a glass of chartreuse apiece, among friends such weaknesses are forgiven, and we began to walk down Saint-Germain-des-Prés because Johnny had insisted that he could walk fine and I'm not the kind of guy to let a friend drop under such circumstances.

We go down the rue de l'Abbaye as far as the place Furstenberg, which reminds Johnny dangerously of a playtheater which his godfather seems to have given him when he was eight years old. I try to head for the rue Jacob afraid that his memories will get him back onto Bee, but you could say that Johnny had closed that chapter for what was left of the night. He's walking along peacefully, not staggering (at other times I've seen him stumble in the street, and not from being drunk; something in his reflexes that doesn't function) and the night's heat and the silence of the streets makes us both feel good. We're smoking Gauloises, we drift down toward the river, and opposite one of those galvanized iron coffins the booksellers use as stands along the quai de Conti, some memory or another or maybe a student whistling reminds us of a Vivaldi theme, humming it, then the two of us begin to sing it with a great deal of feeling and enthusiasm, and Johnny says that if he had the horn there he'd spend the night playing Vivaldi, I find the suggestion exaggerated.

"Well, okay, I'd also play a little Bach and Charles Ives," Johnny says condescendingly. "I don't know why the French are not interested in Charles Ives. Do you know his songs? The one about the leopard, you have to know the one about the leopard. 'A leopard . . .' "

And in his weak tenor voice he goes on at great length about the leopard, needless to say, many of the phrases he's singing are not absolutely Ives, something Johnny's not very careful about while he's sure that what he's singing is something good. Finally we sit down on the rail opposite the rue Gît-le-Coeur and smoke another cigarette because the night is magnificent and shortly thereafter the taste of the cigarette is forcing us to think of having a beer at a café, just thinking of the taste of it is a pleasure for Johnny and me. I pay almost no attention when he mentions my book the first time, because right away he goes back to talking about Charles Ives and how numerous times he'd enjoyed working Ives's themes into his records, with nobody even noticing (not even Ives, I suppose), but after a bit I get to thinking about the business of the book and try to get him back onto the subject.

"Oh, I've read a few pages," Johnny says. "At Tica's they talk a lot about your book, but I didn't even understand the title. Art brought me the English edition yesterday and then I found out about some things. It's very good, your book."

I adopt the attitude natural in such a situation, an air of displeased modesty mixed with a certain amount of interest, as if his opinion were about to reveal to me—the author—the truth about my book.

"It's like in a mirror," Johnny says. "At first I thought that to read something that'd been written about you would be more or less like looking at yourself and not into a mirror. I admire writers very much, it's incredible the things they say. That whole section about the origins of bebop . . ."

"Well, all I did was transcribe literally what you told me in Baltimore," I say defensively, not knowing what I'm being defensive about.

"Sure, that's all, but in reality it's like in a mirror," Johnny persists stubbornly.

"What more do you want? Mirrors give faithful reflections."

"There're things missing, Bruno," Johnny says. "You're much better informed than I am, but it seems to me like something's missing."

"The things that you've forgotten to tell me," I answer, reasonably annoyed. This uncivilized monkey is capable of . . . (I would have to speak with Delaunay, it would be regrettable if an imprudent statement about a sane, forceful criticism that . . . *For example Lan's red dress*, Johnny is saying. And in any case take advantage of the enlightening details from this evening to put into a new edition; that wouldn't be bad. *It stank like an old washrag,* Johnny's saying, *and that's the only value on the record.* Yes, listen closely and proceed rapidly, because in other people's hands any possible contradiction might have terrible consequences. *And the urn in the middle, full of dust that's almost blue,* Johnny is saying, *and very close to the color of a compact my sister had once.* As long as he wasn't going into hallucinations, the worst that could happen would be that he might contradict the basic ideas, the aesthetic system so many people have praised . . . *And furthermore, cool doesn't mean, even by accident ever, what you've written,* Johnny is saying. Attention.)

"How is it not what I've written, Johnny? It's fine that things change, but not six months ago, you . . ."

"Six months ago," Johnny says, getting down from the rail and setting his elbows on it to rest his head between his hands. "Six months ago. Oh Bruno, what I could play now if I had the kids with me . . . And by the way: the way you wrote 'the sax, the sex,' very ingenious, very pretty, that, the word-play. *Six months ago. Six, sax, sex.* Positively lovely. Fuck you, Bruno."

I'm not going to start to say that his mental age does not permit him to understand that this innocent word-play conceals a system of ideas that's rather profound (it seemed perfectly precise to Leonard Feather when I explained it to him in New York) and that the para-eroticism of jazz evolved from the washboard days, etc. As usual, immediately I'm pleased to think that critics are much more necessary than I myself am disposed to recognize (privately, in this that I'm writing) because the creators, from the composer to Johnny, passing through the whole damned gradation, are incapable of extrapolating the dialectical consequences of their work, of postulating the fundamentals and the transcendency of what they're writing down or improvising. I should remember this in moments of depression when I feel dragged that I'm nothing more than a critic. *The name of the star is called Wormwood,* Johnny is saying, and suddenly I hear his other voice, the voice that comes when he's . . . how say this? how describe Johnny when he's beside himself, already out of it, already gone? Uneasy, I get down off the rail and

look at him closely. And the name of the star is called
Wormwood, nothing you can do for him.

"The name of the star is called Wormwood," says
Johnny, using both hands to talk. "And their dead bodies
shall lie in the streets of the great city. Six months ago."

Though no one see me, though no one knows I'm there,
I shrug my shoulders at the stars (the star's name is
Wormwood). We're back to the old song: "I'm playing this
tomorrow." The name of the star is Wormwood and their
bodies'll be left lying six months ago. In the streets of the
great city. Out, very far out. And I've got blood in my eye
just because he hasn't wanted to say any more to me about
the book, and truly, I don't know what he thinks of the
book, which thousands of fans are reading in two lan-
guages (three pretty soon, and a Spanish edition is being
discussed, it seems that they play something besides
tangos in Buenos Aires).

"It was a lovely dress," Johnny says. "You do not want to
know how beautifully it fit on Lan, but it'll be easier to
explain it to you over a whiskey, if you got the money.
Dédée sent me out with hardly three hundred francs."

He laughs sarcastically, looking at the Seine. As if he
hadn't the vaguest idea of how to get drink or dope when
he wanted it. He begins to explain to me that really Dédée
is very goodhearted (nothing about the book) and that she
does it out of kindness, but luckily there's old buddy Bruno
(who's written a book, but who needs it) and it'd be great
to go to the Arab quarter and sit in a café, where they always leave you alone if they see that you belong a little to
the star called Wormwood (I'm thinking this, and we're
going in by the Saint-Séverin side and it's two in the
morning, an hour at which my wife is very used to getting
up and rehearsing everything she's going to give me at
breakfast, along with the cup of coffee, light). So I'm
walking with Johnny, so we drink a terrible cognac, very

cheap, so we order double shots and feel very content. But nothing about the book, only the compact shaped like a swan, the star, bits and hunks of things, that flow on with hunks of sentences, hunks of looks, hunks of smiles, drops of saliva on the table and dried on the edge of the glass (Johnny's glass). Sure, there are moments when I wish he were already dead. I imagine there are plenty of people who would think the same if they were in my position. But how can we resign ourselves to the fact that Johnny would die carrying with him what he doesn't want to tell me tonight, that from death he'd continue hunting, would continue flipping out (I swear I don't know how to write all this) though his death would mean peace to me, prestige, the status incontrovertibly bestowed upon one by unbeatable theses and efficiently arranged funerals.

Every once in a while Johnny stops his constant drumming on the tabletop, looks over at me, makes an incomprehensible face and resumes his drumming. The café owner knows us from the days when we used to come there with an Arab guitarist. It's been some time now that Ben Aifa has wanted to go home and sleep, we're the last customers in the filthy place that smells of chili and greasy meat pies. Besides, I'm dropping from sleepiness, but the anger keeps me awake, a dull rage that isn't directed against Johnny, more like when you've made love all afternoon and feel like a shower so that the soap and water will scrub off everything that's beginning to turn rancid, beginning to show too clearly what, at the beginning . . . And Johnny beats a stubborn rhythm on the tabletop, and hums once in a while, almost without seeing me. It could very well happen that he's not going to make any more comments on the book. Things go on shifting from one side to another, tomorrow it'll be another woman, another brawl of some sort, a trip. The wisest thing to do would be to get the English edition away from him on the sly, speak to Dédée about that, ask it as a favor in exchange for so many I've done her. This uneasiness is absurd, it's almost a rage. I can't expect any enthusiasm on Johnny's part at all; as matter of fact, it had never occurred to me that he'd read the book. I know perfectly well that the book doesn't tell the truth about Johnny (it doesn't lie either), it just limits itself to Johnny's music. Out of discretion, out of charity, I've not wanted to show his incurable schizophrenia nakedly, the sordid, ultimate depths of his addiction, the promiscuity in that regrettable life. I set out to show the essential lines, emphasizing what really counts, Johnny's incomparable art. What more could anyone say? But maybe it's exactly there that he's expecting something of me, lying in ambush as usual, waiting for something, crouched ready for one of those ridiculous jumps in which all of us get hurt eventually. That's where he's waiting for me, maybe, to deny all the aesthetic bases on which I've built the ultimate structure of his music, the great theory of contemporary jazz which has resulted in such acclaim from everywhere it's appeared so far.

To be honest, what does his life matter to me? The only thing that bothers me is that if he continues to let himself go on living as he has been, a style I'm not capable of following (let's say I don't want to follow it), he'll end up by making lies out of the conclusions I've reached in my book. He might let it drop somewhere that my statements are wrong, that his music's something else.

"Hey, you said a bit back that there were things missing in the book."

(Attention now.)

"Things are missing, Bruno? Oh yeah, I said there were things missing. Look, it's not just Lan's red dress. There're . . . Will there really be urns, Bruno? I saw them again last night, an enormous field, but they weren't so buried this time. Some had inscriptions and pictures on them, you could see giants with helmets like in the movies, and monstrous cudgels in their hands. It's terrible to walk around between the urns and know there's no one else, that I'm the only one walking around in them and looking for . . . Don't get upset, Bruno, it's not important that you forgot to put all that in. But Bruno," and he lifts a finger that does not shake, "what you forgot to put in is me."

"Come on, Johnny."

"About me, Bruno, about me. And it's not your fault that you couldn't write what I myself can't blow. When you say there that my true biography is in my records, I know you think that's true and besides it sounds very pretty, but that's not how it is. And if I myself didn't know how to blow it like it should be, blow what I really am . . . you dig, they can't ask you for miracles, Bruno. It's hot inside here, let's go."

I follow him into the street, we wander a few feet off and a white cat comes out of an alley and meows at us; Johnny stays there a long time petting it. Well, that does it; I'll find a taxi in the place Saint-Michel, take him back to the hotel and go home myself. It hasn't been so awful after all; for a moment there I was afraid that Johnny had constructed a sort of antitheory to the book's and that he was trying it out on me before spilling it at full speed. Poor Johnny petting a white cat. Basically, the only thing he said was that no one can know anything about anyone, big deal. That's the basic assumption of any biography, then it takes off, what the hell. Let's go, Johnny, let's go home, it's late.

"Don't think that that's all it is," Johnny says, standing up suddenly as if he knew what I was thinking. "It's God, baby. Now that's where you missed out."

"Let's go, Johnny, let's go home, it's late."

"It's what you and people like my buddy Bruno call God. The tube of toothpaste in the morning, they call that God. The garbage can, they call that God. Afraid of kicking the bucket, they call that God. And you have the barefaced nerve to mess me up with that pigsty, you've written that my childhood, and my family, and I don't know what ancestral heritage of the Negro . . . shit. A mountain of rotten eggs and you in the middle of it crowing, very happy with your God. I don't want your God, he's never been mine."

"The only thing I said is that Negro music . . ."

"I don't want your God," Johnny says again. "Why've you made me accept him in your book? I don't know if there's a God, I play my music, I make my God, I don't need your inventions, leave those to Mahalia Jackson and the Pope, and right now you're going to take that part out of your book."

"If you insist," I say, to say something. "In the second edition."

"I'm as alone as that cat, much more alone because I know it and he doesn't. Damn, he's digging his nails into my hand. Bruno, jazz is not only music, I'm not only Johnny Carter."

"Exactly what I was trying to say when I wrote that sometimes you play like . . ."

"Like it's raining up my asshole," Johnny says, and it's the first time all night that I feel he's getting really sore. "A man can't say anything, right away you translate it into your filthy language. If I play and you see angels, that's not my fault. If the others open their fat yaps and say that I've reached perfection, it's not my fault. And that's the worst thing, the thing you really and truly left out of your book, Bruno, and that's that I'm not worth a damn, that what I play and what the people applaud me for is not worth a damn, really not worth a damn."

Truly a very rare modesty at this hour of the morning. This Johnny . . .

"How can I explain it to you?" Johnny yells, putting his hands on my shoulders, jerking me to the right and to the left. (Cut out the noise! they scream from a window). "It isn't a question of more music or less music, it's something else . . . for example, it's the difference between Bee being dead and being alive. What I'm playing is Bee dead, you dig, while what I want to, what I want to . . . And sometimes because of that I wreck the horn and people think that I'm up to my ears in booze. Really, of course, I'm always smashed when I do it, because, after all, a horn costs a lot of bread."

"Let's go this way. I'll get a taxi and drop you at the hotel."

"You're a mother of goodness, Bruno," Johnny sneers. "Old buddy Bruno writes everything down in his notebook that you say, except the important things. I never would have believed you could be so wrong until Art passed that book on to me. At the beginning I thought you were talking about someone else, about Ronnie or about Marcel, and then Johnny here and Johnny there, I mean it was about me and I wondered, but where am I?, and you dish it out about me in Baltimore, and at Birdland, and my style . . . Listen," he added almost coldly, "it isn't that I didn't realize that you'd written a book for the public. That's very fine, and everything you say about my way of playing and feeling jazz seems perfectly okay to me. Why are we going on talking about the book? A piece of garbage floating in the Seine, that piece of straw floating beside the dock, your book. And I'm that other straw, and you're that bottle going by bobbing over there. Bruno, I'm going to die without having found . . . without . . ."

I catch him under his arms and hold him up, I prop him against the railing above the pier. He's slipping into his usual delirium, he mutters parts of words, spits.

"Without having found," he repeats. "Without having found . . ."

"What is it you want to find, brother," I tell him. "You don't have to ask the impossible, what you have found is enough for . . ."

"For you, I know," Johnny says bitterly. "For Art, for Dédée, for Lan . . . You donno how . . . Sure, every once in a while the door opens a little bit . . . Look at the two straws, they've met, see they're dancing, one in front of the other . . . It's pretty, huh . . . It began to open out . . . Time . . . I told you, it seems to me that time business . . . Bruno, all my life in my music I looked for that door to open finally. Nothing, a crack . . . I remember in New York one night . . . A red dress. Yeah, red, and it fit her beautifully. Okay, one night we were with Miles and Hal . . . we were carrying it for about an hour I think, playing the same piece, all by ourselves, happy . . . Miles played something so lovely it almost pulled me out of my chair, then I let loose, I just closed my eyes and I flew. Bruno, I swear I was flying . . . And I was hearing it like from a place very far away, but inside me just the same, beside myself, someone was standing there . . . Not exactly someone . . . Look, the bottle, it's incredible how it bobs along . . . It wasn't anyone, just that you look for comparisons . . . It was the sureness, the meeting, like in some dreams, what do you think?, when everything's resolved, Lan and the chicks waiting for you with a turkey in the oven, you get in the car and never hit a red light, everything running as smooth as a billiard ball. And who I had beside me was like myself but not taking up any space, without being in New York at all, and especially without time, without afterwards . . . without there having to be an afterwards . . . for a while there wasn't anything but always . . . And I didn't know that it was a lie, that that happened because I was lost in the music, and that I hardly finish playing, because after all I had to give Hal his chance to do his thing at the piano, at that same moment my head would fall out, I'd be plunged into myself . . ."

He's crying softly, he rubs his eyes with his filthy hands. Me, I don't know what to do, it's so late, the dampness coming up from the river, we're going to catch cold, both of us.

"It felt like I wanted to swim with no water," Johnny murmurs. "It felt like I wanted to have Lan's red dress but without Lan inside it. And Bee's dead, Bruno. And I think you're right, your book really is very good."

"Let's go, Johnny, I'm not getting offended at what you think's bad about the book."

"It's not that, your book is okay because . . . because it doesn't have urns, Bruno. It's like what Satchmo blows, that clean, that pure. Doesn't it seem to you that what Satch's playing is like a birthday party or a decent action? We . . . I tell you I felt like I wanted to swim without water. It seemed to me . . . no you have to be an idiot . . . it seemed to me that one day I was going to find something else. I wasn't satisfied, I thought that the good things, Lan's red dress, even Bee, were like rat traps, I don't know how to put it any other way . . . Traps so that you would conform, dig, so that you would say everything's all right, baby. Bruno, I think that Lan and jazz, yeah, even jazz, were like advertisements in a magazine, pretty things so that I would stay conformed like you stay because you've got Paris and your wife and your work . . . I got my sax . . . and my sex, like the good book say. Everything that's missing. Traps, baby . . . because it's impossible there's nothing else, it can't be we're that close to it, that much on the other side of the door . . ."

"The only thing that counts is to give whatever one has that's possible," I say, feeling incredibly stupid.

"And win the poll every year in *Down Beat*, right," Johnny agrees. "Sure, baby. Sure. Sure. Sure. Sure."

I'm moving little by little toward the square. With any luck there'll be a taxi on the corner.

"On top of everything, I don't buy your God," murmured Johnny. "Don't come on to me that way, I won't put up with it. If it's really him on the other side of the door, fuck it. There's no use getting past that door if it's him on the other side opening it. Kick the goddamn thing in, right? Break the mother down with your fist, come all over the door, piss all day long against the door. Right? That time in New York I think I opened the door with my music, until I had to stop and then the sonofabitch closed it in my face only because I hadn't prayed to him ever, because I'm never going to pray to him, because I don't wanna know nothing about that goddamned uniformed doorman, that opener of doors in exchange for a goddamned tip, that . . ."

Poor Johnny, then he complains that you can't put these things in a book. Three o'clock in the morning, Jesus Christ.

Tica went back to New York, Johnny went back to New York (without Dédée, now happily settled at Louis Perron's, a very promising trombonist). Baby Lennox went back to New York. The season in Paris was very dull and I missed my friends. My book on Johnny was selling very well all over, and naturally Sammy Pretzal was already talking about the possibility of an adaptation for Hollywood; when you think of the relation of the franc-rate to the dollar, that's always an interesting proposition. My wife was still furious over my passage with Baby Lennox, nothing too serious overall finally, Baby is promiscuous in a reasonably marked manner and any intelligent woman would have to understand that things like that don't compromise the conjugal equilibrium, aside from which, Baby had already gone back to New York with Johnny, she'd decided that she'd enjoy returning on the same boat with Johnny. She'd already be shooting junk with Johnny, and lost like him, poor doll. And *Amorous* had just been released in Paris, just as the second edition of my book went to press and they were talking about translating it into German. I had thought a great deal about the changes possible in a second edition. To be honest within the limits permitted by the profession, I wondered whether it would not be necessary to show the personality of my subject in another light. I discussed it at different times with Delaunay and with Hodeir, they didn't really know what to advise me because they thought the book terrific and realized that the public liked it the way it was. It seemed I was being warned that they were both afraid of a literary infection, that I would end up by riddling the work with nuances which would have little or nothing to do with Johnny's music, at least as all of us understood it. It appeared to me that the opinion of people in authority (and my own personal decision, it would be dumb to negate that at this level of consideration) justified putting the second edition to bed as was. A close reading of the trade magazines from the States (four stories on Johnny, news of a new suicide attempt, this time with tincture of iodine, stomach pump and three weeks in the hospital, working in Baltimore again as though nothing had happened) calmed me sufficiently, aside from the anguish I felt at these ghastly backslidings. Johnny had not said one compromising word about the book. Example (in *Stomping Around,* a music magazine out of Chicago, Teddy Rogers' interview with Johnny): "Have you read what Bruno

V—— in Paris wrote about you?" "Yes, it's very good." "Nothing to say about the book?" "Nothing, except that it's fine. Bruno's a great guy." It remained to be seen what Johnny might say if he were walking around drunk or high, but at least there were no rumors of the slightest contradiction from him. I decided not to touch the second edition, to go on putting Johnny forth as he was at bottom: a poor sonofabitch with barely mediocre intelligence, endowed like so many musicians, so many chess players and poets, with the gift of creating incredible things without the slightest consciousness (at most, the pride of a boxer who knows how strong he is) of the dimensions of his work. Everything convinced me to keep, no matter what, this portrait of Johnny; it wasn't worth it to create complications with an audience that was crazy about jazz but cared nothing for either musical or psychological analysis, nothing that wasn't instant satisfaction and clear-cut besides, hands clapping to keep the beat, faces gone beatific and relaxed, the music that was driving through the skin, seeping into the blood and breath, and then finish, to hell with profound motives.

First two telegrams came (one to Delauney, one to me, in the afternoon the newspapers came out with their idiotic comments); twenty days later I had a letter from Baby Lennox, who had not forgotten me. "They treated him wonderfully at Bellevue and I went to fetch him when he got out. We were living in Mike Russolo's apartment, he's gone on tour to Norway. Johnny was in very good shape, and even though he didn't want to play dates, he agreed to record with the boys at Club 28. You I can tell this, really he was pretty weak"—I can imagine what Baby meant by that after our affair in Paris—"and at night he scared me, the way he'd breathe and moan. The only thing that softens it for me," Baby summed it up beautifully, "is that he died happy and without knowing it was coming. He was watching TV and all of a sudden slumped to the floor. They told me it was instantaneous." From which one inferred that Baby had not been present, and the assumption was correct because later we found out that Johnny was living at Tica's place and that he'd been there with her for five days, depressed and preoccupied, talking about quitting jazz, going to live in Mexico and work in the fields (he'd handed that to everybody at some time or other in his life, it's almost boring), and that Tica was taking care of him and doing everything possible to keep him quiet, making him think of the future (this is what Tica said later, as if she or Johnny had ever had the slightest idea of the future). In the middle of a television program which Johnny was enjoying, he started to cough, all at once he slumped down all of a sudden, etc. I'm not all that sure that death was as instantaneous as Tica declared to the police (Johnny's death in her apartment had put her in an unusually tight spot she was trying to get out of, pot was always within reach, and probably a stash of heroin somewhere, poor Tica'd had several other bad scenes there, and the not completely convincing results of the autopsy. One can imagine completely what a doctor would find in Johnny's lungs and liver). "You wouldn't want to know how painful his death is to me, although I could tell you some other things," sweet Baby added gently, "but sometime when I feel better I'll write you or tell you (it looks like Rogers wants to get me contracts in Paris and Berlin) everything you need to know, you were Johnny's best friend." And after a page dedicated to insulting Tica, you'd believe she not only caused Johnny's death but was responsible for the attack on Pearl Harbor and the Black Plague, poor Baby ended up: "Before I forget, one day in Bellevue he asked after you a lot, he was mixed up and thought you were in New York and didn't want to come see him, he was talking all the time about fields full of things, and after he was calling for you, even cussing you out, poor baby. You know what a fever's like. Tica told Bob Carey that Johnny's last words were something like: 'Oh, make me a mask,' but you can imagine how at that moment . . ." I sure could imagine it. "He'd gotten very fat," Baby added at the end of her letter, "and panted out of breath when he walked." These were details you might expect from a person as scrupulous as Baby Lennox.

All this happened at the same time that the second edition of my book was published, but luckily I had time to incorporate an obituary note edited under full steam and inserted, along with a newsphoto of the funeral in which many famous jazzmen were identifiable. In that format the biography remained, so to speak, intact and finished. Perhaps it's not right that I say this, but naturally I was speaking from a merely aesthetic point of view. They're already talking of a new translation, into Swedish or Norwegian, I think. My wife is delighted at the news.

SECRET WEAPONS

$\cdot$ $\cdot$ $\cdot$ $\cdot$ $\cdot$ $\cdot$ $\cdot$ $\cdot$ $\cdot$ $\cdot$ $\cdot$ $\cdot$ $\cdot$ $\cdot$ $\cdot$

Strange how people are under the impression that making a bed is exactly the same as making a bed, that to shake hands is always the same as shaking hands, that opening a can of sardines is to open the same can of sardines *ad infinitum*. "But everything's an exception," Pierre is thinking, smoothing out the worn blue bedspread heavy-handedly. "Yesterday it rained, today there was sun, yesterday I was gloomy, today Michèle is coming. The only invariable is that I'll never get this bed to look decent." Not important, women enjoy disorder in a bachelor's room, they can smile (mother shining out from every tooth), they fix the curtains, change the location of a chair or flowerpot, say to put this table where there isn't any light wouldn't occur to anyone but you. Michèle will probably say things like that, walk about touching and moving books and lamps, and he'll let her, stretched out on the bed or humped down into the old sofa, watching her through a wreath of Gauloise smoke, and wanting her.

"Six o'clock, the critical hour," Pierre thinks. The golden hour when the whole neighborhood of Saint-Sulpice begins to alter, ready itself for the night. Soon the girls will begin to emerge from the notary's office, Madame Lenôtre's husband will thump his leg up the stairs, the sisters' voices on the sixth floor will be audible, they're inseparable when the hour arrives to buy a fresh loaf of bread and the paper. Michèle can't be much longer, unless she gets lost or hangs around in the streets on the way, she has this extraordinary capacity to stop any place and take herself a trip through the small particular worlds of the shop windows. Afterward, she will tell him about: a stuffed bear that winds up, a Couperin record, a bronze chain with a blue stone, Stendhal's complete works, the summer fashions. Completely understandable reasons for arriving a bit late. Another Gauloise, then, another shot of cognac. Now he feels like listening to some MacOrlan songs, feeling around absently among the piles of papers and notebooks. I'll bet Roland or Babette borrowed the record; they ought to tell somebody when they're taking something. Why doesn't Michèle get here? He sits on the edge of the bed and wrinkles the bedspread. Oh great, now he'll have to pull it from one side to the other, back, the damned edge of the pillow'll stick out. He smells strongly of tobacco, Michèle's going to wrinkle her nose and tell him he smells strongly of tobacco. Hundreds and hundreds of Gauloises smoked up on hundreds and hundreds of days: his thesis, a few girlfriends, two liver attacks, novels, boredom. Hundreds and hundreds of Gauloises?

He's always surprised to find himself hung up over trifles, stressing the importance of details. He remembers old neckties he threw into the garbage ten years ago, the color of a stamp from the Belgian Congo, his prize from a whole childhood of collecting stamps. As if at the back of his head he kept an exact memory of how many cigarettes he'd smoked in his life, how each one had tasted, at what moment he'd set the match to it, where he'd thrown the butt away. Maybe the absurd numbers that appear sometimes in his dreams are the top of the iceberg of this implacable accounting. "But then God exists," Pierre thinks. The mirror on the wardrobe gives him back his smile, obliging him as usual to recompose his face, to throw back the mop of black hair that Michèle is always threatening to cut off. Why doesn't Michèle get here? "Because she doesn't want to come to my room," Pierre thinks. But to have the power to cut off the forelock someday, she'll have to come to his room and lie down on his bed. Delilah pays a high price, you don't get to a man's hair for less than that. Pierre tells himself that he's stupid for having thought that Michèle doesn't want to come to his room. He thinks it soundlessly, as if from far off. Thought at times seems to have to make its way through countless barriers, to resolve itself, to make itself known. It's idiotic to have imagined that Michèle doesn't want to come up to his room. If she isn't here it's because she's standing absorbed in front of a hardware or some other kind of store window, captivated by a tiny porcelain seal or a Tsao-Wu-Ki print. He seems to see her there, and at the same time he notices that he's imagining a double-barreled shotgun, just as he's inhaling the cigarette smoke and feels as though he's been pardoned for having done something stupid. There's nothing strange about a double-barreled shotgun, but what could a double-barreled shotgun and that feeling of missing something, what could you do with it at this hour and in his room? He doesn't like this time of day when everything turns lilac, grey. He reaches his arm out lazily to turn on the table lamp. Why doesn't Michèle get here? Too late for her to come now, useless to go on waiting for her. Really, he'll have to believe that she doesn't want to come to his room. Well, what the hell. No tragedy; have another cognac, a novel that's been started, go down and eat something at Leon's. Women won't be any different, in Enghien or Paris, young or full-blown. His theory about exceptional cases begins to fall down, the little mouse retreats before she enters the trap. What trap? One day or the next, before or after . . . He's been waiting for her since five o'clock, even if she wasn't supposed to arrive before six; he smoothed out the blue coverlet especially for her, he scrambled up on a chair feather duster in hand to detach an insignificant cobweb that wasn't hurting anybody. And it would be completely natural for her to be stepping down from the bus that very moment at Saint-Sulpice, drawing nearer his house, stopping in front of the store windows or looking at pigeons in the square. There's no reason she shouldn't want to come up to his room. Of course, there's no reason either to think of a double-barreled shotgun, or to decide that right this moment Michaux would make better reading than Graham Greene. Instant choices always bother Pierre. Impossible that everything be gratuitous, that mere chance decides for Greene against Michaux, or Michaux against Enghien, I mean, against Greene. Including confusing a place-name like Enghien with a writer like Greene . . . "It can't all be that absurd," Pierre thinks, throwing away his cigarette. "And if she doesn't come it's because something's happened; it has nothing to do with the two of us."

He goes down into the street and waits in the doorway for a bit. He sees the lights go on in the square. There's almost no one at Leon's where he sits down at an outside table and orders a beer. From where he's sitting he can still see the entranceway to his house, so if . . . Leon's talking about the Tour de France bicycle race; Nicole and her girlfriend arrive, the florist with the husky voice. The beer is ice-cold, he ought to order some sausages. In the doorway to his house the concierge's kid is playing, jumping up and down on one foot. When he gets tired he starts jumping on the other foot, not moving from the door.

"What nonsense," Michèle says. "Why shouldn't I want to go to your place, when we'd agreed on it?"

Edmond brings the eleven o'clock coffee. There's almost no one there at that hour of the morning, and Edmond dawdles beside the table so as to make some remarks about the Tour de France. Then Michèle explains what happened, what Pierre should have assumed. Her mother's frequent fainting spells, papa gets alarmed and telephones the office, grabbing a taxi home and it turns out to be nothing, a little dizziness. It's not the first time all this has happened, but you'd have to be Pierre to . . .

"I'm glad she's better now," Pierre says, feeling foolish.

He puts one hand on top of Michèle's. Michèle puts her other hand on top of Pierre's. Pierre puts his other hand on top of Michèle's. Michèle pulls her hand out from underneath and lays it on top. Pierre pulls his hand out from under and places it on hers. Michèle pulls her hand out from the bottom and presses the palm against Pierre's nose.

"Cold as a little dog's."

Pierre admits that the temperature of his nose is an insoluble enigma.

"Dope," says Michèle, summing up the situation.

Pierre kisses her on the forehead, kisses her hair. As she ducks her head, he takes her chin and tilts it to make her look at him before he kisses her on the mouth. He kisses her once, twice. She smells fresh, like the shadow under trees. *Im wunderschönen Monat Mai,* he hears the melody distinctly. He wonders vaguely at remembering the words so well that make total sense to him only when translated. But he likes the tune, the words sound so well against Michèle's hair, against her wet mouth. *Im wunderschönen Monat Mai, als* . . .

Michèle's hand digs into his shoulder, her nails bite into him.

"You're hurting me," she says, pushing him off, running her fingers over her lips.

Pierre sees the marks of his teeth on the edge of her lip. He pets her cheek and kisses her again, lightly. Is Michèle angry? No, she's not. When, when are they ever going to find themselves alone? It's hard for him to understand, Michèle's explanations seem to have to do with something else. Set on the idea of her coming some day to his place, that she's going to climb five flights and come into his room, he doesn't follow that suddenly everything's solved, that Michèle's parents are going down to the farm for two weeks. Let them, all the better, because then Michèle . . . Then it hits him all at once, he sits staring at her. Michèle laughs.

"You're going to be alone at your house for fifteen days?"

"You're a dope," says Michèle. She sticks one finger out and draws invisible stars, rhomboids, gentle spirals. Of course her mother is counting on faithful Babette to stay those two weeks with her, there've been so many robberies and muggings in the suburbs. But Babette will stay in Paris as long as they want.

Pierre doesn't know the summerhouse, though he's imagined it so often that it's as though he were already in it, he goes with Michèle into a small parlor crowded with antiquated furniture, he goes up a staircase, his fingers grazing the glass ball on the banister post at the bottom. He doesn't know why he doesn't like the house, he'd rather go out into the garden, though it's hard to believe that such a small cottage would have a garden. It costs him effort to sweep away the image, to find that he's happy, that he's in the café with Michèle, that the house will be different from the one he imagines, which would depress him somewhat with its furniture and its faded carpets. "I'll have to get the motorcycle from Xavier," Pierre thinks. He'll come here to meet Michèle and they'll be in Clamart in half an hour, they'll have two weekends for excursions, I'll have to get a thermos jug and buy some nescafé.

"Is there a glass ball at the bottom of the staircase in your house?"

"No," Michèle says, "you're confusing it with . . ."

She breaks off suddenly, as if she had something bothering her in her throat. Slumped on the stool, his head back against the tall mirror with which Edmond tries to multiply the number of tables in his café, Pierre acknowledges vaguely that Michèle is like a cat or an anonymous portrait. He's known her such a short time, maybe she finds him difficult to understand too. For one thing, just to be in love never needs an explanation, you don't have to have friends in common or to share political opinions to be in love. You always begin by thinking that there's no mystery, no matter who, it's so easy to get information: Michèle Duvernois, age twenty-four, chestnut-colored hair, grey eyes, office worker. And she also knows: Pierre Jolivet, age twenty-three, blond hair . . . But tomorrow he'll go to her home with her, half an hour's ride they'll be in Enghien. "Oh, fuck Enghien," Pierre thinks, brushing the name away as if it were a fly. They'll have fifteen days to be together, and there's a garden at the house, likely very different from the one he imagines, he'll have to ask Michèle what the garden's like, but Michèle is calling Edmond, it's after eleven thirty, and the manager'll give her the fish-eye if he catches her coming back late.

"Stay a little longer," Pierre says. "Here come Roland and Babette. It's unbelievable how we can never be alone in this café."

"Alone?" Michèle says. "But we came here to meet them."

"I know, but even so."

Michèle shrugs, and Pierre knows that she understands and that she's sorry, too, at bottom, that friends have to put in such a punctual appearance. Babette and Roland have their usual air of quiet happiness that irritates him this time and makes him impatient. They are on the other side, sheltered by a breakwater of time; their angers and dissatisfactions belong to the world, to politics or art, not to themselves ever or to their deep relationship. Saved by force of habit, though, by the automatic gesture. Everything smooth, ironed out, numbered and filed away. Happy little pigs, poor kids, and good friends. He's on the point of not shaking the hand Roland reaches out to him, swallows his saliva, looks him in the eye, then puts a grip on his fingers as if he wanted to break them. Roland laughs and sits down opposite them; he's got the schedule from some cinematheque, they can't miss the show on Monday. "Happy piglets," Pierre gnaws away at it. All right, I'm being an idiot and unjust. But a Pudovkin film, oh come on, couldn't he look around and find something new?

"New?" Babette teases. "Something new. You're such an old man, Pierre."

No reason to not want to shake Roland's hand.

"And she had on that orange blouse and it looked so good on her," Michèle's talking.

Roland offers his pack of Gauloises around and orders coffee. No reason to not want to shake Roland's hand.

"Yes, she's a bright girl," Babette is saying.

Roland looks at Pierre and winks. Tranquil, no problems. Absolutely no problems, placid little pig. Pierre loathes their tranquillity, that Michèle can sit there talking about an orange blouse, as far from him as ever. He has nothing in common with them, he was the last one to come into their crowd, they barely tolerate him.

As she talks (it's about shoes now), Michèle runs a finger along the edge of her lips. He can't even kiss her nicely, he hurt her and Michèle is remembering. And everybody hurts him, winks at him, smiles at him, likes him very much. It's like a weight on his chest, a need to get up and go, to be alone in his room wondering why Michèle hasn't arrived, why Babette and Roland took a record without telling him.

Michèle takes one look at the clock and jumps up. They set the date for the cinematheque, Pierre pays for the coffee. He feels better, he'd like to talk a little more with Roland and Babette, says goodbye to them affectionately. Nice piglets, good friends of Michèle's.

Roland watches them going off, going into the street full of sun. He drinks his coffee slowly.

"I wonder," Roland says.

"Me too," says Babette.

"Why not, after all?"

"Sure, why not. But it would be the first time since then."

"It's about time Michèle did something with her life," Roland says. "And if you ask me, she's very much in love."

"They're both very much in love."

Roland looks thoughtful.

He's made a date with Xavier at a café in the place Saint-Michel, but he gets there much too early. He orders beer and leafs through the newspaper; he doesn't remem-

ber too clearly what he's done since he left Michèle at the
door to her office. These last few months are as confused
as a morning that isn't over yet and is already a mixture of
fake memories, mistakes. In that remote life of his, the
only absolute certainty is that he's been as close as possible to Michèle, waiting and being aware that he's not
content with that, that everything's vaguely surprising,
that he knows nothing about Michèle, absolutely nothing,
really (she has grey eyes, five fingers on each hand, is un-
married, combs her hair like a little girl), absolutely nothing really. Well, if you know nothing about Michèle, all
you have to do is not see her for a bit for the emptiness to
turn into a dense, unpleasant thicket; she's afraid of you,
you disgust her, at times she rejects you at the deepest
moment of a kiss, she doesn't want to go to bed with you,
she's horribly afraid of something, just this morning she
pushed you away violently (and how lovely she was, that
she crushed up against you when it was time to say goodbye, that she'd arranged everything to meet you tomorrow
and go out together to her place at Enghien) and you left
tooth-marks on her mouth, you were kissing her and you
bit her and she bitched, she ran her fingers across her
mouth and complained, not angry, just a little surprised,
als alle Knospen sprangen, you were singing Schumann
inside, you sonofabitch, you were singing while you bit
her on the mouth and now you remember, besides you
were going up the staircase, yes, climbing the steps, your
hand grazing the glass ball on the banister post at the bottom, but Michèle had said later that there was no glass
ball at her house.

Pierre slides down the bench, looking for his cigarettes.
After all, Michèle does not know much about him either,
she's not at all inquisitive, though she has that attentive
and serious way of listening when he unburdens himself,
an ability to share any given moment in life, oh anything,

a cat coming out of a garage door, a storm on the Cité, a leaf of clover, a Gerry Mulligan record. Attentive, eager, and serious at the same time, listening as easily as being listened to. As though from meeting to meeting, from one conversation to the next, they've drifted into the solitude of a couple lost in the crowd, some politics, novels shared, going to the movies, kissing more passionately each time, letting his hand run down her throat and touch her breasts lightly, repeating the endless question without an answer. It's raining, let's get under that doorway; the sun's burning down on our heads, we'll go into that bookstore, tomorrow I'll introduce you to Babette, she's an old friend of mine, you'll like her. And it turns out that Babette's boyfriend is an old buddy of Xavier's who is Pierre's best friend, and the circle will start to close, sometimes at Babette and Roland's place, sometimes at Xavier's consultation room, or at night in the cafés of the Latin Quarter. Pierre will be grateful, without knowing why, that Babette and Roland are such close friends of Michèle's and that it feels as though they are protecting her discreetly without any particular reason for Michèle's needing protecting. In that group nobody talks much about the others; they like the larger subjects, politics or trials, and more than anything else to exchange satisfied looks, pass cigarettes around, sit in cafés and live their lives feeling that they're surrounded by friends. He'd been lucky that they'd accepted him and let him in; they're not easy to make friends with, and they know all the ways of discouraging newcomers. "I like them," Pierre thinks to himself, and finishes the rest of his beer. Maybe they think that he's already Michèle's lover, at least Xavier must think so; it would never occur to him that Michèle would have been able to hold him off all this time, without any definite reason, only hold him off and go on seeing him, going out together, talking or letting him talk. You can get used to some weird things, get to think that the mystery will explain itself and that you end up living inside the mystery, accepting the unacceptable, saying goodbye on street corners or in cafés when everything could be so simple, a staircase with a glass ball at the bottom of the banister, that leads to the meeting, to the very truth. But Michèle said that there isn't any glass ball.

Tall and scraggly, Xavier brings along his regular working face. He talks about some experiments, of biology as a provocation toward skepticism. He looks at his tobacco-stained middle finger. Pierre asks him:

"Does it ever happen to you, all at once thinking about things completely different from what you've been thinking?"

"Completely different is a working hypothesis, that's all," Xavier says.

"I feel pretty weird these days. Maybe you ought to give me something, you know, some kind of objectifier."

"Objectifier?" Xavier says. "There's no such thing, old buddy."

"I think too much about myself," Pierre says. "It's stupid."

"And Michèle, doesn't she objectify you?"

"Right, yesterday it so happened that . . ."

He hears himself talking, sees Xavier looking at him, sees Xavier's reflection in the mirror, the back of Xavier's neck, sees himself talking to Xavier (but why do I have to think there's a glass ball at the bottom of the banister), and from time to time notices how Xavier's head moves, a professional gesture that looks ridiculous outside a consulting room when the doctor doesn't have on the white coat that sets him on another level and confers other powers.

"Enghien," Xavier says. "Don't bother about it. I'm always confusing Le Mans with Menton. Probably due to one of your schoolteachers back in your childhood."

Im wunderschönen Monat Mai, Pierre's memory hums.

"If you aren't sleeping well, let me know, I'll give you something," Xavier says. "In any case, these fifteen days in heaven should settle you, I'm sure of that. There's nothing like sharing a pillow, it clarifies ideas marvelously; sometimes it even gets rid of them, which is very restful."

Maybe if he worked harder, if he tired himself out more, maybe he should paint his room or make the trek to the university on foot instead of taking the bus. If he had to earn the seventy thousand francs his parents sent him every month. Leaning on the railing at Pont Neuf, he watches the barges going by underneath and feels the summer sun beating on his neck and shoulders. A bunch of girls laughing and playing, he can hear a horse trotting; a redheaded cyclist cruises past the girls with a long-drawn-out whistle, they laugh even harder, and it's as if the dry leaves were coming up to meet his face and were eating it in one single horrible black bite.

Pierre rubs his eyes, straightens up slowly. There'd not been any words, not even a vision; something between the two, an image decomposed into so many words like dry leaves on the ground (that came up to hit him smack in the face). He notices that his right hand is shaking against the railing of the bridge. He makes a fist, fights to control its trembling. Xavier will already be too far away, useless to run after him, add one more illustration to this senseless catalogue. "Dry leaves," Xavier would say, "there are no dry leaves on Pont Neuf." As if he didn't know that there were no dry leaves on Pont Neuf, that the dry leaves are at Enghien.

Now I'm going to think about you, sweetheart, only about you all night. I'm going to think only about you, it's the only way I'm conscious of myself, to hold you in the center of myself like a tree there, to loosen myself little by little from the trunk, which sustains me and guides me, to float cautiously around you, testing the air with each leaf (green, we are green, I myself and you yourself, trunk full of sap, and green leaves: green, green), without being away from you, not letting the other thing come between you and me, distract me from you, deprive me for a single second of realizing that tonight is swinging towards, into, dawn, and that there on the other side, where you live and are asleep, when it will be night again we'll arrive together and go into your house, we'll go up the porch steps, turn on the lights, pet the dog, drink coffee, we'll look for a long time at one another before I take you in my arms (hold you in the center of myself like a tree) and carry you to the stairs (but there's no glass ball at all) and we begin to go up, climb, the door's locked, but I have the key in my pocket . . .

Pierre jumps out of bed and sticks his head under the cold-water tap in the bathroom. Think only about you, but how can it be that what he's thinking is a dark, stifled desire in which Michèle is no longer Michèle (hold you in the center of myself like a tree), where he can't manage to feel her in his arms as he ascends the stairs, because he's hardly taken the first step, has seen the glass ball and is alone, he's going up the stairs alone and Michèle is upstairs, locked in, she's behind the door not knowing that he has another key in his pocket and that he's on his way up.

He dries his face, throws the window open all the way on the early morning freshness. A drunk is conducting a friendly monologue in the street, swaying as though he were floating in water as thick as paste. He's humming, going and coming back and forth, completing a sort of suspenseful and ceremonial dance in the grey light that bites into the cobblestones, the locked-up doors, little by little. *Als alle Knospen sprangen*, the words draw themselves onto Pierre's dry lips, they adhere onto the humming down in the street which has nothing to do with the melody, they come like the rest of it, they adhere to life for a moment and then there's something like bitter anxiety, holes that tip over to show through pieces that hook onto anything else, a double-barreled shotgun, a mattress of dry leaves, the drunk dancing a kind of stately pavane, with curtsies that turn into tatters and stumblings and vaguely mumbled words.

The cycle roars out the length of the rue d'Alésia. Pierre feels Michèle's fingers grab his waist tighter every time they pass a bus close or swing around a corner. When a red light stops them, he throws his head back and waits for a caress, a kiss on the hair.

"I'm not afraid any more," Michèle says. "You ride it very well. You have to take the next right, now."

The summerhouse is lost among dozens of houses that look much the same on a hill just beyond Clamart. The word "summerhouse" for Pierre sounds like a hideaway, an assurance that everything will be quiet and isolated, that it'll have a garden with wicker chairs and, at night, maybe a firefly.

"Do you have fireflies in your garden?"

"I don't think so. You've got such odd ideas."

It's hard to talk on the motorcycle, you have to concentrate on the traffic, and Pierre's tired, he got only a few hours of sleep toward morning. He'll have to remember to take the pills Xavier gave him, but of course he won't remember, and besides, who'll need them? He throws his head back, and grumbles when Michèle is slow in kissing

him, Michèle laughs and runs her hand through his hair.
"Just cut out the nonsense," Xavier had said, clearly disconcerted. Of course it'll pass, two tablets before bedtime,
glass of water. How does Michèle sleep?

"Michèle, how do you sleep?"

"Very well," Michèle says. "Sometimes I have nightmares like anyone else."

Right. Like anyone else, except that when she wakes
up, she knows she's left the dream back there, without getting it mixed up with the street noises, friends' faces,
something that infiltrates the most innocent occupations
(but Xavier said that everything'd be all right, two tablets), she'd sleep with her face buried in the pillow, legs
drawn up a little, light breathing, now he's going to see
her like that, hold her sleeping like that against his body,
listening to her breathe, defenseless, naked, when he
holds her down by the hair with one hand, and the yellow
light, red light, stop.

He brakes so violently that Michèle screams and then
sits very quietly in back, as if she were ashamed of having
screamed. One foot on the ground, Pierre twists his head
around and grins at someone not Michèle, and stays lost
in the air, smiling. He knows that the light's going to turn
green, there's a truck and a car behind the motorcycle,
green light, a truck and a car behind the cycle, someone
begins to lean on the horn, twice, three times.

"What's the matter with you?" Michèle says.

The driver of the car, as he passes them, hurls an insult
at him and Pierre pulls out slowly. Where were we, he was
going to see her as she is, naked and defenseless. We said
that, we had gotten to the exact moment when he was seeing her sleep defenseless and naked, that is to say, there's
no reason to imagine, even for a moment, that it's going to
be necessary to . . . Right, I heard you, first to the left
and then left again. There? That slate roof? There are

pines, hey great, what a nice house you have, garden, pines, and your folks gone off to the farm, I can hardly believe it, Michèle, something like this is almost unbelievable.

Bobby, who's met them with a loud volley of barks, saves face by sniffing conscientiously at Pierre's pants as he's pushing the motorcycle up to the porch. Michèle's already gone into the house, raises the blinds, goes back to get Pierre, who's looking at the walls and finding that none of this resembles what he had imagined.

"There ought to be three steps here," Pierre says. "And this living room, but of course . . . Don't pay any attention to me, one always figures on something other than . . . even the details, the furniture. Ever happen to you?"

"Sure, at times," Michèle says. "Pierre, I'm hungry. No, Pierre, now listen, be good and help me out; we'll have to cook up something."

"Sweetheart."

"Open that window, let the sun in. Just stay steady, Bobby will think that you're . . ."

"Michèle . . ."

"No, now let me go up and change. Take off your jacket if you want, there are drinks in that cabinet. I don't know anything about liquor."

He sees her run off, climb the stairs, disappear around the landing. There are drinks in the cabinet, she doesn't know anything about that. The living room is wide and dark, Pierre's hand caresses the newel post at the bottom of the banister. Michèle told him, but it's like an irrational disappointment, all right, there's no glass ball then.

Michèle comes down in old slacks and an unlikely blouse.

"You look like a mushroom," Pierre says with that tenderness every man shows toward a woman wearing clothes much too big for her. "Aren't you going to show me the house?"

"If you want," Michèle says. "Didn't you find the drinks? Wait, never mind, you're helpless."

They take their glasses into the living room and sit on the sofa facing the half-open window. Bobby leaps about hoping for attention, then lies down on the rug and watches them.

"He took to you right away," Michèle says, licking the rim of her glass. "You like my house?"

"No. It's gloomy, middle class, and stuffed with abominable furniture. But you're here, with those terrible pants on."

He caresses her throat, pulls her against him, kisses her on the mouth. They kiss each other on the mouth, the heat of Michèle's hand burns into Pierre, they kiss one another on the mouth, they slide down a little, but Michèle moans and tries to untangle herself, murmurs something he doesn't get. Confusedly, he thinks that the most difficult will be to cover her mouth, he doesn't want her to pass out. He lets go of her abruptly, looks at his hands as if they weren't his own, hearing Michèle's quick breathing, Bobby's muted growling from the rug.

"You're going to drive me out of my head," Pierre says, and the extravagance of the words is less painful than what has just happened. A compulsion, an irresistible desire to cover her mouth so that she won't pass out. He stretches out his hand and strokes Michèle's cheek from a distance, he agrees to everything, to eat whatever there is, yes, he'll have to choose the wine, that it's very hot next to the window.

Michèle has her own way of eating, mixing the cheese with the anchovies in oil, the salad and bits of crabmeat. Pierre drinks white wine, looks at her and smiles. If he married her, he'd drink his white wine at that table every day, and he'd look at her and smile.

"It's curious," Pierre says. "We've never mentioned the war years."

"The less we talk . . ." says Michèle, cleaning up her plate.

"I know, but memories come back sometimes. For me it wasn't too bad, after all, we were children then. Like an endless vacation, totally absurd, and almost fun."

"It was no vacation for me," Michèle says. "It rained all the time."

"Rained?"

"Here," she says, touching her forehead. "In front of my eyes, behind my eyes. Everything was damp, everything felt damp and sweaty."

"Did you live in this house?"

"At the beginning, yes. Later, during the occupation, they took me down to my aunt and uncle's in Enghien."

Pierre doesn't see that the match is burning down between his fingers, his mouth opens, he jerks his hand and swears. Michèle smiles, happy to be able to change the subject. When she gets up to fetch the fruit, Pierre lights the cigarette and inhales as if he were suffocating, but it's already passed, everything has an explanation if you look for it, Michèle must have mentioned Enghien lots of times during their talks at the café, those phrases which seem insignificant and are quickly forgotten, and later turn out to be the subjects of a dream or a fantasy. A peach, yes, thank you, but peeled. Ah, terribly sorry, but women have always peeled his peaches, and no reason for Michèle to be an exception.

"Women. If they peeled your peaches for you, they were as stupid as I am. You'd be better off grinding the coffee."

"Then you lived in Enghien," Pierre says, watching Michèle's hands with the vague distaste that watching a fruit being peeled always gives him. "What did your old man do during the war?"

"Oh, nothing much, we just lived, hoping that it would all be over soon."

"The Germans didn't bother you at all?"

"No," Michèle says, turning the peach with her wet fingers.

"It's the first time you've mentioned to me that you lived in Enghien."

"I don't like to talk about those days," Michèle says.

"But you must have talked about it once," Pierre says argumentatively. "I don't know how I knew, but I knew you lived in Enghien."

The peach falls onto the plate and pieces of the skin stick to its flesh. Michèle cleans the peach with a knife and Pierre feels the distaste again, starts grinding the coffee as hard as he can. Why doesn't she say something? She looks like she's suffering, busy cleaning the horrible runny peach. Why doesn't she talk? She's full of words, all you have to do is look at her hands, or the nervous flutter of her eyelids that turns into a kind of tic sometimes, all of one side of her face rises slightly, then goes back, he remembers once on a bench in the Luxembourg gardens, he noticed that the tic always coincides with a moment of uneasiness or a silence.

Michèle is preparing the coffee, her back to Pierre, who uses the butt of one cigarette to light another. They go back into the living room, carrying the porcelain cups with the blue design on them. The smell of the coffee makes them feel better, they look at one another, surprised by the period of silence and what went before it; they exchange a few casual words, looking at one another and smiling, they drink the coffee distractedly, the way you drink love potions that tie you forever. Michèle has partly closed the shutters and a warm, greenish light filters in from the garden and wraps around them like the cigarette smoke and the cognac that Pierre is sipping, lost in a mild loneliness. Bobby is sleeping on the rug, trembling and sighing.

"He dreams all the time," Michèle says. "Sometimes he barks and wakes up all at once, then looks at all of us as if he'd just been in great pain. And he's not much more than a puppy . . ."

The pleasure of being there, of feeling so good in that moment, just to close the eyes and sigh, like Bobby, to run his hand through his hair, once, twice, feeling the hand in his hair almost as though it were not his own, the delicate tickle as it touched the back of his neck, relaxed. When he opens his eyes he sees Michèle's face, her mouth half open, her face white as a sheet. He looks at her, not understanding, a cognac glass is rolling across the rug. Pierre is standing in front of the mirror, he sort of likes it, his hair parted in the middle like a silent-film star. Why does Michèle have to cry. She isn't crying, but hands over the face always means someone's crying. He pulls them apart roughly, kisses her on the neck, searches for her mouth. Words are born, his, hers, like little animals looking for one another, a meeting prolonged with caresses, the smell of siesta, the house empty, the stairway waiting with a glass ball on the newel post, bottom of the banister. Pierre would like to lift Michèle into the air, run upstairs, he has the key in his pocket, he'll go into the bedroom, stretch himself out upon her, feel her shiver, begin sluggishly to undo ties, buttons, but there isn't any glass ball on the newel post, it's all far off and horrible, Michèle there beside him, so far away and weeping, her face crying between the wet hands, her body that breathes and is afraid and rejects him.

Falling to his knees, he puts his head in Michèle's lap. Hours pass, a minute or two goes by, time is something filled with whips and spittle. Michèle's fingers caress Pierre's hair, and he sees her face again, a smile peeping through, Michèle's fingers are combing his hair, it sort of hurts him when she pushes his hair back, then she bends over and kisses him and smiles.

"You gave me a scare, it seemed to me for a minute that . . . Oh, I'm so stupid, but you were . . . you looked different."

"Who did you see?"

"Nobody," Michèle answers.

Pierre crouches down, waiting, now there's something, like a door swinging, ready to open. Michèle breathes deeply, something like a swimmer waiting for the starter's gun.

"I was frightened because . . . I don't know, you made me think of that . . ."

It swings, the door swings open, the swimmer; she's waiting for the shot to dive in. Time stretches like a piece of rubber, then Pierre reaches out his arms and imprisons Michèle, raises himself to her and kisses her passionately, his hands reaching under her blouse to find her breasts, to hear her moan, he moans too kissing her, come, come on now, trying to pick her up (there are fifteen stairs and the door's on the right), hearing Michèle's moan, her useless protest, he stands up holding her in his arms, he can't wait any longer, now, right this minute, it won't do her any good to try to grasp the glass ball or the banister (but there isn't any glass ball at the banister), all the same he has to carry her upstairs and then like a bitch, all of him is a single knot of muscle, like the bitch that she is, she'll learn, oh Michèle, oh my love, don't cry like that, don't be sad, love, don't let me fall again into that black pit, how could I have thought that, don't cry Michèle.

"Put me down," Michèle says in a low voice, struggling to get loose. She has finally pushed him away, looks at him for a moment as if he were someone else and runs out of the living room, closes the kitchen door, a key turns in the lock, Bobby is barking in the garden.

The mirror shows Pierre a smooth, expressionless face, arms hanging like rags, a shirttail outside the trousers. He rearranges his clothes mechanically, still looking at himself in his reflection. His throat is so tight that the brandy burns his mouth, refuses to go down, so he forces himself and drinks directly from the bottle, swallowing interminably. Bobby has stopped barking, there's a silence of siesta about the place, the light grows greener and greener in the house. A cigarette between his too-dry lips, he goes out onto the porch, down into the garden, walks past the motorcycle and toward the back. There's an odor of bees buzzing, of a mattress of pine needles, and now Bobby has begun to bark among the trees, is barking at him, has suddenly started to growl and bark without coming too close, but each time a bit closer, and barking at him.

The rock catches him in the middle of his back; Bobby lets out a howl and runs off, begins to bark again from a safe distance. Pierre takes aim slowly and lands one on a back leg. Bobby hides in the underbrush. "I have to find some place to think," Pierre tells himself. "I have to find a place to hide and think right now." His shoulder slides down the trunk of a pine, he lowers himself slowly. Michèle is watching him from the kitchen window. She must have seen me throwing stones at the dog, she's looking at me as though she didn't see me, she's watching me and not crying, she's not saying anything, she looks so alone at the window, I have to go to her and be nice, I want to be good, I want to take her hand and kiss her fingers, each finger, skin so soft.

"What are we playing, Michèle?"

"I hope you didn't injure him."

"I threw a stone just to scare him. He acted like he didn't know me, same as you."

"Don't talk nonsense."

"And you, don't lock doors with keys."

Michèle lets him in, accepts without resisting the arm he takes her around the waist with. The living room is darker, you can almost not see the bottom of the stairs.

"Forgive me," Pierre says. "I can't explain it to you, it's so stupid."

Michèle picks up the brandy glass from the floor and corks the bottle of cognac. It's getting hotter all the time, as though the house were breathing heavily through their mouths. A handkerchief that smells of moss wipes the sweat off Pierre's forehead. Oh Michèle, how can we go on like this, not talking to one another, not trying to figure this thing out that breaks us up every time we start . . . Yes, sweet, I'll sit beside you, I won't be stupid, I'll kiss you, lose myself in your hair, your throat, and you'll understand that there's no reason . . . yes, you'll understand that when I want to take you in my arms and carry you with me, go up to your bedroom, I don't want to hurt you, your head leaning on my shoulder . . .

"No, Pierre, no. Not today, love, please."

"Michèle, Michèle . . ."

"Please."

"Why, tell me why?"

"I don't know, forgive me . . . Don't blame yourself, it's all my fault. But we have time, so much time . . ."

"Let's not wait any more, Michèle, now."

"No, Pierre, not today."

"But you promised me," Pierre says feeling stupid. "We came out here . . . After all this time, waiting so long so that you'd love me a little . . . I don't know what I'm saying, it all comes out so dirty when I say . . ."

"If you could forgive me, if I . . ."

"How can I forgive you when you don't talk, I hardly know you? What's there to forgive?"

Bobby growls out on the porch. Their clothes are stuck to them with the heat, the tick-tock of the clock sticks to them, the hair sticks to Michèle's forehead, she's slumped down on the sofa looking at Pierre.

"I don't know you very well either, but that's not it, you're going to think I'm crazy."

Bobby growls again.

"Years ago . . ." Michèle says, and closes her eyes. "We were living in Enghien, I already told you that. I think I mentioned that we were living in Enghien. Don't look at me like that."

"I'm not looking at you," Pierre says.

"Yes you are, it hurts."

But that's not so, how can he hurt her by hanging on her words, unmoving, waiting for her to go on, watching her lips barely move, now it's going to happen, she's going to join her hands and beg, a flower of delight opening while she pleads, wrestling and weeping in his arms, a damp flower that's opening, the pleasure of feeling her struggling in vain . . . Bobby comes in, dragging himself over to a corner to lie down. "Don't look at me like that," Michèle just said, and Pierre answered, "I'm not looking at you," and then she said yes, it hurt, someone looking at her like that, but she can't go on because Pierre's standing up now looking at Bobby, looking at himself in the mirror, runs his hand down his face, breathes with a long moan, a whistle that keeps going, and suddenly falls on his knees against the sofa and buries his face in his hands, shaking and panting, trying to pull off the images that stick to his face like a spiderweb, like dry leaves that stick to his drenched face.

"Oh Pierre," Michèle says in a whisper of a voice.

His sobbing comes out from between his fingers that cannot hold it back, fills the air with a clumsy texture, obstinate, starts again and keeps up.

"Pierre, Pierre," Michèle says. "Why, love, why."

She caresses his hair slowly, reaches him his handkerchief with its moldy smell.

"I'm a goddamn idiot, forgive me. You . . . you were t-telling me that . . ."

He gets up, he sinks onto the other end of the sofa. He hasn't noticed that Michèle has swung back to it again suddenly, she's looking at him again as she did before he ran away. He repeats, "You were . . . you were telling me," with great effort, his throat's tight, and what's that, Bobby is growling again, Michèle's on her feet, retreating step by step without turning, looking at him and walking backwards, what's that, why is that now, why is she leaving, why. The door slamming leaves him indifferent. He smiles, sees his smile in the mirror, smiles again, *als alle Knospen sprangen,* he hums, his lips compressed, there's a silence, the click of a telephone being taken off the hook, buzzing sound of the dialing, one letter, another letter, the first number, the second. Pierre stumbles, tells himself vaguely that he should go explain himself to Michèle, but he's already out the door next to the motorcycle, Bobby growling on the porch, the house rattles violently with the sound of the starter, first, up the street, second, under the sun.

"Babette, it was the same voice. And then I realized that . . ."

"Nonsense," Babette answers. "If I were out there I think I'd give you a good hiding."

"Pierre's gone."

"It's about the best thing he could have done."

"Babette, if you could come out here."

"For what? Sure, I'll come, but it's idiotic."

"He was stuttering, Babette, I swear to you . . . It's not my imagination, I already told you before that . . . It was as if again . . . Come right away, I can't explain like this on the telephone . . . Now I just heard the cycle taking off and I feel awful, how can he understand what's happening with me, poor thing, but he's acting crazy himself, Babette, it's so strange."

"I thought you'd gotten over that whole business," Babette says in a very indifferent voice. "After all, Pierre's not foolish, he'll understand. I thought he'd known already for some time."

"I was going to tell him, I wanted to tell him and then . . . Babette, I swear he was stuttering, and before, before . . ."

"You told me that already, but you're exaggerating. Roland combs his hair anyway he wants to sometimes, and you don't get him confused with anyone else, what the hell."

"And now he's left," Michèle repeats dully.

"He'll be back," Babette says. "All right, cook up something tasty for Roland, he's getting hungrier and hungrier every day."

"You're ruining my reputation," Roland says from the doorway. "What's wrong with Michèle?"

"Let's go," Babette says. "Let's go right away."

The world is steered by a little rubber tube that fits in the hand; turning just a little to the right, all the trees become a single tree spread out at the side of the road; then turn the slightest bit to the left, the green giant splits into hundreds of aspens that race backwards, the towers carrying the high-tension wires move forward with a leisurely motion, one at a time, the march is a cheerful cadence, even words can get into it, tags of images, nothing to do with what you see along the road, the rubber tube turns to the right, the sound gets louder and louder, a wire of sound extends itself unbearably, but there's no more thinking now, it's all machine, body set onto the machine and the wind against the face like forgetfulness, Corbeil, Arpajon, Linas-Montlhéry, the aspen trees again, bus dispatcher's sentry shack, the light turning more violet, cool air that rushes into your half-open mouth, slower now, take a right at this crossroad, Paris 18 kilometers, *Cinzano*, Paris 17 kilometers. "I haven't killed myself," Pierre thinks, swinging slowly into the road on the left. "It's incredible, I haven't killed myself." Exhaustion weighs him down, like a passenger leaning on his shoulders, something that gets softer and more necessary every minute. "I think she'll forgive me," Pierre thinks. "We're both so absurd, it's necessary that she understand, that she understand, that she understand, you don't know anything until you've made love together, I want her hair in my hands, her body, I want her, I want her . . ." The woods start at the roadside, dry leaves invade the highway, drawn out by the wind. Pierre looks at the leaves the motorcycle is eating up and whipping back; the rubber tube starts to turn to the right again, a little more, more. And suddenly it's the glass ball that gleams faintly at the bottom of the stairs. Don't have to leave the motorcycle too far from the house, but Bobby will start barking so you have to hide the bike in the trees and go up on foot with the last of the daylight, go into the living room looking for Michèle, who will be there, but Michèle's not sitting on the sofa, there's only the cognac bottle and some used glasses, the kitchen door is wide open and a reddish light's coming in through there, the sun that's setting at the bottom of the garden, and just silence, so the best thing to do is head for the stairs, steering yourself by the glass ball that's shining, or they're Bobby's eyes, he's stretched out on the bottom step with his hair bristling, growling a bit, it's not hard to step up over Bobby, to climb the stairs carefully so they won't creak and Michèle won't get scared, door half-open, the door shouldn't be half-open and he not have the key in his pocket, but if the door is ajar he won't need the key now, it feels good to run his hands through his hair walking toward the door, you go in leaning on your right foot lightly, lightly edging the door that opens soundlessly, and Michèle sitting at the side of the bed looks up and sees him, puts her hands to her mouth, looks like she's going to scream (but why isn't her hair loose, why doesn't she have the pale blue nightgown on, she's wearing trousers now and looks older), and then Michèle smiles, sighs, stands up and stretches out her arms to him, says, "Pierre, Pierre," instead of wringing her hands and begging and fighting him off, she says his name and is waiting for him, she looks at him and trembles as if out of happiness or shyness, like the double-crossing bitch that she is, as if he could see her in spite of the mattress of dry leaves that again cover his face and that he tears away with both hands while Michèle steps backward, trips on the edge of the bed, looks behind her desperately, screams, screams, all the pleasure that rises and drenches him, screams, like this, her hair between his fingers, like this, I don't care if you beg, like this then, you bitch, just like this.

"For God's sake, that business is more than gone and forgotten," Roland says, taking a turn at top speed.

"I thought so too. Almost seven years. And it has to pop up just now . . ."

"You're mistaken there," Roland says. "If there was any time it was going to pop up it's now, given that it's absurd, it's really very logical. Even I . . . you know, sometimes I dream about all that. The way we killed that guy, you don't forget things like that very easy. Anyway, you couldn't handle things any better in those days," Roland says, pushing the gas pedal to the floor.

"She doesn't know a thing," Babette says. "Just that they killed him shortly afterwards. It was right to tell her at least that much."

"I guess. But it didn't seem right to him at all. I remember his face when we pulled him out of the car in the middle of the woods, he knew immediately he was a goner. He was brave, sure."

"It's always easier to be brave than to be a man," Babette says. "To force himself on a child who . . . When I think that I had to fight to keep Michèle from killing herself. Those first nights . . . It doesn't surprise me that she's feeling the same thing again now, it's almost natural."

The car enters the street on which the house is located, doing seventy.

"Yeah, he was a pig," Roland says. "The pure Aryan, that's the way they saw it, those days. Naturally, he asked for a cigarette, the complete ceremony. Also, he wanted to know why we were going to liquidate him, we explained it to him, boy, we certainly explained it to him. When I dream about him, it's that moment especially, his disdainful air of surprise, the almost elegant way of stuttering. I remember how he fell, his face blasted to bits among the dry leaves."

"Don't go on, please," Babette says.

"He had it coming, besides, we didn't have any other weapons. A shotgun properly used . . . It's on the left, down there at the bottom?"

"Yes, on the left."

"I hope there's some cognac," Roland says, coming down hard on the brake.